Keith Dixon was born in Yorkshire and grew up in the Midlands. He's been writing since he was thirteen years old in a number of different genres: thriller, espionage, science fiction, literary. He's the author of seven novels in the Sam Dyke Investigations series and two other non-crime works, as well as two collections of blog posts on the craft of writing.

When he's not writing he enjoys reading, learning the guitar, watching movies and binge-inhaling great TV series. He's currently spending more time in France than is probably good for him.

On his website you can download a couple of free books and find out more about the others: www.keithdixonnovels.com.

ONE PUNCH

KEITH DIXON

Semiologic Ltd

To Pat and Keith, who lived it.
Well, nearly.

CHAPTER ONE

WHEN NORTON SAW Storey walk into the bar he knew straight away the type of man he was dealing with: alert, cagey, possibly dangerous.

He was maybe six feet tall, had black hair curling on his collar and seemed restless. Norton noticed a couple of women turn their heads to take him in, as though he'd brought a different kind of energy into the place.

But Norton knew all that from the clippings he'd read about Storey before contacting him. He'd been plastered over the newspapers a few weeks ago—hero ex-cop, saving lives, foiling smugglers. Norton's boss, Bran Doyle, liked that. Said Storey would be a good man to have on board now they'd got rid of Monks.

Norton wasn't so sure, thought Doyle was buying into the hype. Look at the way Storey stood at the bar, smiling at the barmaid, struggling to get his wallet from his jacket pocket. Playing the fool, getting a laugh from the girl. He could have done with a shave and his jeans were faded, though he seemed fit: slim and broad in the shoulders, moved well, probably not yet forty.

He wore a brown leather jacket over an open-neck blue shirt, with a name on the pocket Norton couldn't read, and his shoes were scuffed at the front, as though he'd been kicking stones.

He didn't look at ease in this place—maybe it was too high class.

Which is why Norton had chosen it, give Storey a glimpse of what was coming if he took the job. Let him taste the atmosphere, the possibilities. Norton didn't mind if Doyle wanted to hire Storey, but that didn't mean he got an easy pass.

———

Now Storey had seen Norton staring at him and was walking over, pint of beer in his hand, looking down at the shiny table-top, glancing at the other people in the bar before speaking.

'Norton?'

'Yes, take a seat.'

Storey sat in the chair on the far side of the table, still wary. He said, 'Posh place, this. Your local?'

'You think it's posh?'

'Fancy weddings and so on, isn't it? Horse-drawn carriage taking the bride and groom away to a fortnight in Bermuda.'

'We're not here to talk about weddings,' he said. Noticing Storey registered the rebuke but didn't react. 'We've got a proposition for you.'

'So you said. You and your mysterious boss. I'll drink this beer and listen to your pitch but I'm not guaranteeing anything.'

'Understood. You should know this is completely legit, nothing dodgy. You'll be on salary and some benefits.'

Storey was still staring at him. Then he said, 'Were you in the services?'

Norton feeling himself drawing back, surprised. 'Irrelevant.'

Storey shrugged, looking away, taking in the high windows of the bar, the well-toned young couples possibly discussing wedding plans. The talk was low, the surroundings refined. Norton could see the disapproval in his eyes.

Turning back to him, Storey said, 'There's something in your skin-tone, your hair-cut. The way you sit. You're controlled. It was just a guess.'

Norton felt unnerved but before he could speak Storey was talking again.

2

'You said it was something to do with security. What kind of security?'

Norton took a sip from his whisky and counted to five, steadying himself. He said, 'My boss is a businessman, quite well-known in the city. He has a high profile, you might say. He needs someone to take him from place to place—'

'Like a chauffeur?'

'Well, more than that. There'd be some driving but other general duties.'

'Standing around pretending to be alert but actually bored as shit.'

Norton felt himself growing frustrated, the other man seeming to enjoy being contradictory, pushing him. He said, 'It's not like that. It's interesting work, lots of variety, working for a good family.'

'Why me? You can pick up drivers at the Job Centre.'

'Coventry isn't teeming with people with your qualifications.'

Now Storey was grinning, as though Norton was suddenly comical.

'You read my CV in the papers, didn't you, and thought you'd get a thug for cheap. You'd be amazed the offers I had after that little event. TV interviews, book offers. A couple of women wanted to marry me, show their gratitude for my service to the city. I don't know, you shoot someone and people either want to bury you under a ton of shit or make you the new pope.'

Norton shook his head. 'I look at you and I don't see anything special. Admittedly it took some balls doing what you did. But I suppose you'd done it before, shooting someone. I read you were a specialist when you were in the police. Firearms. Must have known what you were doing but still a risk. My job, I never took risks. Anything went wrong, you got a bollocking and maybe half a dozen men dead in the street, dogs licking their ears. Know what I mean?'

Storey looking at him again, his eyes still, like he was thinking something through.

He said, 'When I went down to London I went for the excitement. Coventry was dead. Didn't have all these students, this buzz it's got now. I come back and the place is changed, like it's had a transplant, something new in the bloodstream. I don't know what it is and I don't know whether I like it. You like it, don't you? Makes you think you're still back in Iraq or wherever the hell you were.'

'It was—'

'Well I don't need that buzz any more. I had enough of it in London and now I'm back here I want to be still. I don't want to wake up every morning with my head already pounding because of the noise I can hear in the background, a noise I don't know whether it's really there or not, or whether it's just my imagination gearing me up to deal with the day.'

'I think you've got the wrong idea of what we're asking you to do.'

'I don't think I have. I know exactly what you want me to do. Drive a car, open doors, keep a straight face, say Yes, sir, No, sir.'

'This place needs people like Bran Doyle—people with energy and vision, people who can get things done.'

'I've never heard of him.'

'He wants to meet you.'

'So why didn't he come in person?'

'He wanted me to meet you first. Sound you out.'

'First interview. See if I'll spit on the carpet. So what do you think?'

'I think you won't last forty-eight hours.'

'I'd better meet him then, hadn't I, while I've still got the chance?'

———

Outside, Storey watched Norton drive out of the hotel's car park, then followed. Norton had said it was only a few minutes' drive but be sure to keep up or he'd miss the entrance.

By now he was interested to meet the guy, Doyle, see what he was like and whether he could work for him. He didn't want to work for anyone, but he couldn't afford to live without some income and at least this sounded interesting, so far as it went. After the business with the Syrian he'd laid low for a while, let things settle down. His former boss in London would still take him back but he thought he was past that now—he'd been his own boss for a while, in a manner of speaking, and he found he liked it. So he wanted to keep his freedom but he needed money and he didn't want to prostitute himself for it. Besides, Norton had said it would only be for a couple of months so maybe he could stomach it for that long.

The hotel had been on the edge of town but now the route Norton was taking him had become more countrified. Without city lighting the road suddenly grew darker, so Storey turned on the Volvo's main beams. He didn't know this part of Coventry and was surprised to see the dim outlines of flat fields to his left, while on his right a succession of expensive-looking executive houses with their own driveways slipped by, their living-room lamps just flickering on, the executives well insulated from whatever was happening outside.

Storey wondered what he was going to find. Who was Bran Doyle and what impact was he going to have on his life?

———

Five minutes later Norton's brake lights glowed and he turned and disappeared behind a stand of trees that edged the road. When Storey arrived he saw a wide metal gate was still swinging open, Norton waiting for it to complete its arc before driving through. Storey followed.

Jesus, he thought, looking ahead. *How the other half lives.*

They'd entered a compound, the drive paved in grey slabs, and at the end of its arc, beyond a raised circular decking area, he could see the main house, looming grandly against the night sky. The house seemed in fact to be two identical structures, perhaps barns in a previous life, that were now connected by an entrance foyer made entirely of glass and lower in height than the buildings either side. This entrance and the building on its left were lit up while the other was dark.

As he followed Norton to the parking spaces in front of the house he passed three self-contained cottages, perhaps stables at one time, and looking further, beyond the house, he could see a tennis court, lit-up by lights on tall poles, and what looked like a covered swimming pool next to it. He could tell the house was set in several acres of its own grounds, though in the growing dark he couldn't see the property's furthest limits.

He pulled in next to Norton's car.

Norton was already out and was waiting by the glass door of the entrance.

He seemed to know what Storey would have been thinking, because he said, 'Valued at one and a half million last year. Not that I think he'll ever sell it. Put too much work into getting it right.'

The door opened and a woman somewhere in her fifties stood there, looking first at Norton and then at Storey. He saw she was still shapely and was attractive in a natural way, slim and with a single loop of gold around her neck, her dark hair cut to reach her shoulders and showing traces of highlight here and there.

She said, 'Bran's upstairs. Can this wait?'

'I told him I'd bring Mr Storey tonight, if he'd come,' Norton said. 'Mission accomplished.'

The woman gave him a look then turned a smile on Storey and stepped back.

'I'm Charlotte Doyle, the missus,' she said. 'Please come in.'

Her voice was well-modulated and had the kind of accent Storey usually associated with blue-rinsed stockbrokers' wives from Kent. He'd begun to form some ideas about Bran Doyle but was already having to change them.

He followed Charlotte Doyle across a tiled foyer and through a door into the largest sitting-room he'd ever seen. The walls and ceilings were white, the floor pale wood and the leather chairs a chocolate brown. A huge television was showing a natural history programme but she flicked it off and threw the remote control clattering onto a low glass table.

Now she was turning to him again with her bright smile, saying, 'You boys sit here while I fetch him. He'll be asleep by now, mouth open in front of his television. Norton, try not to get your shoe-polish on the rugs.'

She clipped out of the room and Storey walked further into it, passing the two huge sofas and rounding a table set with six upright chairs, then approaching a dozen or more black and white photos ranged in a display on the far wall.

Norton had followed him and began to explain. 'Doyle in his pomp. That's Sean Connery, without his wig. That one's the man from Eastenders. The one sitting there is Felicity Kendall. I don't know the others.'

The photos were all taken in clubs or restaurants, people grinning in the background, faces pale in the photographic flash. Storey noticed the man who appeared in all the photos was tall and solidly-built, as tall as Connery but broader across the shoulders. He didn't recognise the man's face but saw that it had a definite character. In the photos he was perhaps in his thirties but his features were large, raw, as though they'd been pushed out of shape and then re-formed. It was an eager face, the face of a man who enjoyed life and looked like he wanted to swallow it whole.

He said over his shoulder, 'You haven't told me what he does yet. An actor or something?'

'In a manner of speaking. He'll tell you himself. Try and stop him.'

Storey was about to reply when someone else came into the room at the far end, a girl in her twenties, he guessed, by the lithe way she moved.

Norton saw Storey looking past him and turned around.

'Felicity. We're just waiting for your dad.'

The girl came forward and now Storey could see her better. She had her mother's clear features and direct eyes but there was a colour to her skin that her mother lacked. She wore tight black jeans and a white Fruit of the Loom tee-shirt and her red hair was tied back in a short pony-tail.

Without holding out her hand, she said, 'I'm Fliss. Are you the new man?'

Storey said, 'That depends on whether your dad passes the interview. Too soon to say but it's not looking good so far.'

A smile flitted over her face but she didn't give in to it completely, turning to Norton instead to say, 'Tell Dad I'm out with Darren, will you? I'll be back later.'

'Your wish, etc.'

She looked at them both again, one after the other, as if checking they'd understood their instructions, then turned and left.

Storey said, 'She still lives with mum and dad?'

'You've seen the place. Why would you move out? She's practically got a wing to herself.'

'A bird's got to fly the coop eventually. Otherwise the coop gets torn apart.'

'You do Chinese wisdom?'

'Only in my spare time. When I'm not practising my levitation.'

———

Storey heard voices outside the room, Felicity talking to someone, then an older version of the man from the photos walked in. Bran Doyle. He wore a black shirt with a wide collar and green cargo pants with big pockets. He was as large as Storey expected, having seen the photos, but moved swiftly with a contained energy. Storey thought he was probably in his early sixties but appeared ten years younger. He had a broad, firm chest and hands like a bricklayer.

He was standing now with those hands on his hips, about ten feet from Storey, looking him up and down.

He said, 'I'm Bran Doyle and this is my patch. Nice of you to come. I read about you in the paper and told Norton I wanted to meet you. Been banned from driving for twelve months, bloody stupid. Said I'd get myself a driver. I did my research and read up on you but on second thoughts I reckon you ain't up to it. Ran away from your job with the cops then got yourself caught up in something tasty. Ratted out your gang and shot a bloke in

8

the 'ead. What use is that to me? I could just as soon get one of our own up here. There's a lad in Brixton wants to come up and work for me. Why should I go outside, especially as you was one of them rotten bastards what worked in the police? Hey, come back 'ere. I ain't fuckin' finished talking to you yet.'

Storey was nearly out of the room. Stopping, he turned back and said, 'I'm loving your interview technique but I've got another engagement.'

Doyle grinning. 'Good. What else?'

'I don't like rich people who are full of themselves and I won't work for you if I'm like one of those lucky charms you hang around your neck.'

'I'm not rich.'

Storey laughed. 'You're not poor.'

'Nothing wrong with being poor.'

'I never said there was. But if you live in a place like this and say you're not rich you've got a weird view of the world.'

Doyle paused, glanced at Norton, who looked as though he'd been enjoying the conversation.

'Fetch us a couple of whiskeys, Craig, there's a good 'un.'

———

Norton left and Doyle watched him, then sat on one of the brown sofas. Storey noticed he still had all his hair but his face was lined, with scars showing around the eyes.

Doyle said, 'You give as good as you get, don't you? I like that in a lackey. Sick to death of people who tell you what you want to hear. Norton's a good man but he's still scared of me. You're not, are you? No use to me if you are. But I expect you knew that.'

'I don't play games.'

'Sit down. Take the weight off your principles.'

'I might not be stopping.'

'Were you looking at my photos? A bit old now. I should get new ones, though I don't meet the same people up here as I did in London. You haven't asked what I want you to do—or did Norton lay it out?'

Storey sat facing him, enjoying the man's ability to dance around the subject as if it were all part of the same conversation, the subject being himself. Doyle sat on his sofa like a ton weight, not just owning it but laying claim to everything in the room through it—the coffee table, the magazines scattered on its shiny surface, the unlit logs in the marble fireplace, the patterned stretcher that lay lengthwise on the dining table ... Everything he looked at, he owned, and Storey wondered what it must be like to have that power. Or at least to think you had it.

Doyle said, 'You met the missus, didn't you? She liked you. Said you'd do. Tonight must be like one big interview, from your perspective.'

'I don't think I want the job.'

'The fuck do you know? You haven't talked to me about it yet. I haven't had chance to exercise the full extent of my fucking charms on you. Incidentally, you don't mind bad language, do you? Can't help meself. What you get being brought up in a London armpit. Eloquence comes second to a punch in the gob.'

———

Norton came in with two glasses, handed one to each man then moved away.

Doyle said, 'What's your opinion, Craig? You've had a chance to see Mr Storey here at close quarters.'

Norton glanced at Storey, then said to Doyle. 'He can drive, so he's qualified. Thinks a lot of himself, but so do you, so you're square.'

'He says he doesn't want the job. Do you think we could persuade him?'

'All the press articles said he was a man of principle. Perhaps he's making a point.'

Doyle said nothing, swirling the liquid in his glass, and Storey took this as a cue and tasted his drink—he knew nothing about whiskey but it was smooth and burned the back of his throat in a way that suggested it was a good brand.

Doyle said, 'You've gone quiet.'

'You two are doing all the talking. I'm just enjoying the view.'

'So do you want to play with us or not? Nice big car to drive, you can live in one of the cottages for a couple of months, we'll feed you and a woman will come in and do your laundry and cleaning. All you have to do is smile at me and make sure the petrol tank's full.'

'What happened to your previous driver?'

Doyle glanced at Norton, saying, 'Difference of opinion. We had to let him go. Now you're looking at me as if I left him face down in a fuckin' ditch. Don't worry—I can give you his phone number if you want to talk to him.'

'What did you do? I mean, for a living? Why all those photos with famous people?'

Doyle looked away for the first time. Storey thought maybe he was embarrassed.

'People wanted to be near me,' Doyle said. 'I was famous in some circles because I was a fighter. A boxer.'

'I've never heard of you.'

'You wouldn't have. I wasn't on telly. Started out, I'd show up at a fair where people were selling cars. There'd be a challenge and I'd knock down a couple of people and walk off with five hundred quid in my pocket. Then it escalated. By the time I finished I was fighting in working-men's clubs and the back rooms of pubs. Five grand a time, or more. These famous people would roll up at the door, watch me fight for a couple of minutes—that's how long it usually took—then they'd want to rub the top of my head for luck.'

'Looking at this place you had a lot of fights at five grand a piece.'

'You've got the wrong end of the stick, my man. I didn't make money from boxing. I made it from property. Investments. Done well in London then moved up here, bought this place when it was a shithole and done it up. And I'm still ducking and diving.'

Storey said, 'Well, thanks for the whiskey and the biography, but I don't think I'll fit in here.'

'Sorry to hear that.'

Storey put his glass down and stood up. He said, 'Were you a good boxer?'

11

Doyle was also standing now. 'Terrible boxer. Good fighter. Do you know what they called me?'

'No idea.'

'I'd knock 'em down so quick they called me One Punch Doyle. Bear that in mind.'

CHAPTER TWO

S TOREY WAS WASHING his car the next morning when
Jackie West called. He stood with one hand on the roof of
his Volvo and the other gingerly holding his phone between
wet fingers.

She surprised him by saying, 'So are you going to take the job
or not?'

'What job's that?'

'Don't be coy, Storey.'

'Excuse the hell out of me, but I thought I was exercising
my right to privacy by not sharing my thoughts with the state
apparatus.'

'Where are you?'

'At home.'

'Can I come visit you? We have to talk.'

Storey saw himself briefly as the neighbours might see him,
standing with a bucket of water next to a wet car holding his
phone by his ear as if it were a bomb.

He said, 'No, say what you have to say now. And you can
start by telling me how the hell you know what I've been doing.
Are you stalking me?'

She laughed. 'You wish. I can't tell you what I know, or how,
but here's a piece of advice: stay away from Bran Doyle.'

Jackie West was the woman police officer he'd rescued from the Syrian arms dealer. There'd been a moment when he'd considered going out with her on a permanent basis, but he'd realised in the end she was too wrapped up in her job, and if he saw her more frequently then he'd be drawn into her circle and be mixing with coppers again.

He didn't want that.

So he'd allowed the relationship—if that's what it was—to drift away. She hadn't seemed too upset and still called him occasionally to pass the time—or check up on him, he wasn't sure which.

———

Now he said, 'I had every intention of staying away from him but now you've changed my mind.'

'Why did he come to you? Who made first contact?'

'You've been listening in, you must know that. Where are the bugs, incidentally—phones? Lights?'

'If he came to you first then you're still on safe ground. Tell him you don't want the job. Tell him to find someone else.'

'Why are you listening in? He must have done something serious for you to put bugs in his house. To get the permission.'

She hesitated, then said, 'Yes, we think he's done something serious. I can't say what and you know why. I'm breaking house rules by telling you this much anyway.'

'So why are you?'

'You want me to say I still have feelings for you, make you feel better? Give it up, Storey. We both knew it'd run its course. I'm telling you because I don't want you screwing things up, getting involved. Like last time.'

'You mean that last time when I broke a smuggling ring and helped prevent two suicides? *That* last time?'

Now he heard the exasperation in her voice. 'You can twist it how you want, but you nearly got me killed and we'd have—'

'What? Found those two women? Who you didn't even know existed?'

Storey heard himself arguing with a woman he liked and closed his eyes. He didn't want to do this, give himself credit for something he'd got involved in almost by accident. And he didn't want to put Jackie West on the defensive.

He said, 'Look, I need the money. They're telling me it's a proper job, mostly driving, and if you've got the place bugged you'll know all that anyway.'

'I thought you weren't going to take it?'

'Well your powers of persuasion have worked wonders. I'll try not to mention your name when I'm telling my new employers about this conversation.'

'You better not—'

'Gotta go. Something's come up.'

Charlotte Doyle was driving a cream coloured Alfa Romeo sports car, two seats, soft top, black leather interior. She parked behind Storey's Volvo and opened the door, gathering her bag.

Storey put away his phone and squeezed out the sponge he'd been using.

Charlotte Doyle climbed out and smiled at him. She was wearing a short black leather jacket with a high collar over a pale blouse and cream skirt. It was as though she was trying to match the colour scheme of the car. She moved towards him, saying, 'Can we go inside, Mr Storey? I don't like being stared at.'

He nearly told her not to drive a car like that, then, but instead led the way across the short expanse of grass to his garden gate and then inside the house, seeing it as she would—cramped, under-furnished and in need of a couple of coats of paint.

He smelled her perfume behind him as she entered and felt a strange frisson that was almost sexual. He ignored it and led her into the living-room.

She barely glanced at her surroundings, saying, 'I want you to take the job with Bran. He left all these cuttings lying around about you, which I read, and I think you'd be good to have at the house.'

Storey looked down, avoiding her eyes, amazed at all the advice he was getting recently. He wondered whether he came over as indecisive so people thought they needed to give him a push.

He said, 'I've already said no, Mrs Doyle.'

'So he told me. And that's why I want you there.' She glanced at the room and saw the sofa and sat down on it, her shapely legs suddenly appearing from beneath the hem of her skirt. 'It's because you don't want the job that I want you to take it.'

'I know where you're going with this.'

She was surprised. 'You do?'

'He already told me he was surrounded by lapdogs so he wanted someone who'd say no to him.'

'That's what he says, but it's not true. He actually wants people to agree with him, though he doesn't know it.'

'So you don't agree with him and you're saying it's in his best interests if someone's there to argue with him?'

She smiled at him and said nothing.

———

He said, 'I'M not a nursemaid, Mrs Doyle. It's not my job to look after him and stop him getting into trouble. Besides, I've never worked security before, not like this, anyway, so I wouldn't know where to begin.'

'Forget the security. Craig Norton largely takes care of that. What they've done, they've tried to make your job sound bigger to interest you, but mostly you'll be driving him around, meetings and so on. He's always having meetings. Anything else you need to know about security or suchlike you'll learn as you go along.'

Storey sat in the single armchair by the window. He said, 'Why is it important to you I take the job?'

Her eyes slid away. 'He needs someone who can give him good advice. Unfortunately that's not me any more. At least, when I give it he doesn't listen.'

'You're not expecting me to report to you, I hope.'

'Of course not, you'll be working for Bran. Craig will try to boss you around a little but you can always refer upwards to Bran.'

Storey wondered how long he could keep this up. After Jackie West's call he'd decided to take the job anyway—if Doyle was interesting to the police then he'd probably be interesting to work for. Now he realised he didn't like deceiving this woman any longer.

But before he could say anything, she added, 'You can stay in one of the cottages. Rent this place to someone, then you wouldn't have to drive out to us every morning. That was one of the problems with Monks—he was never there when Bran needed him, which is hopeless in a driver.'

Storey stood up and looked out of his front window, wanting to show that he was giving it some thought. If they wanted to try hard to recruit him he wasn't going to appear a pushover.

He said, 'Does he know you're here? Or Norton?'

'I very much doubt it. Bran probably thinks I'm out spending his money.'

'I'm not promising anything, but I'll talk to Norton.'

'You don't have to talk to him, you can tell me.'

'If he's going to be my boss it's probably best if I talk to him direct, isn't it?'

The brightness of the previous evening had returned to her eyes, as though he'd taken a burden from her. She stood up and offered her hand. It was small and delicate and one finger held a single ornate ring containing a large blue stone. He took her fingers briefly and then let go: she was so delicate it felt like an infringement of privacy.

She said, 'It would be nice if you could start tonight. We're having a bit of a celebration so it would be a good opportunity for you to meet some people, get settled in. You can bring some things and I'll get Norton to show you your cottage.'

'You don't waste any time, do you?'

She grinned, moving away and not answering the question. 'You were teasing me, weren't you? You were going to take the job all along.'

'What makes you say that?'
'We're a very persuasive family. You'll see.'

CHAPTER THREE

H E'D BEEN TOLD by Norton to turn up at six, but when he arrived at the house he saw the party had already started. The entrance gate was open and as he drove into the compound he saw a dozen cars were parked at angles in front of the house like puppies trying to find a teat. He noticed a few balloons had been stuck to the windows of the house and to the crossbar of the fake lamppost that stood near the deck. This was a large circular area facing the entrance and made safe by a waist-high wooden bar, the whole thing overlooking an overgrown pond surrounded by tall reeds. Two striped chairs faced the water.

He parked by the cottage nearest to the house, the one Norton had said would be his. He'd been told to park, then come through the side door of the main house, via the kitchen, to get the key and receive further instructions.

He pulled up his shirt collar and walked the fifty yards or so to the house. Before he arrived at the side door he could hear the noise from inside. It sounded like a live band were playing sixties hits but he could hear voices talking loudly over the music as well. He peered through the glass of the kitchen door, saw a man sitting at a table, and went in.

The kitchen was almost as big as the living-room he'd seen the night before. An island on wheels at one end of the space was piled high with plates of two sizes, and an assortment of serving dishes, each filled with food under clingfilm, stood on one of the counters. A forest of glasses stood upside down on a separate counter.

Storey nodded at the man at the table, who wore a black high-neck jumper and a thin moustache. His hair was also black and cut short at the sides though longer on top. Storey thought he looked somewhere around twenty-two, twenty-three, his features clear and attractive, though there was something hard in his eyes. He was peeling an apple with a knife, the peel curling around in one piece. He looked up at Storey, said, 'You're the new man.'

He didn't seem to have an attitude about it so Storey wondered why it sounded like an accusation.

He said, 'Norton about? I was told to come here for a key.'

The man had stopped peeling and now cut off a chunk of the apple and knifed it into his mouth.

He said, 'You're the man who shoots people, aren't you?'

'Paul Storey in real life. You are?'

'Darren.' When Storey said nothing he was compelled to add, 'I help out around here. As you see, I'm guarding the food from passing layabouts.'

'Are there many?'

'None. I'm very good at it. What do you think of this place?'

'I've seen worse kitchens.'

Darren snorted. 'The house, the grounds, the mini-empire Bran's set up.'

'It's all very white. Except the grass. And the wood.'

'He bought it three years ago today. That's what we're celebrating. Three-year anniversary. Practically gutted the place, made cottages out of the stables, linked the original farmhouse to the barn next door using that glass entrance hall. Put in that pond or lake or whatever the hell he calls it. The farmer who owned it still lives near here, down the road. Bran brought him in the other day to show him around, show what he's made of it. Know what the guy said?'

'He should have asked for more money?'

'He said he wouldn't let one of his cows live in it. Hated it. Thought Bran had ripped out all the character and replaced it with modern crap.'

'What do you think?'

Darren seemed surprised to be asked. 'Me? I don't care. I don't live here.'

'But you're seeing Felicity Doyle.'

The man's eyes came up and met Storey's warily.

'How do you know that?'

'It was mentioned yesterday.'

Storey thought the other man's pale skin had turned a shade pinker, and now he stood up and walked to one of the counters, pulling open a door to show a rubbish bin attached to it. He dropped the apple peel and core inside, then rinsed his knife under a tap and placed it on the draining board.

He said, 'You go through that door and you'll come out at the foot of the stairs. The door on the other side'll take you where the action is. Norton should be there, watching people over a glass of strong water.'

He walked past Storey and left through the door to the outside, Storey wondering whether he was embarrassed or angry to be accused of dating the boss's daughter.

———

He stuck with Darren's directions but didn't need to—he could have just followed the noise. The last door opened into the same living-room he'd been in the previous night, though it had been reconfigured. A trio of drummer, keyboards and singer/guitarist had been set up against the far wall, next to the black and white photos. They were into a medley of Rolling Stones numbers now, played low-key and jazzed up a little, the rhythm different, perhaps better suited to their audience.

The ages of the people in the room ranged between thirty and seventy, Storey guessed, all of them talking loudly and sipping sparkling white drinks from flutes. A small group was gathered around Bran Doyle, whose voice he heard narrating a convoluted story, while in the opposite corner he saw Charlotte Doyle looking cool in pale blue and surrounded by a group of women who all seemed to be talking to her at once.

A voice in his ear said, 'Welcome to your new world.'

Storey turned, found Norton behind him looking over his shoulder at the crowd. He was carrying a glass containing a liquid Storey thought looked like tap water.

Storey said, 'Is it like this every night?'

'More nights than is good for any of us. Doyle likes a crowd. Let's get you settled.'

He followed Norton through the crowd and out of the room, into the entrance foyer. Norton shuffled through some keys hanging on a rail by the door, said, 'This is the one,' then went outside, Storey close behind.

He asked whether Storey had brought a bag and Storey said it was in the car and they walked along one of the paved paths between the house and the row of cottages until they reached the Volvo. Storey wondering what he'd got himself into as he lifted his bag from the boot, watching Norton fiddling with the door lock before managing to get it open. Thinking to himself it was a different situation and he had to give himself time to get used to it. Take a breath.

They went in and Norton showed him around—a tiny hallway led to a small lounge, with sofa and TV, then through to a well-equipped kitchen, a fair-sized bedroom upstairs and a bathroom with shower. Every room painted white, all the floors and work surfaces in the same blond wood as the main house. Food in the fridge and soap in the bathroom.

Norton gave him the keys and asked whether he knew he'd be on duty tonight.

Storey said, 'How would I know? You didn't mention it when I called to say I'd take the offer.'

Norton looked at him speculatively. 'I wondered if someone else might have talked to you. Convinced you to change your mind. Last night you were pretty definitive.'

Storey all innocent, now, putting the key on his keyring and avoiding Norton's eyes. 'I change my mind on a daily basis. What shall I wear? Do I get a uniform? A peaked cap?'

Norton looked him up and down. 'Take off that bloody leather jacket and you'll do. I'll see you up there in ten minutes, all right?'

An hour later Storey was beginning to admire the patience of Presidential security details. When he'd been an ordinary policeman, before graduating to the firearms division, he'd done his share of crowd control—football matches, ministerial visits to local factories, protecting politicians from protesters. But at least there'd been plenty to look at, usually hundreds of different faces to watch, to follow and track, to lip read.

Here there were maybe fifty people and he thought he knew them all intimately after twenty minutes. He'd spent some time wondering who they were: neighbours from the executive houses down the road? Business associates? Local bigwigs, or people from the council? Given Jackie West's interest in Doyle, were any of them outright crooks? He looked at the men, trying to see signs of villainy in the way they spoke or their body language.

And he overheard them talking, too. Discussing recent holidays. Asking about each other's kids, or parents, or former spouses.

In the end he thought they were just ordinary people, perhaps better-heeled than average, but not especially villainous or exciting.

And then he began wondering why Doyle even thought it necessary to have 'security' on hand for a private party. What did he think was going to happen? Did these parties degenerate into slanging matches, all the grey hair getting mussed, the ties undone, the ladies throwing their jewellery at each other? He

23

thought about the next two months and whether he'd be able to stand it, if this was the level of excitement he was expected to live with.

Then it got interesting when he heard a raised voice outside the main room. He wandered through to the entrance hall, feeling the change in the air as he arrived. The glass door was open and two men were squaring up to each other—one in jeans and a denim shirt with copper buttons, the other obviously a guest in a black suit and white shirt, his ginger hair thick and straggly. They were both in their twenties and by the time he arrived they were further into the row—as Storey watched, the man in the suit grabbed the other man by the throat and marched him out through the door, pushing him on to the paving slabs. The other man tried to stay upright but he lost his footing and fell down on all fours, Storey seeing too late that the man's vulnerable position didn't prevent the first man bending down and punching him on the side of the face.

Now Storey heard yelling and realised it had been there for a while, in the background—a girl in a short black dress and shiny high heels standing back from the doorway, fixated on the pair of fighters, her face bloated and pink, screaming encouragement at the man on the floor.

Storey arrived just as the suited man was drawing back to kick the other one, Storey catching him by the arm so he lost his balance and stumbled backwards, which didn't stop him pivoting and aiming a punch at Storey's head. Storey let it slip by and took the man's arm under his own armpit, straightening him up. He saw briefly the anger in the man's grey eyes before he turned off a switch behind them and calmed down instantly and said, 'All right, all right. This bastard's trying to gatecrash. I'm doing you a fucking favour.'

Storey walked backwards, still with the man's arm under his own, keeping him on his toes, then released him into the house. The girl had stopped yelling but still hadn't moved, her face ripe with exertion. He bent down to the man in jeans, saying, 'You okay?'

Then standing back as the man rose to his feet, brushing down the front of his shirt and rubbing his jaw. His eyes were as small and hard as peashell. 'Fuck off, and tell Billy Jenkins I know where he lives.'

'Next time take the fight there.'

The man said nothing, threw a look at the door behind Storey, seized the girl's arm and walked off, Storey watching them climb into a dusty Vauxhall with orange stripes painted down its side.

He turned and Norton was there, studying him.

'I can't turn my back two minutes and you're in trouble.'

'I was waiting for my manager to arrive. He never did.'

Norton waved him inside then closed the door behind them, gesturing towards the man Storey had restrained, who was now in the main room again, visible from where they stood, and apparently having a good time, probably talking about the fight.

Norton said, 'Not a good idea to get on Billy Jenkins' bad side.'

'Is he important?'

'Not as much as he thinks he is. Which is the problem. Get back in there and show your face. Everything's all right, nothing to worry about. You needn't tell Doyle about this.'

Storey checked his clothing before moving back into the room, brushing down his own shirt, pulling out his cuffs, wondering why Norton was already helping him conceal unpleasant news from their boss.

He had two more encounters that night which, when he thought about them later, struck him as odd.

An hour after the fight a woman his own age walked up to him and smiled. She had large eyes in an oval face and blonde hair that was straight and hung mostly to one side, perhaps like a film star from the thirties, and he'd seen her across the room and noticed she had a nice shape. He'd watched her because it was easy to do, and saw she often hovered on the edge of conversations without getting involved. She seemed to be on her own because she never stood by a solo male for any length of time, no one who seemed to pay her undue attention, anyway.

Now she was saying, 'Who are you, then? Watching me from the other side of the room like a stalker and not even coming over to talk to me. Your wife here somewhere?'

'I'm staff. If I'm seen talking to guests they take me out back and horsewhip me.'

'Staff? Oh, you mean like one of Norton's men. Security.'

'He has men? I was led to believe I'd be the star of the show.'

She smiled, showing good teeth, and two dimples appeared on her cheeks. Storey thought it was a very girlish feature and wondered whether she was aware of it. He knew his height was attractive to some women, and the way his hair curled on his collar, but he'd never found a way to take advantage of these natural features. If that was what he wanted.

She said, 'I say men ... there was someone called Monks, but he doesn't seem to be around any more. Apart from that, you're right. Maybe I've been exaggerating his manpower in my head. Oh, I'm staff too. Katherine, everyone calls me Kate.'

Storey wanted to ask what she did but felt it was too obvious a question and he never liked being obvious with women. He thought it was probably why all his relationships were short and not often sweet.

She seemed to know what was going on for him, though, because she added, 'I'm Doyle's tame decorator. I've done all his houses. We usually argue about which shade of white he wants to use.'

'Glad you cleared that up before I asked.'

'It's not so much the colour scheme he wants from me, it's the kitting out—finding the kitchen cabinets, the sofas, the lamps, the bookcases. He hates doing all that and Madam's not much better.'

'She seems to have an eye for clothes.'

'You've noticed. Tell her from time to time, you'll get a raise.'

Storey wanted to carry on talking to her but thought he should at least act like a professional. So he shifted his position and looked past her into the room, which she noticed straight away, saying, 'Oh, sorry, you're working, aren't you?'

'It's hard to work when you're distracted.'

She poked him in the chest with a finger. 'I believe that's the nicest thing ever said to me by a security guard.'

'Watch out, here's the boss.'

He'd seen Doyle moving towards them through the crowd and gave him a small nod, Doyle snaking an arm around Kate's middle and pulling her towards him. Storey thought he was drunk.

Raising his voice above the music, Doyle said to him, 'Watch this one, Storey. Maneater at large. Stay on your guard, am I right, darlin'?' — aiming this last question at Kate so closely she pulled her face away from his.

Looking him in the eye, she said, 'You're always right, Bran. You can never be wrong.'

Doyle turned and raised his eyebrows at Storey as if to say, 'See what I mean?' then let go of her waist. He said, 'Enjoy yourselves, I've got to circulate,' and moved away. Storey thought he seemed hurt.

Watching him leave, Kate said, 'I shouldn't have said that.'

'What, will he have words with you later?'

'Bran? No—I meant he'll worry about it, wonder whether he's upset me. He acts like a sexist pig sometimes but in fact he's protective towards me. What he's just said to you is probably his way of warning you off. Are you warned?'

'Not especially.'

'Good. One day I'll show you what he's having me do in the loft. '

'Does it involve white paint?'

'Far from it. See you around.'

She was moving away as she said this, looking over her shoulder at him, making sure he was intrigued.

It was hard for him to say he wasn't.

The second event was when Charlotte Doyle approached him as the evening was winding down, people saying their goodbyes, scurries of cold air swirling into the room from time to time as the front door was opened and closed.

She leaned close, so close he could see the powder on the tops of her breasts, and said, 'Thank you for taking the job.'

Storey shifted backwards to what he thought was an appropriate distance, saying, 'I needed the money.'

'You don't give anything away, do you? You don't take any prisoners. Very insular young man.'

'I'm sorry if I seem ungrateful.'

'It's not a matter of gratitude,' she said quickly, her voice snapping out the words. 'You could loosen up. Or is that poker fixed permanently up your backside?'

'Are you all right?'

'Why, are you suggesting something?'

'Of course not.'

'I hope not. You can be gone as quickly as you came.'

'I know.'

'My husband's a powerful man.'

'Everyone tells me.'

'He's still got friends, contacts. Get your hands off me.'

'I thought you'd be more comfortable in some fresh air.'

She stood upright. 'And away from these people ... all right, all right, you can let go. I'm calm now. Look at me, aren't I calm?'

'Very.'

He'd managed to walk her into the entrance hall but she didn't seem to have noticed.

'My husband is a very powerful man. People in London still look up to him. Because he's still got something they want.'

'Are you sure you should be telling me these things?'

She looked at him as though she didn't know who he was. 'Bran and I have no secrets. Been married twenty-eight years come July and he still loves me.'

'Why wouldn't he? You're a very attractive woman.'

'Am I?' Now there was doubt in her face and Storey wished he'd said nothing. She said, 'Do you think that's all it is, though? Being attractive? Is that enough to keep a marriage together — mutual attraction?'

'It can't hurt.'

Then Felicity was there, talking in her mother's ear and leading her gently away, throwing a glance back at Storey but saying nothing to him, moving slowly through the guests now putting their coats on, murmuring and nodding to them as she continued to lead her mother to the rear staircase. He realised it was the second time a woman had glanced over her shoulder at him.

Storey realised he liked her. Strangely, he liked her mother, too.

By one o'clock he'd helped the caterers clear the tables and pack up their dirty dishes and glasses in the plastic boxes they'd brought for the occasion.

Doyle was sitting on one of the sofas with a glass in his hand, alternately watching the tidying activity around him and dropping off into a brief nap. Storey thought his voice would be hoarse from all the talking he'd done, but he'd seemed to be in his element, touring the room, talking to everyone, telling stories about the famous people he'd met, drinking an unending supply of liquor.

Storey noticed that Norton had vanished when the clearing-up had started but now he reappeared, as neat as ever, tie done tight to the throat, little band of white handkerchief showing above the breast pocket of his tweed jacket, trousers sharply creased. He was like a mannequin brought out to demonstrate what an ex-soldier of a certain kind should look like. Storey wondered if he had friends from his time in the army who still called him Major.

He told Storey he could go, and take some of the cake from the kitchen if he wanted. There was far too much left for the family to deal with.

Storey said, 'I like cake.'

'Saturday tomorrow. Nothing immediately in the agenda. Be around after ten, in case.'

Storey went through into the kitchen and saw that Darren had returned and was sitting at the table again, this time with Billy Jenkins, the man involved in the fight he'd broken up earlier.

When Jenkins noticed Storey a light came into the back of his eyes, Storey remembering the man had been drinking all night, off in a corner with a group of men his own age and younger than all the other guests.

Jenkins said, standing up, 'You're the bastard nearly broke my arm.'

'I did you a service.'

'How do you reckon that?'

'If you'd have caught him with your boot, that boy, you'd be up before the magistrate Monday morning for Actual Bodily Harm. At least six months in the nick, probably more. Ruins your day.'

'What are you, a fucking copper?'

Storey grinned. 'No, I'm the bastard who nearly broke your arm. Want to try again?'

Despite the confusion in his face Jenkins was coming around the table when he suddenly stopped. Storey sensed someone behind him and turned.

Bran Doyle was standing in his characteristic pose, hands on hips, frowning. He said, 'Raised voices, boys, when my good lady wife is upstairs catchin' forty winks? That's not nice, is it?'

———

Storey stood aside as Doyle came further in. He walked up to Jenkins and said, 'You … it's Billy, isn't it?'

'Yes, sir, Billy Jenkins, sir.'

'You don't have to Sir me … just don't let me catch you squaring up to a man in my kitchen again. Got it? You want to fight, you do it elsewhere. Darren, take him home.'

'I was going to have a word with Felicity …'

'Never mind that. I'll tell her you said hello. Now fuck off, the pair of you.'

Storey made to leave with them but Doyle caught his arm, holding him till Jenkins and Darren had left.

Then he turned face on to Storey and glanced around the kitchen. It was empty and quiet apart from the chugging of a dishwasher. He said, 'You did all right tonight. I give it the *mein host* routine but I used to work as a bouncer when I was a kid so I know what you was up to, keeping things in check.'

'It's not brain surgery.'

'Take the compliment, don't be an arsehole. And look, take no notice of Darren and his mates but watch him.'

'Jenkins?'

'No, not him, he's just a fuckin' dimwit. Darren. He's young, younger than Felicity, and he doesn't know what he's up to yet. What you don't know is he's Craig Norton's nephew. We're doing him a favour by having him around, running errands, letting him find his feet. And Fliss seems to like him, so we'll see how that goes.'

He reached out a hand and patted Storey on the shoulder. 'Keep it up. See you tomorrow.'

Back in his room Storey laid on his bed and ate a piece of lemon cake, wondering why he was feeling guilty about the listening devices spread around Doyle's glistening white mansion, and also wondering what it was that Doyle was supposed to have done.

CHAPTER FOUR

T HE NEXT MORNING Storey ate some cornflakes and drank some orange juice, then sat in his living room for half an hour learning how his television functioned. As for work, was he supposed to wait for a phone call? Or would Doyle knock on the door with car keys dangling from his thick fingers, waiting to be driven somewhere?

He had no idea what his duties were supposed to be.

Looking out of his front window towards the house he thought it looked dead. He expected to see some signs of life in the house by eleven o'clock, and there was nothing.

When he went outside the air was chill and he could hear the traffic from the centre of town—like London, the noise never ended, there was always movement, something happening. He breathed deeply and walked towards the house.

———

He pushed open the kitchen door and called out a Hello, but got no reply so went in anyway. He wondered why the air after parties was always vaguely pathetic—it smelled of alcohol and was underpinned by the dank odour of stale bread.

The place seemed empty. Deserted. As though it had all been a con-trick and he was about to discover the whole evening was a lie created for a TV show, Doyle was a TV presenter and the women—Charlotte, Felicity, Kate—had been tasked with trying to seduce him while being secretly filmed. One of them had nearly succeeded, though when he thought about it, he didn't know which one.

He went out the rear exit of the kitchen and stood at the foot of the stairs, listening intently. Then he started to walk up the stairs, trying to look casual, wondering whether the bugs Jackie West's people had planted also included miniature cameras and idle coppers were currently pointing at their screens and laughing, look at him, the old man, still thinks he's in uniform, keeping the peace ...

The stairs opened to a wide landing and a corridor with five doors, two of which were open, one showing the end of a bath, the other an unmade bed, its clothing thick and expensive, a couple of paperbacks on the bedside table nearest to him. On the walls of the landing and along the corridor were more black-and-white photos, this time Doyle posing in shorts and boxing gloves, staring at the camera and trying to frighten it.

He stood and glanced down the corridor, wondering what he would say if one of the doors were wrenched open and he was confronted by Charlotte Doyle in a dressing gown, her hair in curlers. Could he say he was looking for her husband? Or the toilet? Or would she just smile shyly and retreat into the room crooking a finger ...

There was another flight of stairs at the end of the corridor, and as he was standing looking up at it, a head appeared over the banister.

Kate, the decorator, her hair pushed back under a band.

She said, 'I thought I heard someone—was that you?'

'I like to give a warning before I burgle a place. Where is everyone?'

'Emergency shopping expedition. Shoes to be bought. And I suppose bread and meat and stuff. Even Doyles have to eat.'

'I thought driving was my job.'

'Charlotte drives when they go out together. Come up, I said I was going to show you something, didn't I?'

33

Now validated, he went up the stairs and came out immediately into the loft, boarded underfoot and with three large mansard windows angled into the roof. There was one of Doyle's customary brown sofas already up there, and as he turned he saw a pool table covered in blue baize and a digital projector attached high on one of the roof beams, aimed at the end gable, which had a still-rolled projection screen suspended in front of it.

Kate had seen where he was looking. 'All electronic. Press a button the screen comes down. Another one, the home theatre system revs up. But none of that is what you're here to look at.'

He turned again and knew immediately what she meant. On the far wall, opposite the door, a huge mural had been painted on the brickwork. It looked to Storey like the New York skyline, with some changes. So the Statue of Liberty and Brooklyn Bridge and the Empire State Building were all visible together, painted as if the scene were a night-time view—Liberty lit from beneath, the Empire State filled with little squares of office light, the sky turning to a pink dusk behind them.

Kate said, 'Before you say anything, don't say a word. Not my idea. Not even Bran's. It was Felicity who came up with it. She went there a couple of years ago and persuaded Bran to have this monstrosity done up here, like a memento. This'll be his room and she won't see much of it, but I don't suppose he cares one way or the other.'

'Other than the fact it's not white.'

She'd been standing next to him, looking at the scene, Storey aware of her physical presence, and now she said, 'Thank Christ it's nearly finished. That's why I'm here today, in case you were wondering. I want to finish the damn thing and go.'

'I don't know much about painting.'

'Don't worry about it, nobody does. It's a complete mystery, even to professionals like me.' She said it with absolute seriousness but he knew she was joking—but at least she was laughing with him, not at him. She went on, 'Murals are my thing but I prefer to do what I want, not according to other people's designs. I've realised I don't like working to order.'

'It seems to me you don't fit here.'

She was amused by this. 'You know me so well already?'

'You're obviously artistic. I'm not so sure about the Doyles. Not much art on the walls downstairs. Other than photos of himself.'

Now she gave him a longer look, as if she were analysing what he'd just said. 'You sure you work in security? You're not a bohemian sent along by Greenpeace to solicit donations?'

'As I said, I don't know anything about art or painting. But I can tell when it's not there.'

She said, 'Anyway, I'm out of here when this is done.'

'Doesn't he pay well enough?'

'I don't like the atmosphere.'

'What sort of atmosphere?'

'Male testosterone gone to seed.'

'Doyle? I'm shocked.'

'Not just him. Norton. Darren and his friends.'

'I'm thinking I'm included in that lot.'

Now she grinned slyly up at him, and he saw the dimples again, and liked them again.

She said, 'Until you prove otherwise, yes. Let's go have a drink.'

He agreed, because he'd realised now he liked Kate the best of the three women.

'So my business is going nowhere, I'm struggling to pay myself and my one staff member, when this man Doyle comes into the shop, looks at some of the photos of my work, and tells me he's got three properties he needs doing up and decorating. Just like that. I nearly kissed him. This was what, seven years ago now, and I shut the shop anyway—the girl I had with me got married and I had all the work I could do but no more, and you reach the moment when you have to make a decision: do I just work for me, or do I make a business? Well, I hadn't done great at making a business so I thought maybe I'll just take the work day by day, see how it goes. If it all goes to shit then I'll get a job packing cheese or something and paint watercolours at the weekends. You did ask.'

They were sitting at the kitchen table with coffees, the house still empty around them, Storey wondering from time to time what he was doing. That thing where a wheel turns and suddenly you're in a strange place, talking to a strange person as though you'd known them forever. Still wondering whether listening devices were installed in the pot-rack hanging over the table or in the halogen downlighters.

He said, 'Your accent's North London, isn't it?'

'Good detective work, Mr Storey. I came to college up here and stayed. I'd be in Brighton if I'd gone to their art school, but I didn't. I tend to stick where I land, like a fly in treacle.'

'So where were Doyle's properties? Here in Coventry?'

'Yes. I didn't know it at the time, but one of the three properties I did up for him was theirs, I mean, where they were going to live. He bought that and the other two all at the same time, with the idea of living in one and renting out the others. So it was a kind of test for me — screw up on the house where he was going to live and he'd probably have cancelled me on the other two. Of course he wasn't long there before he sold up and bought this place and we had to start all over again.'

'He told me that's how he made his money.'

'Property? Yes, as far as I know. I'm sure he had his earnings to begin with, you know, the purses or whatever they call them. But mostly it's been buying, redecorating, selling. I'm not the only decorator he uses. There's a man he has in London. In fact,' she raised her coffee cup as if toasting him, 'he's talking about a big job in London for me. I think his other guy has retired. So rather than looking for someone else he wants to send me down there.'

'What kind of big job?'

'Nosy bugger ... I don't know. I'll be sure to fill you in when I find out.'

She was smiling at him but there was something distanced about her now, as though her story had been well-rehearsed. Perhaps she'd told it so many times it had lost its freshness.

He pushed his sense of unease aside, saying, 'I just like to know who I'm working for.'

'Well don't ask too hard.' Still smiling. 'You might not like what you hear.'

———

There was a noise at the front door and moments later Charlotte and Felicity Doyle came into the kitchen, carrying shopping bags, both shining like athletes after a race. They glanced at Storey and Kate, sitting there nursing coffee, Storey thought, like long-lost friends, then they dumped the bags on to one of the kitchen counters.

Charlotte said, 'Well good morning, glad to see you've made yourself at home.'

'I'm sorry—' Storey began.

'I'm joking. Jesus, you don't have any sense of humour, do you?'

Storey sensing Kate watching him, wondering what he was going to say, how he was going to react.

Before he could reply Felicity saved his embarrassment, saying to Kate, 'I'm going to try these on upstairs. You want to come see?'

Charlotte had been unpacking a shopping bag and placing cans and jars and bottles and bread on the counter. She watched Kate stand up and peer inside the bag that Felicity was holding out, an expression Storey couldn't read on her face. Then Kate said, 'Try and stop me. I like the look of this blue top.'

The younger women left and Charlotte continued unpacking, giving Storey her back but he knew she was aware of him watching.

He said, 'Can I help?'

'No, all done,' she said, turning to face him. 'So do you get on with her, Kate?'

'She seems nice. She showed me the room upstairs. I like the mural.'

Charlotte pulled a face. 'I can't stand it. Thank god that's going to be somewhere for Bran to go with his mates and play. I won't need to see it every day.'

'Kate was saying she's done several houses for you and Mr Doyle.'

'She's one of his favourites but I think we need a change now. Get someone else in, next time he buys another house.'

'Is that on the cards? Another house?'

'Maybe, when the current project's finished.'

'What's that—the attic?'

She folded her hands in her lap, leaning backwards against the counter. 'Oh, you don't know about that yet, do you?'

Bran Doyle walked in from the entrance hall, nodding at Storey. He was still wearing an outdoors jacket. He said to Charlotte, 'Doesn't know about what?'

'Your project.'

'He's about to find out. Get your coat, Storey, we're going visiting.'

CHAPTER FIVE

D OYLE TURNED LEFT out of the front door and led them to the garages behind the house. It was the first time Storey had seen them. There were three in a row, concrete structures connected by a single tiled roof and with three individual metal roller-doors. Doyle pressed a button and the door of the middle garage began to roll upwards and fold inside.

He said, 'You ever driven a Mercedes before?'

'Will it matter if I haven't?'

'Not really, I'm stuck with you, aren't I? Now get in the fuckin' front and drive.'

Storey liked the feel of the car, which was probably the most comfortable vehicle he'd ever driven. Doyle directed him to cut north along roads that seemed to Storey like the edge of the city, one side fields, the other rows of redbrick houses, the sun casting flickering shadows on the road ahead.

Doyle uttered brief instructions to turn here or cross there but didn't say much else until they passed through a small estate of modern houses and arrived at a building site, its perimeter marked by a tall wire fence twice the height of a man. He told Storey to stop in front of its mesh gate while he climbed out and pushed it open, waving the car through and pointing Storey towards an area that wasn't as muddy as the rest of the site, next to a small Portakabin. A rusty red Jeep Defender was already parked there, its driver seated inside and talking into his mobile phone. Storey saw him signal to Doyle through the windscreen, a familiar gesture, but didn't get out.

Storey looked at the construction works—a long single-storey building, its roof space covered with blue tarpaulin stretched over straight beams, the breeze-block walls jagged where windows and doors would fit. The tarpaulin covering the beams flapped noisily in the wind. It was Saturday so no one was working and the site looked desolate.

Storey thought Doyle would start describing what the place was intended to be, trying to impress him. But instead the older man came and stood next to him looking at the muddy ground and the unfinished building with a calmness that Storey hadn't seen before. He surprised Storey by saying, 'Things are complicated back home, I know that. Keep your nose out of it and you'll be all right. It's a full house with Felicity still there and Norton having a room and an office and Darren hanging around like a teenager, sniffing after Felicity … I don't want you to get all mixed up in it.'

'It's none of my business.'

'Damn right, but you've walked into it so you should know.' He glanced at Storey, then shifted his stance to take in the site, staring at the earthworks where pipes and conduits led into the building, the broken pieces of yellow wood and stacks of red bricks on pallets, swathed in polythene, the half-covered machinery and rutted pathways. He went on, 'Darren's dad was Craig Norton's brother. Him and his wife, Darren's mum, were killed in a car-crash when Darren was thirteen. So Norton took him in. Good of him to do that, if you think about it. It was difficult for him at his work, in the army, Darren was a little shit even then, and losing his mum and dad can't have been much fun. So when Norton came to work for me, after he quit the army, he asked if there was anything we could do for him, for Darren. I seen lots of youngsters go wrong when I was coming up in the East End, so I give him a chance. He's close to breaking point on that chance now, I have to say. But we'll see how it goes.'

He didn't know what to say to Doyle so he backed off from the door a few paces, taking in the size of the building. Doyle watched him, hands on hips. Storey said, 'I give in. What is it?'

Doyle grinned at him and spread his arms, the master in charge of his estate. 'When I was starting out I 'ad no training, nothing. I was just a big bastard with a good punch. I'd fight anyone for tuppence. Then, when I started making money, I thought I better develop some skills—know what I mean? Learn to box. I was starting to come up against blokes who knew what they was doing. When I was doing it on the cobbles it didn't matter, we was all as bad as each other. But when we was in a ring with a timekeeper and these skinny gloves they give us, it was different. So I thought, I'll get a trainer, find somewhere to practice, go a few rounds with a likely lad to build up my puff. Could I find somewhere? Could I bollocks. Took me bloody ages to find somewhere local, and a sparring partner willing to get knocked around the 'ead by me for three rounds.'

Storey realised where he was heading. 'You're building your own gym.'

'I am.' He stepped forward now and started to walk towards the periphery of the site, patting a concrete mixer as he went by it and stepping around a big puddle that was yellow and oily in texture. Storey followed. Doyle went on, 'That's the noble reason, if you like—making something that kids like me will be able to use. Sixteen, seventeen-year-olds with time on their hands. Cheap membership, safe environment, proper training so they don't knock themselves silly too young.'

'And there's another reason?'

Doyle had stopped near the wire fencing that surrounded the site and was looking at the estate houses on the other side, beyond an untidy hedge, the houses neat and orderly. He said, 'This was just a bit of wasteland when I bought it. At least it'll be useful now.' He turned back towards the car. 'The other reason is that it's going to be my legacy, something I can be proud of. Is that stupid or what?'

'Not necessarily.'

41

'Fuckin' diplomat. Right, here's Rod.'

The driver's door of the Jeep was opening and a man in his mid-forties climbed out and nodded at them. His hair lay in tight grey curls close to his head and his skin was weathered and creased. He had the look of someone who worked outdoors and didn't give way for wind, rain or hailstorms. He lit a cigarette then shook hands with Doyle, who introduced Storey and added, 'He's the new driver, till he fucks up. Storey, this is Rod, the main man on this site. Anything needs doing, Rod organises it.'

Storey shook hands with Rod, who said, 'You've not been here before.'

Storey looked around at the site. 'I'm sure I'd have remembered it.'

Doyle cleared his throat. 'I've brought Rod here because I wanted him to meet you.'

'Okay.'

'The reason being I'm giving you a promotion.'

Storey felt himself tightening up and his mouth creasing into a thin straight line. He wondered when the manipulation had begun—the interview with Norton? The visit from Charlotte Doyle? When had they begun to manoeuvre him into position?

He said, 'I don't like promotions I haven't earned.'

'Just listen, will you? Yes, I need a driver. You'll still be doing that, and other things, besides security. We always had you in mind for bigger duties, having read about your checkered career. And one of those other duties is going to be here.'

'Doing what?'

Rod said, squinting through his cigarette smoke, 'This is what happens. I look after this place. I tell the men what to do, where to work. I order the materials and look after the rotas, all that shit. Then I tell Darren what's going on and when he feels like it, he tells Mr Doyle here. When he doesn't feel like it, he sods off somewhere else and I can't get hold of him.'

'Why would you need to?'

'Because I asked him to do a job,' Doyle said. 'I give him this work because of Craig Norton. Something to do. Management. Only he's not fuckin' managing. The fact that Rod doesn't need managing is neither here nor there. It's the principle.'

Storey said, 'I don't understand. If he's not doing what he's supposed to do, get rid of him. Or give him something else to do.'

'It ain't that simple,' Doyle said with a pained expression. 'Rod, show him round, will you? I've got a phone call to make.'

Storey followed Rod back into the half-finished building, Rod telling him where not to tread, pointing out where there was going to be a lounge bar so people could have a drink, where the boxing ring was going to be erected, where the changing rooms and showers were going to be.

'Rest of the roof's going on next week, starting Monday,' he said. 'Then we get utilities connected up, get the doors and windows in and start on the plumbing and electrics.'

'How long's it going to take to finish off?' Rod shrugged, saying, 'Couple of months, weather permitting.
We've got a good bunch of lads.' He lit another cigarette and offered one to Storey, who shook his head. 'Mr Doyle uses the same people if he can. He knows they'll do well for him and he treats them all right.'

'So you've built properties for him before?'

'Not built—restored. You've been to his house?'

'That's where I'm working.'

'That's right, you're the gunman, aren't you?' He fired an imaginary gun with his finger, grinning. 'Anyway, I did that for him. Me and most of the same lads. Was a right mess before we got in there. Took us nearly two years to get it put right, the Doyles living in a couple of caravans in the grounds, like gypsies.'

He took Storey outside and around to the back and showed where they were going to lay the works for the geothermal heating system, using pipes laid underground to gather heat before it was pumped into the building as warm air. 'State of the art,' Rod said, looking down at the patch of ground as if he could already see the elaborate plumbing in place.

Storey said, 'You like this stuff, don't you?'

Rod looked up, grinning again. 'Love it. He always wants to try new things, so long as they're not too expensive.'

Storey found himself liking the man, feeling he could trust him, and said in a quieter voice, watching Doyle thirty yards away, by the cars, talking loudly on his phone, 'What's all this business with Darren? You and I both know I'm an idiot as far as construction's concerned. What's Doyle doing?'

Rod's face turned sombre and he also glanced towards Doyle. 'He's fed up with Darren arsing around but he thinks he's got to be fair to him, because of Norton. If he kicks him off the project altogether it'll sour things with Norton and he might bugger off. Doyle can't manage without him, so he's got to keep him sweet.'

'So what am I supposed to do that you're not already doing?'

Rod's eyes flicked away, past Storey. 'You'll find out in a minute. He's here.'

———

A green mini with a Union Jack on its roof was driving through the gateway and turning in next to the other two cars. Darren got out, looking across at them as he bent down to take his jacket from the passenger seat. He was wearing jeans and a grey sweatshirt. With his pencil moustache and brushed-back dark hair he looked like a matador out of uniform and seemed faintly ridiculous. Walking up to Doyle, Storey felt sorry for Darren and thought his day was going to get worse.

Doyle hung up on his phone and waited till everyone was standing in front of him, then said to Darren, 'Thanks for coming. Just wanted to talk over a couple of things.'

Darren nodded at Rod and glanced at Storey. He said to Doyle, 'I got your text. What's up?'

'How are things going? Here, I mean?'

'In what way?'

'Don't be fuckin' difficult, Darren. How are you getting on, you know, working between me and Rod here?'

Darren looked at them each in turn, frowning, then said, 'Well it's a system, isn't it? It's working so far, isn't it?'

He didn't seem to realise the conversation was about him, Storey thought. Perhaps he believed he'd been summoned for an idle chat.

Now Doyle turned, perhaps trying a different approach, softening a little, walking them away from the cars and back towards the unfinished building, saying, 'I appreciate what you've been doing, but I know it's a stretch for you to be here helping Rod supervise the work and at the same time reporting back to me. You can't be in two places at once, can you?'

'I don't mind the drive. It's only ten minutes.'

'True, but it's not fair. Half the time you're hanging around here, the other half you're trying to find me.'

'Like I've told you before, I could just phone you.'

'And like I've told *you* before, I don't want that. I'm a face-to-face person. Besides, you've got to bring the delivery notes and stuff back so your uncle can check them off against the invoices.'

Darren stopped and Storey and Doyle halted with him, Storey realising that Rod had drifted away, had unlocked the Portakabin and gone inside, perhaps not wanting to be part of this conversation. Now Darren was saying, 'What's this about? Have I done something wrong? If I have, just tell me.'

'You haven't done anything wrong but I'm going to give you some help. I don't want you coming backwards and forwards from the site. I want you here, understand? So Rod has someone he can turn to for a decision.'

Darren seemed surprised and relieved. 'Oh, okay.'

'And to make it easier for you, Storey here is going to come along every now and then and get a heads-up from you as to progress. It'll give you more time to think about what's happening on-site without having to worry about reporting back.'

Storey watched Darren register this. It didn't take him long to get the implications.

'Hang on … so Mr Been-here-five-minutes is going to come out and check up on me? Is that it?'

'Not the point—he's going to get a progress report, not do your job.'

'Just seems like wasted effort to me.'

'I'll be the judge of that.'

'So, how often will he be here?'

'Every day if necessary.'

'Sounds like you don't trust me to get on with it.'

Doyle paused just a fraction and Storey knew the truth was going to come out now.

Doyle said, '*Can* I trust you? I heard a load of bricks went missing. You know anything about that?'

'Who told you that?'

'Never mind who told me—is it true?'

'That fucking Rod, isn't it? Going behind my back. Turns out they didn't go missing but they weren't delivered when they were supposed to be. Came on the next delivery but invoiced on the previous one. See? I'm on top of things and I don't need a minder—'

'I'm not a minder,' Storey said.

'I wasn't talking to the monkey.'

'Hey, watch your mouth. He works for me same as you do.'

'Yeah, well, seems to me my job just got downsized.'

Darren looked away and Storey wondered whether he was actually hurt or was just going through the motions. But then the younger man said, 'Ah, fuck it,' and walked to his car and drove out of the gate.

Doyle said, 'See what I mean?'

CHAPTER SIX

S TOREY HAD DECIDED he was going to spend Saturday in his little cottage and watch TV. He never watched TV so thought it would be a nice change—catch up on all the reality and game shows he didn't recognise, just so he could mingle with ordinary people and know what the hell they were talking about.

He fried some chicken and poured a curry sauce over it and ate it with a naan bread he'd bought that afternoon, after he'd got back with Doyle and Doyle had told him he could have the afternoon off, he wasn't doing anything for the rest of the day. Then he sat with a can of Heineken and watched ten minutes of a dating show before switching it off and picking up the book he was reading—a biography of John Lennon. He liked biographies, liked to be inside someone else's head and try to understand why they did what they did.

It was after nine o'clock when his mobile rang. Norton.

'We've got a treat for you,' he said. 'Come on over. Come to the kitchen.'

'I was thinking of going to bed. It's been a hard day on security.'

'I'll meet you there. You drink beer, don't you?'

'Incessantly.'

Norton was waiting in the kitchen for him. He'd taken his jacket off but didn't look any more relaxed. Storey noticed for the first time that the other man's eyes were dark around the sockets, as though he didn't get much sleep.

Norton threw a beer can at him, which Storey caught. 'Guinness. You can do without a glass.'

'Glasses are for beer snobs.'

'Doyle's upstairs. He wants to show you one of his fights. Someone's put them all on YouTube. Go along with it. Don't be critical. And watch out if he has too much to drink.'

'How do I know what's too much?'

'You'll know.'

Storey followed him from the kitchen and up the stairs, realising as he went there were still parts of the house he hadn't visited. The other 'wing', for one, the identical building on the far side of the entrance lobby, where he thought Felicity might have her bedroom and her own quarters.

Norton looked over his shoulder, saying, 'The missus is watching a film on TV,' as though Storey might be wondering where she was. In fact he had wondered whether she'd be watching the fight with them but had decided she'd probably seen them all before, and was probably there when they took place.

They went into the loft and Storey glanced at Kate's mural of the New York skyline. It still looked as out of place as it had that morning, though it wasn't as visible in the muted lighting. The room still smelled of paint.

Doyle had lowered the projection screen and Storey noticed there were a couple of armchairs here now, not just the brown sofa he'd seen earlier. Perhaps Doyle had spent the afternoon moving furniture, preparing the room for the show. Storey still had the sense that Doyle wanted to impress him in some way. Perhaps it was an ego thing—he had to match up to the man who killed people with guns. And the only way he could do that was by showing himself in combat.

Doyle was already seated facing the screen, a table with a bowl of crisps and a half-finished pint of beer on it. He nodded at Storey, then pointed him towards one of the armchairs. Norton took the third.

———

Doyle said, 'I had a series of fights against one man, thirty plus years ago. This is the first fight. I was already cock of the walk and this young feller starts knocking on my door. Handsome Frank Ivory. Been shooting his mouth off like Cassius Clay, saying how he was going to take me down in three rounds. Watch.'

He picked up a small remote control and pressed a button. The white screen had been showing a paused title card: 'Bran "One Punch" Doyle vs. "Handsome" Frank Ivory, Leicester Drill Hall, 1985.' Now it began to flicker and the film started, garish colour from an old Super-8 camera, Storey thought, the sound very tinny. It showed a view from seating twenty yards from the ring, the cameraman moving slowly to get closer for a better view. The crowd was raucous but didn't seem particularly loud. He said to Doyle, 'Was this a legal fight?'

'Not exactly. Unlicensed. Unofficial. Just watch the fuckin' thing, will you?'

An announcer in a pale blue suit and a flouncy dress-shirt stood in the centre of the ring and said something that was unintelligible, though Storey heard the words 'Doyle' and 'Handsome Frank', both phrases greeted with a mixture of boos and cheers.

Then the announcer left the ring and a referee in a white shirt and black dickie-bow brought the two fighters together. Doyle was slimmer than he was now but had the same general shape, thick with muscle around the waist, the same hair, the same forward-leaning stance. Handsome Frank Ivory was maybe an inch taller, slimmer still, and looked a few years younger, perhaps 25 to Doyle's 30.

They touched gloves and the bell rang and Ivory took a step back, perhaps to prepare himself.

To Storey's right, Doyle said, 'Watch this,' and Storey knew he was grinning.

On the screen, as Ivory stepped back, Doyle went forward. Ivory raised his arms but it was too late. Doyle had launched a looping right-hand that went over Ivory's meagre defence and caught him flush on the cheek.

An enormous cheer went up from the crowd as Handsome Frank Ivory's knees buckled then gave way and he fell to the floor. The camera wobbled, the cameraman presumably jostled by crowd-members celebrating. The referee counted Ivory out while Doyle stood over him, shouting something Storey couldn't hear above the cheers and taunts.

'What were you saying?' he asked Doyle.

'I was telling him to get his handsome fuckin' face off the canvas and fight like a man. I was charged up for that one. Couldn't stand what he'd been saying about me, what he was going to do to me. I learned him a lesson, didn't I? One punch.'

Doyle picked up his remote control again and pressed more buttons. Another film started, this one with a steadier camera filming from further away and outdoors, a blue sky and what looked like a football stand behind the ring. There was no caption this time and the film began with a girl in a bathing costume walking round carrying a board showing 'Round 1'.

Doyle said, 'This was Woodford Town's ground, an afternoon set up by Rotten Sal Severino. They was all there: Roy Shaw, Lennie McLean, Mad Barry Dalton. Six months after the one you just seen. I'd been lazy, not taken care of business, thought I could beat anyone.'

The fight began the same way, with Ivory backing off and Doyle shuffling forward, but Storey saw that Doyle had put on weight and wasn't as limber as he was in the first film. He tried the same kind of swinging knock-out punch but Ivory was ready for it and brushed it off easily.

'Been doing his homework,' Doyle said.

Storey saw Doyle had finished his first pint and was already half-way down the second.

Norton said, 'This was the one where—'

'Yeah, yeah, just watch it.' He took another draw from his drink. 'Gets me fuckin' mad just watching him. Look, see that? Got me in the face and just twisted his thumb in my eye.'

Norton said, 'All legal, though, in these fights.'

'Everything was fuckin' legal. Or nothing was *ill*egal's a better way of putting it.'

The end of the round came and the camera zoomed in on Frank Ivory's corner, where two squat men with dark hair wiped him down and gave him liquids.

Doyle said, 'Look at them, Charlie and Bert Tate. They called Bert "Truckie", never knew why. Pair of evil bastards, cousins. They was the ones who turned him, made him mean. He was a fair man till they got their 'ands on him.'

'I've heard of them,' Storey said. 'They're still at it round the East End.'

Doyle glanced at him, curious. 'You ever meet them when you was down there?'

'No, but I heard people talking about them. Into property now. If there were still such things as slum landlords, that'd be them.'

'Funny you say that.'

'Why?'

'I've got a nice bit of land down there in Fulham they're after. Got planning permission and everything. They want it off me so they can build another fuckin' slum. But fuck 'em. Give 'em an inch and they take ten fuckin' miles. Here we go, now watch this.'

Round Two was starting as Storey turned his attention back to the screen. The younger Doyle and Ivory seemed wary of each other now, both going sideways rather than forward.

Doyle said, 'That was so boring, I couldn't stand it. I work on adrenaline, me, I get angry and clobber people. That was my thing—I took all the punches and just went forward till I could batter them. And here he was, just biding his time. Watch out.'

Storey flinched as Doyle punched the air and then kicked out, grunting. On the screen Ivory had got inside Doyle's defence and a big uppercut caught him on the chin. Doyle staggered back and then fell to the canvas, the referee on him immediately, counting … and instead of going to a neutral corner, Ivory stepped forward and started kicking him in the ribs.

In the attic room, Doyle sprang to his feet, shouting at the screen. 'You fuckin' bastard! We said no boots!' He turned to Storey. 'We said no boots, not like when we met outside, on the cobbles. Anything went then, it was all in.' He turned back to the screen. 'You're gonna get yours, you fuckin' wanker!' He turned to reach for his drink, his hand clawing at the glass, and it toppled off the table and smashed on the polished wooden floor. Norton stood up immediately and went round to a trolley on the other side of the room. He came back with napkins, dabbing at the spilled liquid on the floor and picking up shards of glass.

Doyle ignored him, still staring at the screen, where the younger version of himself had stood up and dusted down his gloves.

Storey caught Norton's eye behind Doyle's back and saw Norton display the first hint of emotion he'd seen from the man—a look of resigned misery, his mouth turned down, his eyes blank.

Yes!' Doyle said, turning to Storey. 'Did you see that?'

Storey saw that young Doyle had charged at Ivory and backed him up, and as he watched the younger version of his new master lashed out a fierce right hand and caught Ivory flush on his jaw. For the second time that night, Ivory collapsed and Doyle both on the screen and in the attic raised his arms and danced a little jig.

The scene on the film deteriorated into a scrum as more people entered the ring, surrounding Doyle and lifting Ivory, helping him to his corner. In the attic, Doyle began to cough, bending over and retching for a while before finding his way back to the sofa, where he collapsed with his head back, staring at the ceiling. Norton took his parcel of glass shards to a waste bin in the corner and dumped them.

Within a few minutes Doyle was snoring softly and Norton said, 'Let's get him to bed.'

'Does he do this often?'

'Watch the films? Couple of times a year. This was for your benefit, so you'll know where he came from, who he was.'

'It's impressive but wasn't necessary.'

'It was for him. Take his other arm.'

They got him through the door and then Norton took the weight on the narrow stairs down from the attic. On the next floor Storey took the other side again and they walked Doyle down a corridor until Norton pushed open a bedroom door.

Storey saw it was sparsely decorated—no dressing-table with chair-height mirror, no clothing hanging from a wardrobe door, no hand-creams on the bedside table. Instead a couple of motor magazines, an electric clock, a scale model of a Mercedes that looked like the one he'd driven that morning. A man's bedroom.

'We don't have to undress him, do we? That wasn't in my unwritten contract.'

'Just lay him on the bed. He'll wake up in the night and sort himself out and never mention it again. If he even remembers it.'

'Does the missus have a separate bedroom then?'

'I'll forget you asked that question. Undo his shoe-laces then you can go. I think you've got tomorrow off.'

Storey did as he was told, then slipped out of the house and walked back to his cottage. The night was cold, the stars sharp against a black sky.

Today had been strange. He had the feeling the days to come were going to be stranger.

CHAPTER SEVEN

H E WAS HALFWAY to the building site the following morning when he realised he didn't have the gate key to get inside. He'd been so keen to have a look at the place by himself, without Doyle breathing down his neck, he'd forgotten that when they went the first time the site had been unlocked by Rod before they'd arrived and presumably locked by him when they left.

Instead of going back for the keys he drove around until he found the housing estate that backed on to the building site. He parked in a dead-end street, seeing the wire fence surrounding the site on the far side of the houses, behind their gardens, and giving the impression that each house had a private tennis-court. He walked back out of the dead-end, along another short suburban road, skeletal trees lining either side, and eventually found an alley-way leading to the site. It was nine o'clock Sunday morning, no one around.

At the end of the alley he came out on the other side of the back-gardens of the estate houses, in a metre-wide gap between their rear walls and the site's own fence. He walked this perimeter, passing the back gates of half a dozen houses, occasionally grabbing the wire fence between his fingers to steady himself on the rocky ground. The fence was twice his height and topped with barbed wire and it would have needed nimble thieves to climb over it and not be seen by the house-owners.

———

When they arrived he was on the far side of the gym, where the flattened area of the site behind the building ran up against overhanging oak and chestnut trees. The fence defining the edge of the building site continued all the way around it, but here there were no garden walls, no convenient gap, just waist-high scrub and then the heavy branches of tall trees making passage difficult. He was pushing his way through brambles and thick shrubbery when he heard a car approaching ... no, two cars.

He stood still, panting a little, and heard the cars come to a halt, their engines running, then the squeal of the tall gate being swung back. The cars came on to the site and Storey shifted his position, moving back and crouching so he could see past the corner of the building without being seen himself.

One of the cars was Darren's green Mini, now pulling into the parking slot next to the Portakabin. The other was a standard white Transit van, rusty on the sills and driven by Billy Jenkins, the young man who'd wanted to fight him in Doyle's kitchen. Darren was leaning against his car now as Jenkins climbed out and looked around, then went to the rear of his van and opened the doors. He wore full-length blue overalls and work boots, his ginger hair wild, a pencil behind one ear and white iPod earbuds draped around his neck.

He called to Darren, 'What is it this time?'

'Over there,' Darren said, pointing to the part of the building that would become the bar, according to what Rod had told Storey. 'There's some nice timber and new roof tiles under a tarp. Go wild.'

'Are you gonna help or just give fucking orders?'

'Hey, it's your profit. I'm doing you a favour just unlocking that bloody gate. Be quick. I'm not happy about doing this in daylight.'

'It's Sunday. You won't get any builders working on Sunday.' He added with a grin, 'They'll all be in church,' then strode towards the gym, and Storey.

Storey considered standing up and letting himself be seen but thought it would be better to learn where this was heading. Besides, until Jenkins drove off with the materials, nothing illegal had taken place. What were the odds they'd deny everything and say they were doing a little extra work, checking up on the site? Storey knew he needed evidence of some kind.

So he ducked low behind the rear wall and watched Jenkins take out half a dozen thick joists and lay them in his van, carrying them two at a time, then go back in, making several trips to bring out a hundred or so red roof tiles, laying them down carefully on the corrugated floor of the van so they didn't shatter.

Darren had been standing with his arms folded, watching. Now he called out, 'I hope you left some. Rod finds out they're all gone someone will be in shit, and it'll probably be me, the way things are going.'

'I spread out the tiles a bit so you couldn't tell. There's still twenty or more joists in there. He'll think he's miscalculated.'

'You don't know Rod. He never miscalculates.'

Jenkins threw up his hands, 'Well, fuck him then.'

He closed the van doors then climbed inside and started the engine, reversing and turning the van before halting. He leaned out of the window.

'You around tomorrow?'

'Maybe, why?'

'Just asking. Stay in touch. Don't forget to lock up after yourself.'

He drove through the gate. Darren watched, then climbed into his Mini and drove to the far side of the gate, getting out to rattle it shut and lock the chain behind him before moving off again.

When he was out of sight, Storey stood up and raced around the fence and past the still-quiet back gardens to the alley-way. He'd memorised the plate number of the van and doubted he'd find it, but it didn't look like it was capable of going particularly fast and there were maybe three routes out of the estate. If he could make a couple of lucky choices he should pick him up.

As he ran back to his car, he wondered what the hell he was doing, still playing cop. By the time he arrived at the Volvo he'd convinced himself this was part of his job description: security. Of a kind. He unlocked the car and climbed in and fired it up.

He found Jenkins again as he was turning north on Holbrooks Lane, heading out of the city towards Ash Green. They went past the Honda garage on the right and after five or six minutes turned on to a narrow leafy road that finally left behind the redbrick estates they'd been driving through. Storey kept well back and eventually saw the van brake, pull into a lay-by and stop behind another truck with its tail-gate already lowered. He pulled up two hundred yards back and took out his mobile phone, activating its camera. He knew his car would be seen so he reached for a folding map and opened it out and stood it on the dashboard to cover half the windscreen, leaving a gap he could see through. Maybe they'd think he was lost.

Zooming in the camera he saw two men come from the truck. One was enormous, probably about six feet six inches tall, with wide shoulders and a broad chest. He wore a dark suit and tie over a white shirt, like an undertaker. Storey also noticed the thickness of his neck and his long arms but he moved easily enough. He stayed by the truck's cabin and leaned with his back to its door, looking both ways along the road, his arms folded.

The other man who came towards Jenkins was older, wearing a long beige overcoat like a car dealer, and had a full head of black hair that looked unnatural even at this distance and magnified on a phone screen. He began a conversation with Jenkins even as the younger man started to pull the joists from the back of his van and walked them round to lay them on the bed of the other vehicle. The conversation went back and forth between them as Jenkins continued to work, transferring all the wood and then carefully taking the tiles and laying them gently in the truck. When he'd finished he raised the tailgate and locked it, then went back, jumped into the rear of the Transit and swept the floor, pushing the detritus on to the road so the older man had to step back to avoid being caught in the sweepings.

Storey thought the big man, who'd kept out of the conversation, but was apparently listening, was probably a driver or a bodyguard. *A lot of us about*, Storey thought, without feeling any affinity with him. The older man was obviously Jenkins' client.

He took photos, zooming in as far as he could, holding the phone steady with his hand on the dashboard of the Volvo, occasionally ruffling the map to make it look as though it were in use.

Finally Jenkins finished, closing his van doors and now giving his full attention to the other man, who was still talking. When at last he stopped, he pulled a wallet from his inside pocket and gave Jenkins a wad of notes. Jenkins didn't count them but stuffed them into one of the pockets of his overalls.

The two unknown men climbed into the truck and it drove off. Jenkins started up the van then performed a three-point turn in the road and headed back in Storey's direction. He ducked down as the van went past. His Volvo was a distinctive sand colour but he wasn't sure Jenkins was watching too closely with all that money in his pocket.

As for the other two men, he thought he recognised the older one but he needed verification before he could be sure. If he was right, his job had suddenly become a lot more interesting.

CHAPTER EIGHT

A S HE DROVE into the parking slot next to his cottage he saw Norton open the kitchen door and walk towards him, his tweed jacket flaring open in the wind.

Storey was out of the car and waiting as Norton arrived, looking unhappy.

'Where have you been?' Norton said. 'I've been looking for you.'

'On my days off I tend to do what I want.'

'Besides the point. You should have told me.'

'I have a phone. You have a phone. One can contact the other. You should try it.'

Norton stared at him, his skin moist and his eyes intense and dark. *Great*, Storey thought, *another control freak on my case.*

He said, 'So now I'm here, what do you want?'

'Doyle asked where you were and I couldn't tell him. Don't put me in that position again. You got this job because we needed someone available at all times.'

'I heard Monks wasn't reliable.'

Norton shook his head. 'Irrelevant. Yes, you have time off, but you have to let us know where you are so we can make arrangements.' He looked away and seemed to relax, putting his hands in his pockets and shifting his weight on to his heels. He watched the trees on the far side of the compound waving in the wind. He said, 'I know it sounds like I'm giving you a hard time and you've barely been here a couple of days. I suppose I'm passing on Doyle's tension. There's a lot going on with the gym and other stuff.'

'Like what?'

'I can't tell you that. It's not important from your perspective. It's up to Doyle what he tells you, anyway.'

Storey thought of asking why Doyle wanted him to supervise Darren at the building site. Doyle said it had been on their agenda before Storey was even hired. Then he thought Norton might resent questions about Darren as he was more or less sponsoring him in the household.

Now he was confusing himself and he began to get angry. He liked to think and act in a straightforward manner and the manipulation they'd used on him was beginning to make his brain ache.

He said, 'I'm going to need a key for the site.'

Norton was startled. His eyes came back to Storey, who saw in them a fearfulness he hadn't noticed before. He wondered what Norton's men had thought of him in combat, whether they'd trusted him or believed he might do or say something stupid. He didn't seem convinced of his own worth.

Now he was saying, 'Is that where you've been? The site?'

'I wanted another look. But it was locked up.'

'I'd have come with you, shown you around.'

'I've had the official tour. I wanted to check it out for myself.'

Norton looked him up and down. 'You went there anyway.'

Storey looked down at himself—his shoes were muddy and his jeans had short lengths of bramble still sticking to them. He plucked them off carefully, saying, 'Doyle suggested something had been stolen. I was looking for holes in the fence.'

'Rod's already done all that. We're not a complete bunch of amateurs.'

That was when Storey almost told him about Darren and Billy stealing materials, wipe the smug look from his face … but he held back. What he did instead was turn to go into the cottage before saying something he'd regret later.

Norton said to his back, 'What are you doing now?'

Unlocking his door, Storey said, 'Changing my shoes then going home to fetch some more stuff. I need my computer and some books.'

'Don't be long,' Norton said, coming to the door as Storey went through to his kitchen at the back of the cottage.

———

Storey sensed Norton's presence behind him and wondered what he really wanted. It was as though he felt some responsibility for Storey's actions even though Doyle was the one who'd made the decision to hire him.

He took a glass from one of the cabinets and ran water into it, then turned back to the door.

He said, 'What do you know about Billy Jenkins?'

'Why, what about him?'

'He's got an attitude problem.'

'That's not Darren's fault.'

'I never said it was. You don't have to defend him just because you're his uncle.'

Norton was almost a silhouette in the door but Storey sensed his surprise. There was a pause, then Norton said, 'Doyle told you.'

'He thought I should know you were related. Does it matter?'

'Not really.' He came further into the house, pushing the door closed. 'I'm probably too soft on him. Did Doyle say that?'

'No. Well, in a manner of speaking he did. But he knows it's complicated. He said he admired you for taking him in. But he thinks he's a little shit. Just so you know.'

'Doesn't give you the right to get on his back.'

'Unless he deserves it.'

'What are you getting at?'

'I don't know. Probably nothing. Is there anything to be got at?'

'I don't think he's a bad kid, if that's what you mean. He's twenty-three, for Christ's sake, and doesn't have a clue what he wants to do. Stevie, my brother, was what they call a steadying influence but when he and Meg were hit by that other car

Darren kind of lost it for a bit. At the moment I'm just glad he's not fighting for ISIS in West Africa or putting drugs in his arm. A bit of laziness and occasional incompetence I can cope with.'

'Can Doyle?'

'We'll see, won't we?'

CHAPTER NINE

H E'D BEEN AWAY from his house only a couple of days but it seemed abandoned already.

Storey was surprised by his ability to change locations without feeling any attachment. He'd left his flat in London with most of its furniture still in it, dumping the responsibility for selling it on one of the other lodgers, Millie. He hadn't spoken to her in a couple of weeks but didn't feel like being the butt of her ironic carping right now.

He had too much to think about.

He packed his small suitcase with more socks, underwear and a couple of tee-shirts he'd left out the first time. His bedroom was cold—he'd turned the central heating off when he left— and he stood looking at the meagre furniture for a moment. Would he come back here after the job with Doyle had ended, or not? He'd had a major plan once to sell it and move into an apartment closer to the town centre, but this was the house where he'd grown up and where his father had lived alone for the last twenty years, so it was hard to get rid of it. Besides, he'd already pissed off one estate agent by refusing to sell to a client he'd found. He wanted to be certain before he went down that route again.

Outside the cold wind had turned into a wintery squall, rain snapping sideways against the windows. He went downstairs and put his laptop in its bag then made a cup of Yorkshire tea, realising too late he didn't have any milk so drinking it black, the dark taste of the strong brew like medicine in his mouth.

He sat at the table in the 'dining area' of the lounge, keeping his hands warm on the mug. He went through a couple of scenarios in his mind: Option one, tell Doyle about Darren and Billy Jenkins. It was the right thing to do and would probably be best for Darren in the long run—keep the theft low-key, deal with it in-house, don't get the police involved.

The downside: it makes things awkward for Norton. First, because Darren's partly his responsibility and he's been let down. Secondly, because it screws up the relationship between Norton and Doyle. Would Doyle blame him? Maybe not. But he'd probably insist on sacking Darren on principle and then give Norton the option of staying. Darren was a grown man after all—Norton couldn't be held responsible for every misstep he made.

The upside, it gets Darren and Jenkins out of the way and lets the gym get built more efficiently and, without the thefts, more cheaply. Why was he even thinking about it? What was stopping him picking up the phone and calling Doyle now?

Right ... the other business. Whatever Jackie West and her listening spies were waiting for. If he stuck his oar in, would it upset the investigation? Without knowing what it was about he couldn't risk getting in the way. In principle he didn't mind— the police could look after themselves and shouldn't rely on overheard conversations anyway—but for such a minor offence as stealing a few planks of wood and some tiles it didn't seem right to upset any apple carts.

Option two: tell Norton and let *him* deal with it. That could work, Storey thought, but he wondered whether Norton would implode under the pressure. He hadn't given any signs yet that he could deal with difficult situations so telling him might make things worse. Besides, although he could probably deal with Darren, the only way Norton could handle Jenkins and his customer in the white truck would be to involve the police. Again, that was potentially difficult.

He drank the last of his tea and washed the mug. He realised he needed to talk to someone to get his thoughts in order, so he hunted down his jacket and took his mobile phone from its inside pocket.

———

The Toby Inn he'd suggested was quieter at three o'clock than it would have been at midday, he thought, people finishing their Sunday lunches before heading back home to watch television.

Jackie West was out of uniform and looked uncomfortable in civilian clothes. He wondered whether he'd been the same when he was a copper—did the uniform make you feel more at ease, more yourself? Or did it simply put you on duty and made you act more formally when dealing with civilians, and then that turned into the way you dealt with people generally?

She was seated in one of the raised sections in the far corner of the room and caught his eye when he came in. He noticed she'd cut her hair even shorter, almost in a man's style, but it suited the shape of her face. Her grey eyes, always a little distant, watched him sit opposite her before she said, 'I shouldn't be talking to you at all, so make it quick.'

'Can I get you a drink? We look more suspicious without one.'

She sighed and asked for an orange juice and he fetched it and a half of Guinness for himself, slipping back into his seat and saying, 'Did we ever go on a proper date?'

'I don't remember. You nearly blowing my head off wasn't much of an aphrodisiac.'

'Ah, come on, you never felt so good as when you realised you were alive and Algafari was dead.'

She tasted her drink and frowned at it, then said, 'Okay, you're my hero. You got me into the situation and you got me out. Can we move on?'

Storey recognised the tone in her voice, the one she probably used with the men in her unit to get something done. It was patient but slightly irritated at the same time, as though she knew she was playing a game with children who had to be cajoled.

He said, 'I know you can't tell me anything about Doyle—'

'True.'

'—but I've found something and I want to run it past you. It's your choice whether you tell me anything after you've investigated.'

She was leaning back now, her cool eyes giving nothing away, holding her glass in front of her mouth, her elbow propped up by her other hand. He noticed how slender her fingers were— women's hands always surprised him. She said, 'So tell me, don't be such a bloody drama queen.'

He told her about the gym that Doyle was building and that Craig Norton's nephew was acting as a kind of on-site liaison between the foreman and Doyle.

She said, 'We picked that up, thanks. Anything else?'

'Just hang on. Without naming names, I can tell you one of the men working on the site is stealing materials and selling it to someone else.'

'Who?'

'Who's selling or who's buying?'

'Either. Both. Jesus, you're not much of a snitch, are you?'

'I've just said I'm not going to name names. I've got too much integrity to spill the beans. People keep telling me that so it must be true. I know who's selling and actually it's probably not important.' He took out his phone and found the best photo of the man in the beige coat who Billy Jenkins had delivered the timber and tiles to, turning the phone to show her. Jenkins wasn't visible in the shot. 'This is the buyer. I think I know who he is but if you could find out for certain it would be very helpful.'

Jackie West's expression hadn't changed, it was still sceptical and wary. She waited a moment, thinking, then said, 'You've got a bloody cheek, haven't you? I told you not to take this job and now you're in danger of ruining all our work.'

'I meant to ask about that—how did you get the bugs into the house? Is it just listening or are you watching, too? Do I have to watch my underwear rituals?'

'Get your head out of your backside, Storey. This isn't a game. We've gone to a lot of trouble over this and I'm going to get a right bollocking if it goes tits up.'

'You sweet talker. Can I Bluetooth this photo to your phone? Would that be easier?'

She sighed again, her expression getting darker. 'Just email it to me. I don't know what you expect me to be able to do with it. It's grainy and only three-quarters profile.'

'You're so high-tech now I'm sure you've got software that'll cough him up.'

'Only if he's in the database.'

'We're all in the database now, aren't we? What's the matter with you? I thought you'd like this helping hand.'

'You're doing exactly what you did last time around, getting mixed up in something you have no idea what's going on. Whether it's this petty theft or something bigger.'

Storey sipped his Guinness and wiped his top lip, not liking the way the conversation had turned. He'd thought he could jolly her along, use a bit of charm, but she wasn't having any of it. Now she was looking away and he watched her profile, the lift of a nostril as she breathed, the flicker of an eyelid. He became aware of her again as a woman, a rekindling of the feeling he'd had when he'd grown closer to her several weeks before. Then he remembered why he'd asked to see her, and said, 'So come on, what's your advice?'

She turned back to him, frowning. 'What advice can I possibly give the great Paul Storey, the newspapers' darling and well-known crime-fighter?'

'Don't be like that … look, between you and me, I'll tell you what's going on.' He put his phone back in his pocket, giving himself time to think. 'It's actually a young man called Darren who's involved, Norton's nephew, helping someone else steal the stuff. He's got the key and he lets him into the site. Then the guy loads up in his van. They're clever about it, they don't take so much stuff that it's immediately obvious.'

'What do you want me to tell you? You know full well it's theft. You're concealing the commission of a crime. If you saw it, report it to your local nick.'

'At the moment it's my word against theirs.'

'You've just shown me a photograph.'

Storey shrugged. 'That doesn't prove anything, does it? Just some building materials being transferred from one vehicle to another.'

'You didn't take photos at the scene? Where they were being nicked from?'

'I couldn't move for fear of being noticed.'

She'd started to lean forward to listen more intently. Now she was moving back again, thinking.

'What do you want to do?'

Storey laid his hands palm up on the table. 'I don't know. That's why I'm here. I could shop both of them but at the moment I don't really have any proof. Even that photo's not conclusive. Plus, as I said, Darren is Norton's nephew and I actually like Norton, despite his best efforts to piss me off. I don't want to do anything that puts him in shit unless I absolutely have to.'

'So why exactly are you telling me all this?'

'I thought you might have a view, being a serving copper and all that.'

As he said it, he realised this sounded like an accusation and wanted to take it back. But it was too late. It was as if he'd triggered her to move. She stood up and reached for a jacket and handbag on the chair next to her and was ready to leave.

She said, 'I'm not your conscience, Storey. It looks like you're not going to quit working for Doyle, like I asked, so there's nothing I can do. Make up your own mind and stop looking for others to back you up. I've got enough on my plate without constantly having to defend you to my boss.'

'I didn't ask you to do that.'

'No, you didn't, but if I hadn't you might have found yourself yanked out of bed at six o'clock one morning so you wouldn't have been reporting to work for Mr Bran Bloody Doyle.'

Storey watched as she slipped sideways from behind the table and made room for herself to put on her short jacket, which she then buttoned up the front.

He said, 'Jackie?'

'What?'

'You're still going to look into the photo, aren't you?'

CHAPTER TEN

T HE PROBLEM WITH TV, Charlotte Doyle thought, was that it wasn't 'real' enough.

Documentaries, news, even reality shows ... she could tune them out because they didn't touch her. Ever since she was a girl she'd liked contact with real people, people she could sit next to and talk to about things. Distractions like television and films and even books didn't give her that connection.

So to be stuck at home again, this time alone, watching some stupid talent show, was driving her up the wall.

Growing up in Guildford she'd been shielded, she knew that. Her parents treated her like a doll, and it's true she was pretty and knew it early on. She couldn't help herself smiling at men, testing herself, testing their ability to resist her. It was a kind of power she'd never expected to have, so when she hit fifteen, and the equipment arrived, she took advantage. Went off the rails, her parents said. Tried to enrol her in secretarial school, give her a trade until the right man came along.

Well, she remembered, come along they did. The right men for her because they were absolutely the wrong men for the fuddies back home.

So the secretarial school was ditched and just when punk arrived she was there, age sixteen, down in the pit at the

Marquee, watching The Stranglers and Eddie and the Hot Rods and Generation X, screaming and spitting her lungs out ...

Cut to eleven years later: two abortions, one failed marriage, a minor career as a backing singer with Fine Young Cannibals and Simple Minds ... then meeting Bran Doyle.

That night she'd been taken to a fight by one of Culture Club's roadies. She didn't know it was going to be a fight until they walked through to the back room of the Green Man pub in Peckham and saw the ring they'd constructed. It wasn't up high, on a sprung floor. It was just laid out on the concrete, four wooden fence posts jammed into buckets and fixed in with poured concrete, then roped together to make the square and each post tied back to a fixture on the walls to stop them moving.

Doyle had come in like a film star, not bad-looking still, despite a nose that had been hit too often. It was his swagger, his confidence, that made her mouth dry, the way he ducked into the ring and walked around all four corners, looking at the yelling crowd and yelling right back at them.

His opponent, a young Italian, didn't stand a chance. Doyle had him down in the first thirty seconds. Not quite One Punch but near enough.

That night she'd ditched the roadie and made her way to the back room where the fighters were sitting together, talking it over, neither seeming to have much animosity towards the other. Half a dozen other men in there, too, handing over money, drinking from hip-flasks, laughing with each other. She'd found Doyle and introduced herself, saying it was her first fight and she liked the way he fought.

He'd looked her up and down, the wild hair she had then, slim with good breasts, and said, 'You talk posh for a rough-looking bird, don't you?'

She didn't know his first wife had left him a month before, but it didn't matter anyway because six months later he was divorced and she married him and Felicity was on the way.

Now Felicity was the same age as she'd been when she met Bran and she worried about her all the time. What must it have been like for her own mother, married to a bank manager in Guildford, the vicar's daughter from Reading, when her daughter hooked up with a half-Irish tearaway who punched other men in the back rooms of pubs?

———

She'd seen Storey drive in a couple of hours earlier, just after her husband and Craig Norton had left for one of their occasional nights with 'the boys' in the town centre. Bran seemed incapable of giving up whatever limelight he still attracted, and Norton was a faithful batman, ready to look after his boss even when it wasn't in his job description and when he was probably dying inside the whole time.

Pity he wasn't with him when Doyle pranged the car, hitting a lamp-post full-on while several milligrammes over the limit. Luckily no one was hurt but it was enough to get him banned for a year, which his lawyer said was a good result.

So now when the doorbell rang she thought it might be Storey and it was, standing there in running shoes, sweatpants and a zip-up shirt with a number on the front, a little sweaty, his hair sticking to his forehead. Not a bad look on him, actually.

He said, 'Sorry for the state I'm in. Been for a run. Are Norton or your husband here?'

'No, but you can talk to me. Come in.'

He hesitated then walked in and she closed the door behind him, catching a faint whiff of male energy.

Before he could turn she said, 'Go through. Do you want a drink? Beer? Water?'

'Water would be good. Sorry, I just wanted a quick word with them about tomorrow. Didn't want to bother you.'

She fetched a glass of water from the kitchen and when she came back he was in the lounge, watching a girl singer on the TV. She said, 'I wish they'd all give up and get proper jobs, working in supermarkets and clothes shops where they belong.'

He took the glass from her but she saw he was thinking about her remark. He said, 'Not everyone has it easy.'

'Meaning what? I did? You think because I talk like a Rank starlet from the fifties I didn't have to work for a living?'

'I didn't say that. But times change, don't they? Some things get easier, some get harder. If I could sing I might go on one of these things. Try to make some quick money.'

'No you wouldn't,' she said, moving towards the leather couches so he'd follow her. 'You don't give a shit for this kind of thing. You just think I'm a high-class married woman with a chip on her shoulder.'

She thought he'd say something like, 'Well aren't you?' but he didn't, instead sitting opposite her, sipping from his glass and apparently cooling down. She saw the dark hair sprouting above the neck of his shirt and on his wrists and wondered whether he was hairy all over. Bran's Irish blood tended towards ginger skin and she'd rarely seen a body hair on him.

He finished the water and said, 'I'm sorry if I was rude the other night, the party.'

'I'd had a snoot-full,' she said. 'You were probably right. In the past I loved those get-togethers. Now I'm just bored after twenty minutes and let my fingers do the walking to the bottle. You were bored too, don't lie.'

'It's my job now, isn't it? I'll get used to it. For a while. Do you know whether Doyle, sorry, your husband, will want me tomorrow?'

'Who knows? Certainly not me. I suggest you hang around from eight o'clock and something's bound to happen. It usually does. Will you have a drink with me? I mean, alcohol?'

She saw him think it over briefly before saying, 'I'd better go back and shower. Where are they, by the way, Norton and your husband? I texted Norton but he didn't reply.'

She knew he was bringing them back into the conversation as a safety measure, so she wouldn't forget who she was married to. Pretty forward of him to think she was coming on to him. But maybe she was, a little. She told him they were in town, drinking with friends.

He'd seemed ready to go but now he changed his posture and relaxed, sitting back and asking where she was from, originally, and when she told him Guildford he asked how she'd met Doyle and what she thought of living in this house, in Coventry, away from the bright lights of London.

So because she'd been thinking about it before he arrived, she told him how she met Doyle and how they'd been married quickly and how they'd lived in a friend's house in Fulham while the friend was away doing a couple of years in prison in Lewes. Then she explained how he'd had a fight up here, in Coventry, and for once she'd come up with him and they must have caught it on a good day—there was a buzz about it and property was much cheaper than London, even then, so they'd decided when the time was right they'd move up here, away from the stale smoke and razzmatazz of the capital.

She must have said this in a particular tone because he picked up on it, saying, 'But now you're not so sure?'

'Let's just say we could have carried on up the motorway and stopped at Manchester. At least the shops are decent there.'

'There's always Birmingham.'

'As no one in a romantic comedy ever said.'

———

Then she found herself asking him about the gym and whether it could work. Was there a market for it?

'I've no idea,' Storey said. 'But if he can afford it, why not? So long as it gives him more pleasure than stress.'

'He could do without the stress,' she said, then moved on before he could comment on that. 'He could afford it better if he sold the land in London.'

'Why won't he?'

'He's saving it for Felicity and he doesn't want those mobsters the Tates getting their hands on it. They've been after it for years. But Bran's being his usual awkward self and won't sell it to them.'

She watched him digest this, then he said, 'He still thinks a lot about the past.'

'The films he made you watch?'

'That's one thing. Other stuff. He won't let go, will he?'

'It made him what he is. He doesn't want to go back to London but London's still in him.'

'But not you?'

'I was always a visitor to London. A visitor from another planet.'

There was a pause, then he said, 'You can have a drink, if that's what you want. Don't let me stop you.'

'I won't. Did you think I was being subtle by asking whether you wanted one?'

'You're the boss, you can have one without my permission.'

She looked at him closely but couldn't work out what he was thinking. His eyes didn't let you in. Now she wanted a drink but couldn't have one because it would seem like he'd won something.

She said, 'Norton said you came back here because your father died. Is that true?'

'It's true, but it's not the only reason I'm here. I was a visitor to London too. It didn't really stick.'

'He said you're trying to sell your father's house.'

'I had a buyer but I put her off. Now I'm not sure I want to sell.'

'You could rent it out while you're staying here.'

'That's not going to happen,' he said.

'Why not?'

'Because I'm selfish. It's my home now, it's where I was brought up. I can't imagine other people living in it.'

'It won't be permanent. A short let won't kill you.'

'The problem is, I don't know how long that's going to be, do I?'

'Maybe longer than you want,' she admitted.

'Maybe shorter,' Storey said, and this time there was a smile in his eyes.

She wondered what he meant.

———

She was seeing him out of the door when Doyle's Mercedes came through the gate and its headlights swept over the house, the car swishing almost silently in an arc before them. The vehicle went past them slowly, then stopped after it had travelled another thirty metres, as though Norton, driving, had changed his mind about going round the back. The cabin lights came on as the two men climbed out.

Charlotte said quietly to Storey, 'Don't hang around, he'll be drunk.'

Storey saw it was too late, Doyle already waving his arm in the air, shouting, 'Oy, you, Paul Fuckin' Storey, what you doing with my wife? Have you been giving her comfort and solace?'

Storey said nothing and watched Charlotte step in front of him, all smiles, to embrace her husband and then lead him past and into the house without acknowledging his presence.

Norton arrived next to him, saying, 'I've been thinking about what you said. Earlier.'

'I said a lot earlier. Can you narrow it down?'

'You said Billy Jenkins had an attitude problem.'

'Glad you were paying attention.'

'Don't be smart all the time. What were you talking about, when you mentioned Jenkins?'

'I didn't like him, that's all.'

'No it's not. You barely met the man on Friday night. I see you coming back from the building site on Sunday lunchtime and you mention him to me, out of the blue. What's going on?'

Storey hesitated. He knew this was the first step away from being an ordinary employee and moving into something new. He'd be conspiring with someone, but he didn't know why or even who he'd be conspiring with.

Norton saw his hesitation. 'Look, if it's to do with Darren, tell me anyway. I'm his uncle not his father confessor. If he's doing something with Jenkins that's going to get him, or me, in the shit then I need to know. You don't get to come in here with your puffed-up moral righteousness, deciding what to say and who to say it to. You're just an employee.'

'Right, and so are you,' Storey said, pulling his shoulders back. 'You don't pull rank on me, you don't have any stars or bars on your arm to tell me what to do. I can walk away any time.'

He saw Norton weighing this up, perhaps realising Storey was right but still trying to find a way to exercise power over him. He didn't take into consideration that Storey had eighteen years dealing with officers pulling rank to get their way, making stupid decisions to cover their own backsides or to suck up to the next backside above them. Now he was a civilian he was damned if he was going to let anyone claim superiority on the basis of an invented hierarchy.

And then he saw Norton make the realisation, and change tack, turning to stand next to him, looking in the same direction over the compound, the decking and its handrail casting shadows from the lamp-post over the driveway's grey slabs. He thought he heard frogs from the pond but couldn't be sure, given it was so late in the year.

Norton said, 'I apologise. I've been out of uniform years now but I sometimes think I'm still wearing it, especially where other ranks are concerned. I never expected to be in this kind of position, a kind of *aide-de-camp*. I thought I might get myself a law degree, actually, get involved in legal work for ex-soldiers, that kind of thing. I fancied the law might have a kind of logic to it that I'd work well with.' He glanced up at Storey. 'Instead, Bran Doyle found out I was on civvy street and got in touch and, well, here I am. Living in the boss's house, acting like a fucking secretary. He paid for me to do some accountancy exams so I'm now a pen-pusher and leader of men. Life's twists and turns, eh?'

'How did he know you in the first place?'

'Family. His father knew my father back in the Smoke. I know you probably think Doyle and I come from different backgrounds, even different classes. But I was brought up three streets away from him, went to the same school, but with fifteen years between us so we didn't really know each other. Turns out his dad and my dad used to rob garages and betting shops together. His was caught and sent down for ten years. Mine got away with it and gave it up. Earned enough to send me to a decent school and eventually I signed up wih the army and here I am. Family means a lot to Doyle. The one thing he didn't like about coming up here, which to be honest was more Charlotte's idea than his.'

'There's more to her than meets the eye.'

Norton grinned. 'She told you, did she? The punk queen of Guildford. Now frozen butter wouldn't melt in her mouth. But all those bankers' wives you saw the other night would spit out their sherry if they knew some of the things she'd done.'

Storey continued staring over the deck and the pond. He said, 'What was it like bringing up Darren by yourself?'

Norton glanced at him. 'You've never had kids?'

'Never got near to it. I'm not the sort to have them.'

Norton took a long time before continuing and Storey thought he wasn't going to bother. Perhaps it was too difficult. Then the other man said, 'Nightmare. When his mum and dad were killed he was put with some foster people until I could sort out the paperwork and take him home. He resented everything and everyone. Thank Christ I was posted back here by then.'

'He seems a bit … I don't know, adrift.'

'He's basically a good kid. He went to catering school in Henley Green when we first got here. But he was a young sixteen and he couldn't hack it. Too repetitive. Not exciting enough. Fancies himself as an international Casanova or something. You'll have noticed the little moustache.'

'Is that what it is? I thought a slug had landed on his top lip and hadn't been able to escape.'

They listened to the activity in the pond.

After a moment, Norton said, 'Doyle wants you to drive him tomorrow.'

'Where to?'

'He'll tell you. Eleven o'clock departure.'

'Where will you be?'

'None of your fucking business, is it?'

That's how Storey knew their moment of intimacy was over.

CHAPTER ELEVEN

S TOREY DIDN'T KNOW where Doyle was taking him until he said slow down and turn right, through the entrance. The sign on the half-height brick wall said it was a Marriott Hotel and Country Club and before they arrived at the car park Storey had guessed it was an expensive golf club with leisure facilities and hotel attached. Various signs pointed to the Spa and to the clubhouse and Doyle told him where to park and when they climbed out led him towards the entrance — a brick construction apparently intended to replicate a Gothic arch. Storey hung back, saying, 'Can't I stay out here, in the fresh air?'

Doyle stopped and looked at him, hands on hips. 'Don't give me shit today, Storey. I want you to come in and meet my friends.'

'Your wife said you were drinking with them last night.'

Doyle hesitated only a fraction, but Storey saw it, the confusion in his eyes, before he recovered and said, 'Different bunch of lads. Don't be a pain.'

'I don't play golf.'

'Who said we're playing golf?'

'It's a golf club.'

'Look at my hands. Do you think I can play golf? Stop pissing about and come in.'

They passed through an entrance lobby dominated by huge round pillars and Doyle marched purposefully over the broad marble flagstones and led them into a large and airy dining-room that gave on to a patio, the windows closed against the chill. There was a bar to their right, a waistcoated barman polishing glasses and smiling at them briefly. More tiles here, and four huge chandeliers overhead with a dozen small lamp-shades nestled on each one.

Three men sitting next to the window turned their heads towards them. They were in their fifties, Storey judged by their hair and girth, all of them wearing sports jackets over polo shirts. Doyle was also wearing a sports jacket but when he took it off to drape it over the back of a chair he revealed a tight black tee-shirt. Evidently dress-codes were not relevant here—or not relevant to Doyle.

Now he was shaking their hands, leaning over the table, turning to bring Storey into the group.

'This is Paul Storey, he's driving me around. And I'm probably driving him nuts.'

The men laughed, and Storey realised that Doyle had some power over them. Perhaps it was just charisma and force of personality, or maybe there was something else, something dependent on their knowledge of him and his history.

Doyle saw the question in his face. He said, 'I come up to Coventry to fight Big Jerry Finch. That's when me and Charlotte first saw it. These reprobates was my crew—Alf was the promoter, looked after me, showed me around, made sure I was fed and watered. George and Derek here were in my corner. When we come back here to live I looked 'em up. Now we meet what, every five, six weeks?'

The one called George said, 'Whenever you can drag yourself away from that gorgeous wife of yourn,' and they all laughed again.

Doyle had seated himself now and pointed Storey to pull up a chair from the neighbouring table to sit with them. Looking around, Storey saw the place was nearly empty. It was not yet mid-day on a Monday morning in December so he wasn't surprised there were few people around.

A young waitress came and they ordered drinks and food, Doyle instructing Storey to order what he wanted. He chose a Perrier water and what appeared to be a burger designed by a committee of Michelin chefs, given its price. Then he sat and listened as they talked amongst themselves about people they knew, people who'd died, people who'd moved away to be closer to the grandchildren.

Doyle was at ease and didn't perform to the crowd, as Storey had seen him doing the night of the party. Although he was the dominant personality in the group, he took their ribbing in good spirit and didn't pull rank.

After they'd eaten the men ordered whiskeys and brandies and Alf Chamberlain, a red-faced man with bushy eyebrows and a stronger Midlands accent than the others, leaned across the table towards him.

'So what's your secret, Paul? Who are you?'

'I'm just a driver,' he said, conscious of Doyle's eyes on him. He didn't care what Doyle thought, but neither did he want to embarrass him in front of his friends by saying something stupid.

'Just a driver,' Alf repeated. 'You weren't born a driver, though, were you? And you're what, in your mid-thirties? Are you doing this for a living or what?'

'For the moment. I'm in-between careers.'

'Aren't we all? I was hoping to be a ballet-dancer — oh, hello, look what the cat dragged in.'

Storey followed his eyes, half-turning in his seat, and saw two men approaching. The one in front was in late middle-age and was wearing a patterned golfing sweater and pale trousers, his thick hair neatly combed. He was the older man Storey had seen talking to Billy Jenkins and paying for the stolen building materials.

The other man was the huge bodyguard or driver who'd leaned against the truck while the goods were being transferred. Storey noted the hardness in his dark eyes and the fact that he didn't seem to blink.

Now the first man had reached their table and everyone had gone quiet. All the men except Doyle were looking away. Doyle had turned his chair to see the newcomer more directly, then he stood up as he realised he didn't want the other man looking down at him.

There was a pause, then Doyle did a strange thing. He gestured to Storey and said, 'Stand up, Paul. Do you know who this is?'

Storey pushed his chair back and stood up. 'Yes. It's Frank Ivory, the man you beat in a couple of fights thirty years ago.'

Doyle let this settle and Storey saw a ripple of irritation cross Ivory's face.

Then Doyle said, 'That's right, Handsome Frank. Though age has taken a bit of a toll, as I think you mentioned the other night. How are you doing, Frank?'

'Well, Bran, very well,' he said, bringing a half-smile back to his face. 'You and I should have a chat at some point. There's something I need to talk to you about. I was saying to Lionel just the other day, I need to talk to Bran Doyle. Isn't that right, Lionel?'

'That's right, boss. You were very keen.'

Storey was now feeling awkward, standing next to Doyle and Ivory, who seemed to be measuring each other up as though exchanging taunts at a weigh-in. Behind him, he sensed the same coiled power in Lionel as he'd seen the day before, an animalistic strength that was more than muscle-power, more atavistic.

Ivory was saying, 'A shame about your driving ban, Bran. The Bran ban, as I like to call it. Means you need someone driving you around because you can't do it yourself, is that right? Is that who this is, this bright young man? You'd be right to point out I've got a driver, too, but of course that's because I want one, not because I need one.' He turned to Storey. 'It must be tough on you, having to obey the whims of your boss. Drive me here, drive me there, just do as I say and don't have a life of your own. Where did he find you, the Job Centre? Is he paying minimum wage? You know his businesses aren't doing so well, are they, Bran?'

Doyle was grinning at him, their faces about eighteen inches apart. He said, 'I'm doing okay, thanks for asking.'

'I'm only repeating what I've heard. I hope you *are* doing well, you being one of the city's leading businessmen. I wouldn't want anything to go wrong for you. Tenants to start leaving your properties, that kind of thing. Or the properties themselves developing problems. That can happen when you invest in old housing stock, no matter how much you spend in renovating them. Isn't that true? An old building is an old building. How many have you got now? Ten, is it? Fifteen? Lot of revenue coming in. Be a shame if they started to fall down. Whereas you see my income is from proper investments. Grown up stuff, international markets, that kind of thing. Safe and secure.'

Storey wondered whether he should say or do something. He was, after all, 'security' and despite the apparent bonhomie in Ivory's tone of voice it seemed to him there was a threat behind every word.

He said, 'Mr Doyle—'

And was cut off immediately by Ivory. 'Oh, it's *Mr* Doyle! That's a true employee for you, Lionel, eh? Something you could learn. A bit of respect for me. Young Paul here obviously knows his place. Come up through the school of hard knocks and knows which side his bread is buttered. Knows when to kow-tow to the master. You've got him well trained, Bran, I'll give you that.'

Doyle glanced at Storey. 'I wouldn't say things like that in front of him, Frank. You don't know where it might lead.'

'Do you hear that, Lionel? Things might get out of hand if I say the wrong thing in front of Bran's *driver*. What a politically-correct world we live in. What's the problem, *Paul*? Am I in danger of hurting your feelings? Being too familiar? Might you do something that I'd live to regret?'

Doyle was grinning again. He said to Storey, 'Tell him. Tell him what you did.'

Storey had known this was coming. He'd felt Doyle manipulating the situation to put him and Ivory in this position. He didn't want to play Doyle's game but neither could he stand the sight of Ivory believing he was playing a superior hand.

While he was thinking this through there'd been a pause, which Ivory seemed to take as fear or hesitation on Storey's part. He half-turned to Lionel, his audience, giving him a small secret smile that probably only Lionel and Storey saw.

So Storey said, 'I used to be a policeman.'

'Oh really?' Ivory said. 'That means you have a nice pension.'

Storey felt the men seated at the table paying more attention, their heads turning towards him.

He said, 'I was a specialist.'

'Oh good. Computers? Filing?'

'Firearms. I was trained in the use of weapons. Interesting job. Out and about, knocking in doors, dealing with low-lifes. I was involved in a couple of well-known incidents. The one people still talk about, because it amuses them, is the one where a naked man ran towards me and I put two bullets in his chest. Here and here.' He tapped Ivory on the chest in two places. 'Then there was the one a few weeks ago, you might have seen it in the press. I broke up a Syrian smuggling ring. Big shoot-out, a couple of people dead. It ended when I put a bullet through the eye of a Syrian arms dealer. He was holding a woman police officer hostage. He was dead before he hit the floor.'

Doyle was still grinning as he turned back to Ivory, seeming to lean in a little further towards the other man. He said nothing.

Ivory lost his certainty. He forced himself to look at Doyle and down at the men at the table, who by now were staring directly at him, as if to see how he'd react to Storey's tale.

Apparently deprived of options, Ivory looked from Storey to Doyle and back again, said, 'Have a nice meal,' then turned and walked away, heading towards the furthest corner of the dining room, Lionel loping slowly behind him.

Doyle turned to Storey. 'You enjoyed that, didn't you?'

'Not particularly,' he said. 'He won, didn't he?'

'How do you make that out?'

'He forced me to tell him something about myself I didn't want to say. Now he knows more about me and I've got nothing.'

On the way home Doyle asked him about the shootings.

'What did it feel like, afterwards? When I'm fighting it's all adrenaline and then there's the downer afterwards. Is it like that?'

'The opposite. What you're doing is trying to combat adrenaline. You don't need that in your body, making you tense.'

'But you can't help it, right? You go in a place, what, half a dozen of you, tooled up, waiting for blokes like that one who ran at you.'

Storey kept his eyes on the road. He'd talked about this over the years and people always had their own ideas of what it would be like to carry weapons into conflict situations. No one really understood unless they'd done it, like other officers or, sometimes, soldiers.

He said, 'The first time I shot someone I was two hundreds yards away, on a roof, looking through a kitchen window at an accountant threatening his wife with a machete. It's easy when someone else is threatened. You're doing a job that someone's got to do, however much you might not like the idea of the bullet going into him.'

'You can't afford to be squeamish, though, can you?'

'The second one was a mistake. My mistake. We'd gone into a house to arrest a man and we knew he had weapons, so we were being careful. I was caught out. He ran at me carrying his dog's chew-toy, a big piece of rope, and in the dark I thought it was a gun or something so I shot him. The bullets went through him in two places and just missed his wife and kids.'

'Bloody 'ell. I think that was mentioned in one of the pieces I read.'

'That one didn't feel good because it went against my training. He surprised me, and I wasn't supposed to be surprised. And that's why I quit, in the end. I couldn't trust myself not to do it again. Plus, you might not believe it, but it was all a bit boring by then.'

Doyle was silent for a few minutes, Storey paying attention to his driving, proving he could be the professional, keep his mouth shut.

Then Doyle said, 'You recognised Frank Ivory soon enough.'

'He hasn't changed much from that video.'

'What did you make of him? And Lionel?'

Storey had known this conversation was coming and had been wondering what to say, whether to reveal that he'd seen the two men the previous day. What would happen if he did? He'd already thought through the answer to that: Doyle would go nuts, fire Darren and Jenkins and maybe set the police on Ivory for receiving stolen goods. Bad for Norton, bad for Jackie West.

So why did he feel guilty keeping the information from Doyle?

Finally he said, 'Ivory sounded like he still had a grudge against you. All that stuff about your business. Sounded like a threat.'

'He's always had a big mouth. He likes to ponce about, throwing his weight around. I ignore it.'

'So what's he do now?'

'All that bollocks about investments … He owns a couple of pubs round and about. He had family here so he come back when he finished fighting. It was just bad luck we ended up in the same place. Mind you, I fought hundreds of people so I couldn't get away from all of them. Pity he's the biggest wanker of the lot and I still have to see his mush from time to time. That's fate for you, as my nan used to say. Drunk Irish witch as she was.'

Storey said, 'And who's that Lionel character? He looks like something from the Munsters.'

'Him? That's Frank's son. There's a rumour he's a bit slow, but he'll he do whatever his dad tells him to.' He paused, then said, 'You haven't talked about that last feller you shot, the Syrian. From what I read it sounded pretty hairy.'

'He was threatening someone I liked, so I shot him. And he was an arsehole.'

'Remind me never to get on your bad side.'

Storey grinned at him. 'Watch what you say about my driving, then.'

CHAPTER TWELVE

H E DROPPED DOYLE in front of the house and drove around the back to put the Mercedes under cover in one of the garages.

He noticed Felicity and Darren standing outside the back of the house and when he'd parked and was closing the garage door he heard them talking loudly at each other, her voice light but cutting against the early evening air.

Darren was staring at him as he walked past them, keeping a respectable distance and making no attempt to catch their eye.

But it wasn't enough for Darren, who turned towards Storey and raised his voice, saying, 'Hey, Mr Driver, how did you do that?'

Storey turning, keeping his face pleasant, not needing this now. He said, 'Sorry, I didn't catch that. Hello, Miss Doyle.'

She smiled quickly, as seemed to be her style, as though a full-on baring of her teeth would give too much away, then lowered her eyes in recognition of Darren's rudeness.

Darren was on adrenaline now, stepping forward, his hair perfectly in place, the delicate moustache still trying to impose itself on his pale features. 'I said, how did you do that? Get to be so high and mighty all of a sudden?'

'I'm just doing a job, Darren. Like Rod. Like you. It's just work.'

'I could be doing what you're doing, driving him around, but he didn't want me, did he? He wanted the killer, two-gun Storey.'

'Why don't you give it a rest?'

'Or what? You'll twist my arm like you did Billy Jenkins'?'

'What do you want me to say? Or rather, what do you want me to do? Do you want me to thump you so you can go off feeling justified that I'm the bad guy? Or do you want me to explain why I'm the better choice, because of my experience, my age and my much better dress sense?'

Now he saw Felicity Doyle covering her mouth behind Darren, unable to stop herself laughing, and he wondered what was really the situation between these two. He knew she was older than Darren and from what little he'd seen of her she had the brains and the sense. Perhaps she went for the Latin Lover type.

Darren also heard Felicity smothering her laugh and he looked back at her, a flash of annoyance on his face, before turning to say to Storey, 'Just don't think you're better than me.'

'I don't. But some people have natural class.'

'And I don't?'

'I didn't say that.'

'You didn't have to. That's what you're thinking. Well don't get too carried away with yourself. You have no idea what's going on in this house—'

'Darren,' Felicity said, and he turned to look at her again before continuing. 'I can see what you're doing. Sucking up to Doyle, telling him stories, getting him to like you so you can get more and more involved. Don't try it. It's none of your business.'

'You're making a lot of assumptions,' Storey said, watching Darren run out of steam. 'If you try to read my mind, you should be careful. You never know what you might see in there. You might not like it.'

He stared at Darren long enough for the younger man to eventually become unnerved, glancing helplessly at Felicity again before brushing past Storey and walking along the stone pathway to the front of the house, where Storey knew his green Mini was parked.

He watched Darren walk away and when he turned back Felicity Doyle was staring at him with an expression he couldn't read.

———

She said, 'Why are you giving him a hard time?'

'I think you'll find he spoke to me first. I was minding my own business.'

'He's twenty-three years old. You're what, in your mid-thirties?'

'Meaning I should know better?'

'Meaning it makes you a bully. Once a cop, always a cop.'

Storey nearly turned and left, then, but something occurred to him. He said, 'What do you know about his friend, Billy Jenkins?'

'What do you mean, what do I know about him?'

'When I met them the other night it seemed to me Jenkins was a bad influence.'

'Jesus, you're beginning to sound like my dad. What does that mean, a bad influence?'

Storey glanced away, at the big house where she lived behind closed doors, still seeing her parents every day, perhaps not even exposed much to the outside world. He shouldn't expect too much of her.

He said, 'I've only been working here two days and I feel like I'm drowning in subterfuge and conspiracies. Do you not see it? What's going on around you?'

'Have you considered it might be the other way around?'

'What?'

'You've only been here two days and you think you know us. Got us sussed. You've been a policeman so you're probably cynical and don't think much of ordinary people, civilians I suppose you'd call them. Why did you say that to me? About conspiracies and whatever.'

'I don't know. I sometimes act as though women are cleverer than men. Maybe that's because I'm a man and I know I'm stupid most of the time. I can't help thinking you've got the edge on us. I was hoping you'd be able to help me out with your family.'

She'd wrapped her arms around herself as the evening had got colder. She was wearing a thin jumper with buttons up the front, her red hair out of its pony-tail and just reaching the nape of her neck.

———

He said, 'You should go inside. It's getting chilly.'

Ignoring this, she said, 'You were trying to tell me something just now. What was it? Something about Billy. You don't have to be polite. I know I've been sheltered but I'm quite strong.'

'From what I've seen I don't like Billy Jenkins. Call it professional instinct, or whatever. I wouldn't want Darren, or you, caught up in anything you shouldn't be caught up in.'

'What the hell are you talking about? Caught up in what?'

Storey was realising that he was saying all this because they were outside, beyond the reach of Jackie West's bugs. He hadn't done it consciously but maybe part of him knew that inside the house he was likely to be heard by forces outside of his control. He wanted to avoid that if he could.

He said, 'I've seen people like Jenkins before. We had a guy called Simmons when I was a beat copper, when I was very young, who was like a magnet for people with shaky morals, or who didn't know who they were. Know what I mean? He gave off certainty like a goat gives off musk. So naive kids stole for him, tried to impress him, made it possible for him to live quite well without doing anything illegal himself. He was like Fagin, only the kids were a bit older, late teens or early twenties, looking for someone to approve of who they were.'

'What happened to him?'

'One of the lads he worked with suddenly realised what was going on, how he was being used. Broke into Simmons' house and stabbed him in the neck. Then called us. I was first on the scene, what a bloody mess. And the guy was sitting on a chair in the corner with the knife still in his hand, saying Simmons deserved it.'

'And you're saying that Billy is like this Simmons character?'

'People who find out they can be persuasive always look for people to serve them. I think he might be someone who enjoys having Darren around but not for good reasons.'

Felicity was shaking her head now. 'Darren's a good guy, trust me.'

'I haven't seen much evidence of that yet.'

'Well you're not looking hard enough.' Giving him a bleak smile and turning on her heel to walk inside and close the door behind her.

He made his way back to the house to drop off the keys. Turning the corner he saw a white van parked in front of the glass entrance, its rear doors open. As he watched, he saw Kate, the decorator, carry a couple of cans of paint to the back of the van and lay them down inside. Her hair was hidden beneath a cloth she'd tied over it like a cleaning-woman from a 1960s film. He thought she still looked good, though, holding herself with a certain elegance, slim in jeans and a short denim jacket.

He knew she'd seen him but she didn't look up from the darkness of the van straight away, saying before she turned around, 'Don't let the boss see you fraternising with the staff. He might dock some of your wages.'

'Would it be worth my while?'

Now she turned to him, smiling, her teeth white in the growing darkness. 'That depends on what you get in exchange, doesn't it?'

He didn't know what to make of this, so he nodded towards the van. 'Packing up?'

She brushed the palms of her hands on the tops of her jeans. 'Nearly finished so I thought I'd start taking some of the heavier stuff back. Still one or two things to titivate but I don't need the ladders or all the brushes and the work-tables and so on. All I need is just a small pot of paint and a narrow brush.'

'So what's next? Contracts lined up?'

'A few things, yes.'

'Time to go for a drink later?'

She hesitated and he couldn't read what was in her eyes. Then she said, 'No. But you could take me for a meal. I warn you, horses have to leave the area when I'm hungry.'

He asked where she'd like to go and she thought for a moment and then told him the name of a place he didn't know. 'But that's no surprise,' he told her, 'I don't know anywhere. Still a stranger in my own town.'

'We'll get you up to speed soon enough,' she said, slamming shut the van doors.

As she drove off he went inside the entrance and hung the car keys on the rack next to the door. Turning to leave, he thought he glimpsed Doyle watching him from the doorway into the lounge. When he moved further inside to say goodnight there was no one there.

CHAPTER THIRTEEN

W HEN NORTON FIRST met Swann and Lethbridge he thought it was an accident. He'd been sitting at the bar of Crosby's, opposite the IKEA car park, when a fat man wearing a white mackintosh sat next to him. His hair was fair and thin but layered neatly over the crown of his head, and the cuffs of his shirt emerged an inch from his jacket. He seemed well-fed and expensively dressed. After a while he started talking to no one in particular, glancing at Norton until he responded and soon they were in conversation, Swann telling him his name as if he should recognise it but not being offended when he didn't.

An hour later they were sitting at a table when another man appeared, a man with narrow, dark eyes that never blinked, introducing himself as Eric Lethbridge, like Swann in his mid-forties or fifties, Norton guessed, both of them having enough money to afford expensive clothes and buy whiskeys as though they were Coca-Colas. Swann was the talkative one, very active with his hands, laying things out, palms up, emphasising with a chop of his right hand, shrugging like a Frenchman inside his white mackintosh.

Lethbridge was the quiet one, those intense eyes not moving far from Norton's, almost as though he were trying to force Norton into agreeing with him by staring him out.

He didn't really put it together until they'd been talking for another hour, when Swann said they had a proposition for him.

Norton had drunk enough to be interested and asked what it was and they told him they both owned betting shops in the city and now they wanted to branch out, set up something that would bring in more money, but it had to be a project related to what they already did professionally, otherwise what was the point? They wouldn't be able to leverage their reputation. Norton wondered what kind of reputation a couple of bookies might have but said nothing.

He got a jolt when Swann told him what the project was: they wanted to build a chain of gyms, focusing on weights and boxing. Swann said Coventry had its fair share of youth who were, let's say, out on a limb. Never mind the students. They might jog or do spinning or yoga ... but they were talking about the youngsters who couldn't find work, who weren't academic enough to go to college or university, who were in danger of winding up in a criminal lifestyle.

Swann and Lethbridge wanted to prevent that, to offer them an outlet, and they understood Craig Norton was the man who could help them.

At this point Doyle had just started to break the ground for his own gym, so Norton's first thought was to wonder whether this was good timing or bad. Or just a coincidence. Somehow they knew of his connection to Doyle—they were old enough to know of the old fighter, hell, they might even have seen him fight thirty years ago. Were they talking to him thinking he might leave Doyle's organisation and join theirs? Or did they just want to borrow him, to find out what Doyle was doing and maybe steal his ideas?

Norton knew himself well enough to know he didn't have many principles. What he'd seen in the army had knocked that out of him. But for the first time in his life he found himself in a moral dilemma. He liked Doyle but he didn't think Doyle was giving him the credit he deserved. They went back a long way, because of the friendship of their fathers, long before he signed up for the army, even with the fifteen years or so between them.

So he couldn't just dump all that history and go work for a rival company. Could he?

But this was a chance to make something for himself. Yes he'd be on a payroll again, working for someone else, but if the plans for franchises around the country came good he might be a big fish in a big pond one day. Didn't he owe it to himself to take the risk?

The problem was, Swann and Lethbridge had their own plans. And they were already well underway. They told him during that first meeting, when he'd grudgingly said he'd think about it, that they saw him as a facilitator for this first gym. They had builders, workmen, accountants, planners ... everything they needed. What they wanted him to do was supervise. Perhaps learn on the job at Doyle's construction and help them out from time to time. Keep them up to speed.

It didn't matter if he didn't go on site much, they said, because he kept the books, didn't he? He must have let that slip, he thought afterwards, though he didn't remember it.

The point was, all they wanted from him was an occasional heads-up on what was going on with Doyle's works, so they could avoid any mistakes.

It was almost a month into the construction before Norton realized what he was doing and what position they'd put him in. Then he wondered what he could do to get out of it.

———

He'd been waiting twenty minutes when they came in, together as usual, reminding him of that couple in the Blues Brothers — the dark glasses, the suits, the difference in their body types. Only they weren't funny.

In addition to owning four betting shops each they also owned and ran this pub in Binley, a small establishment that never seemed very busy. He thought perhaps it was a way to get rid of surplus profit from the betting shops. They certainly hadn't put much into decoration or hygiene. Now they saw him and came over, Lethbridge pausing at the bar to order drinks, Swann scraping out two wooden chairs for them to sit on. Norton was sitting on a green faux-leather banquette, its surface scratched and torn in places and leaking a kind of brown sponge material from the holes.

Swann did his usual social bullshit, asking how he was, saying he and Lethbridge had been busy, it was good of him to come on short notice … Norton knew it was all blah meant to normalise what they were up to.

Because by now he knew what he was doing: he was betraying Bran Doyle.

And he despised himself for doing it, even though he couldn't stop.

They asked about Darren and whether he was still fucking up and before he knew it, Norton was talking about Storey, the new guy Doyle had hired as a driver but had already promoted, giving him some kind of supervisory power over Darren even though he had no experience of construction, as far as he could tell.

Swann was immediately interested, said, 'So that's weird, right? Why do you think he's done it?'

'Who knows what goes through the mind of Bran Doyle?' Norton said, finding himself, as usual, adopting a formal and slightly sarcastic way of talking to the two bookies, as though he could distance himself from what they were doing by pretending to be someone else, someone with higher morals.

'Is he someone we should worry about?' Lethbridge asked. 'I don't have to remind you we're paying for you to keep us in the loop when things like this happen, and it seems to me you've been off your game with this. What've you been doing?'

Swann then coming in as usual to smooth things over, saying, 'It is what it is, so let's move past that. I'm sure you'll keep an eye on this Storey character, right, Craig? And besides, there's something bothering me more, Craig, that I need to ask you about. Something that came to me the other day.'

'What's that?'

Swann's round face turned serious, his pale eyebrows scrunching together as he frowned. He said, 'I have to ask you—does it bother you, us being in competition with Doyle? I mean, are you okay with it? You're like his right-hand man, and this can't sit easy with you.'

Norton asking himself, Why now? Why the sudden concern after two months of secret meetings and quiet conversations in the back of this shitty pub?

But he said, 'I can't say it does. Bother me, I mean.'

Swann seemed relieved. 'Good, good, I'm glad to hear that. Because, you know, if you had second thoughts ...'

'Look, I owe Doyle nothing. He's my employer and that's fair enough. But I learned in the army to respect where the money's coming from, but you can't believe it's going to respect you back.'

Lethbridge said, 'It's got no conscience,' and Norton thought to himself the man had read that somewhere because he'd never said anything remotely philosophical before. And at the same time wondering how he'd managed to find himself here, betraying a former friend—wait, *was* he a former friend? Or was it just that their relationship had changed now Doyle had this new enterprise? Previously, Norton had looked after Doyle's properties, kept them in order, maintained the books, did the tax returns. Set up the office in town and taken on the secretary, Nicki. Then when Felicity had grown old enough to take over that part of Doyle's portfolio, and he'd had the notion to build the gym, Norton had handed over to her and shifted his responsibilities, too. Felicity had become the landlord's agent, working in the office, and he was now a project manager. Or at least project accountant.

Which for some reason had turned Doyle into a client more than a boss. Which meant that Doyle now felt entitled to throw tantrums and stamp his foot and blame Norton when things went wrong.

So he'd been losing respect for Doyle even before the Blues Brothers came along to tempt him into espionage and treachery. Hadn't he?

Swann said, 'The reason I asked is because things are moving along now. We've purposefully kept you away from the build, except for the odd photo we've shown you, obviously, because we wanted to save your blushes.'

Lethbridge said, 'Because you blush like a girl. Did you know that?'

Swann glanced at him, annoyed, then continued. 'Now we're going to have to ask you to step up.'

'Seeing that I haven't done anything yet, it won't be hard.'

'I'm glad you see it that way. We're going to be putting more responsibility on your shoulders. Although we're largely funding this first construction, we're not doing it all by ourselves. We've got some backers—'

'Hold on,' Norton said. 'You told me you were putting up all the money yourselves.'

'We are,' Swann said. 'Mostly. There are some extra expenses we didn't take into account. The price of raw materials has gone up, you know that, with the political situation and everything. We'd budgeted for a certain amount but it's eaten into our contingency. So we've got some other interested parties on board.'

'I can't have anything to do with that. Doyle would literally kill me if he thought I was talking to financiers about your business. It's bad enough dealing with you.'

'Come on, what have you done so far? Mentioned the cheapest place to buy timber. Identified the most efficient heating system. All things we could have found out for ourselves, you've just helped us cut a few corners, speed up our timetable. You've acted like a consultant and been compensated for it.'

'Are you sure you're a bookie?'

'Of course, why?'

'You're beginning to sound like my uncle Fred. My dad's brother. Went down for ten years for laundering money through his jeweller's shop. They called him Fancy Fred because of the way he talked about money, the language he used, like he was talking about holy relics.'

Swann seemed offended, pulling back in his seat. 'So you're saying I'm talking like a criminal? That's a bit rich coming from someone two-timing his boss.'

'Then perhaps I should stop.'

Lethbridge leaned forward, his expression unchanging. 'You can't do that. Check your bank balance. You're in deep. You pull the plug and Bran Doyle will be getting something really interesting in his mail. Bank statements never lie, do they?'

Norton was seeing himself as someone walking into the pub might see him—a middle-aged man talking to two other men of the same age, discussing sensible matters over expensive drinks in a darkened corner of the room. Very ordinary and respectable.

When what he wanted to do was to rip the heads off these bastards and leave them bleeding open-mouthed on the green faux-leather seats.

CHAPTER FOURTEEN

W HAT HAPPENED WAS, Kate had told him to meet her outside the Godiva News at the top of Hertford Street, next to the Lady Godiva clock tower.

He got there just before the hour and when it struck seven o'clock he took a few steps back to watch the yellow doors open, a white model Lady Godiva with long blonde hair go riding by on her white horse, and Peeping Tom emerge from his little niche to watch through his hands. She'd been doing that as long as he remembered and Tom never learned to protect himself before going blind. There was something to be said for not looking at what you're not supposed to see, he thought, as Godiva re-entered the tower through the opposite door.

Kate had turned up five minutes later and said, 'Let's walk,' and taken him down Greyfriars Lane to the Italian restaurant at the bottom of the steps, threading her arm through his in a way that felt natural. She smelled good and seemed taller—she was probably wearing heels, not the flats she wore to work.

She'd reserved a table and they were seated and choosing from an extensive menu within a few minutes.

She said, 'Whatever you do, don't order Chianti. I can't stand the stuff. I'm happy to have a beer if you are.'

He told her he'd drink whatever she wanted and she looked at him with the same sly grin she'd used at the party, that time looking over her shoulder, as if wanting him to know she was working on him. It was a playfulness he liked much more than the type of candour Charlotte Doyle used, that actually ended up hiding who she was. Kate acted as though she wanted you to find the real person beneath the skin. You just needed to try harder.

———

They talked about Doyle and the house again and she asked him what it was like to leave the police force when he'd been part of it for so long.

'I'm still transitioning,' he said. 'I read that word somewhere—good, isn't it? I'm still neither in or completely out. I catch myself still thinking like a copper even though I've got no more authority than that waiter to arrest people or haul them in for questioning.'

'Or shoot them.'

He dismissed that, saying, 'I never had that authority. It was only lent to me on occasion. I was in London, not the Wild West. And before you say anything, yes, there was a difference.'

'So you don't miss having that power, the power to shoot people who were bad people?'

'Absolutely not. It didn't make me any braver or cleverer or more ethical ... it didn't make me anything except a bit more scared from time to time.' He saw the question forming in her eyes. 'Scared I might do something stupid, shoot someone I wasn't supposed to. Which I nearly did. Can we change the subject?'

She smiled, saying, 'Sorry, didn't mean to push any buttons.'

'It's okay. I just get a bit fed up talking about it when I'm trying to move on.'

'Transition.'

'Exactly.'

She said she got it and began to talk about the projects she had in the pipeline with other clients. The newest one had a Victorian folly at the bottom of his garden that he wanted her to restore as a study. 'Which sounds all very well,' she said, 'except there's barely room inside to fit a chair, never mind a table to work at.'

'I'm sure you'll come up with something.'

'Are you?' she said. 'Well it's nice to know someone's got confidence in me.'

'I've seen your mural.'

She laughed. 'Don't start.'

When they'd first arrived she'd looked around and, as the waiter led them to a table, asked Storey if she could sit facing out of the restaurant, through the window, and not into the room. He'd thought it was an interesting choice for an interior designer, but after the first course, when he'd settled down and started to look at the other people in the room, he understood why.

He said, 'That's Felicity Doyle over there.'

She didn't seem surprised. 'I wondered when you'd notice.'

'She's not with Darren, as far as I can see. It's a girl ... oh, I get it.'

As he'd been watching, Felicity Doyle had lightly picked up the other girl's hand and held it briefly to her lips. The other girl, a slim blonde with dark eyes and a broad smile, had enjoyed the gesture and leaned forward to say something.

Storey said to Kate, 'Did you set this up? Did you know they were going to be here?'

She was smiling now, enjoying his confusion. 'What do you think?'

'But why would you want me to see her? Doesn't she want her privacy?'

'You should talk to her about it sometime. Privacy, I mean. Living with Bran Doyle.'

'So she should move. She's old enough. He'd help her out financially.'

'She told me she wanted you to know things weren't as straightforward as they seemed. At the house.'

'What does she want me to do about it? Christ, I've only been around three days. It's like walking into a soap opera and finding out you've got the lead role. I haven't learned my lines yet.'

Kate threw back her head and laughed, showing the delicate muscles in her neck. She was wearing a simple black top that showed her strong shoulders and arms and was scooped on the top of her breasts. She said, 'Why on earth would you think she wants you to do anything about it? She's not a problem to fix.'

Despite himself he found he was annoyed, as though he were the butt of a joke. He said, 'It's not a revelation, it's not something that's going to embarrass me. I just don't understand why you've had to treat it like such a big surprise. You could have just told me and saved me the cost of a couple of meals.'

The smile left her face. 'For once, Paul, this isn't about you. She wanted you to know, to see her as she wanted to be seen. I think she probably likes you. But the real point is about Darren.'

She waited, watching him. Then he understood.

'So he's a ... what do they call it, a beard. He's pretending to be going out with her for the sake of her dad. So they can come into town and she can meet Miss Blonde over there. Is Doyle so bad she has to deceive him about stuff like this?'

'I'll say it again: what do you think?'

He didn't have to think long. 'He's a very old-fashioned man. He wouldn't have tried to stop it—how could he, in this day and age?—but he might have been upset.'

'And while she's been living under his roof she didn't want to upset him. She doesn't think it's the right time to come out ... whenever that time is, I don't know. But it's her call. So she asked Darren to help her, to create a fiction, and he was happy to help out. He's not such a shit as you might think.'

'And her dad doesn't know?'

'Absolutely not.'

'And Charlotte?'

'Felicity hasn't told her outright but she thinks she might know. Putting two and two together.'

'So thanks for the hot potato, with Bran.'

'You'll manage. You're resourceful. Besides, let's face it: who cares what you think?'

At that point Felicity Doyle turned from her companion towards him and waved with her fingers.

CHAPTER FIFTEEN

H E WAS GETTING used to waking in a strange bed, seeing the light come into the room from a different direction, having the sense of being in a separate world, on the compound, further away from road traffic than the thin strip of grass and a pavement that separated him at home.

That morning, Tuesday, he woke to find a text from Norton telling him to be ready to drive by ten o'clock, Doyle would tell him where. *I really should have a peaked cap*, he told himself as he sat on the sofa in his lounge watching breakfast TV and eating cornflakes. Black and with a shiny brim, something that would show how important he was.

He was drinking tea when his phone rang and, assuming it was Norton, he answered with a curt, 'Yes?'

Jackie West said, 'Oh, are we grumpy in the morning?'

'You'll never know, will you?'

'I'm going to ignore that and give you some information.'

'The man in the photo is Frank Ivory. Ex-boxer, local businessman.'

There was a pause. 'Were you fucking with me, Storey? Because that doesn't go down very well in my unit.'

'No, I wasn't,' he said. He explained that before he'd given her the photo he thought he recognised the man because Doyle had shown him a film of one of their fights. But it was thirty years old. Then after he'd sent her the photo he and Doyle had met Ivory in a golf club, and now he was sure it was the same man.

'You met Frank Ivory in a golf club? Was he playing or beating up the barman in the clubhouse?'

'He was dressed for golf but I never saw him on the course. He was with Lionel, his son.'

'Ah, the lovely Lionel. The Godzilla of our times.'

'So what was that about a barman? Has Ivory got form?'

'You think I was joking? Him and Lionel ganged up on a man a couple of years ago, worked in a pub in Earlsdon. Ivory thought he'd been disrespected so he had Lionel drag him over the counter and the pair of them went to town on him.'

'Did it get to court?'

'You'd have thought so, wouldn't you? But a man with Ivory's reach, charges were dropped, it was a misunderstanding, we're all best mates now ... Usual bullshit.'

Storey wasn't surprised—he'd seen the suppressed violence in the younger man's attitude and even the way he stood, as though waiting for a fight to break out so he could join in.

———

He said, 'So is that all you wanted to tell me? Not that I'm not grateful.'

'You in a hurry?'

'Come on, Jackie, don't play games,' he said, standing now and looking through the cottage window at the main house, a light on in the kitchen and one of the bedrooms. He wondered why Doyle had built something so big when there was only his wife and daughter to accommodate. And Norton, he told himself. Don't forget Norton.

Jackie West said, 'I'm interested. So Ivory and Doyle meet in a golf club, what, at the bar? Having a nice drink?'

'You want me to tell you what they talked about? Is that what you're after?'

'Can't blame me for being curious, seeing as we've got his bloody house under surveillance.' There was frustration in there, Storey thought, and then she added, 'Did he mention anyone, any names?'

'No. No names. And you still won't tell me what this is all about?'

'I can't. Stop asking me.'

'Glad you're so trusting of an ex-colleague.'

He heard himself saying this and regretted it at once. But either she didn't care or she was still working him and couldn't allow herself to be provoked again.

She said, 'I'm being told I've got to persuade you to get out of there while you can. Not that there's any danger,' she added, 'but if and when things happen they're going to happen quickly. You might get caught up in it all. You have a habit of finding yourself where you're not supposed to be.'

'Seems to me I've got a couple of choices. Stay here and keep an eye on things for you. Or resign from my job, lose money and deprive you of a valuable contact.'

'I didn't say it was me wanting you to get out. I'm not the only one involved, as I'm sure you know.'

'Do they see me as a loose cannon? Tell me they see me as a loose cannon. I always wanted to be a loose cannon.'

'I think the words "bumbling idiot" might have been spoken. You have to realise that although the press and the people of Coventry saw you as some kind of hero a few weeks ago, my bosses and their bosses saw you as a danger to yourself and to others. When you walked into this operation you should have seen their eyebrows rise.'

'Nice to have fans.'

'Storey, listen to me,' using her serious voice now, and he could see her face in his mind's eye, the knitted brows, 'there are some big hitters involved in this operation. Our end and potentially yours, too. Keep your eyes open and if the opportunity arises, get the hell out. I'm not kidding.'

'I can't do that,' he said. 'I'm having too much fun.'

Half an hour later he was driving parallel to the section of the Coventry Canal that terminated at the dead end of the canal basin, close to the centre of town. Doyle directed him to drive along a narrow lane that ran behind the red-brick warehouses and cottages beside the canal. Those original buildings had mostly been converted into offices, typically gentrified and cleaned up compared to how he imagined they looked a hundred years before. He'd seen a lot of it in London, especially in Docklands, where Victorian wharfs and factories had been re-purposed as high-tech factories or recording studios.

They parked in front of some bollards intended to prevent them driving directly into the canal, and Doyle said, 'I want you to come in and listen. You don't have to say anything.'

'I know my place.'

'I sometimes wonder about that,' Doyle said, slamming the door of the Mercedes.

They went through a door that had 'Biggs and Delvine: Architects' stamped on the glass and Doyle told the receptionist they had an appointment.

They were asked to wait and a couple of minutes later a slim man in his fifties wearing glasses with coloured frames came into the lobby and shook their hands, Doyle introducing Storey as an associate. The man was called Vogel.

In a meeting room containing a large central table, on which plans were laid out neatly, Vogel described what they were looking at. Storey thought he was nervous, watching how he licked his lips, but knew it was because Doyle was a difficult customer and this was probably going to be a hard sell.

Storey learned that the designs had been drawn up to add an extension to the gym that was already under construction. Doyle had asked for another room, a members' lounge that would be separate from the other 'social club' division. It would have its own bar and be configured so that small groups of people could sit together privately. Vogel pointed out with a bony finger where the room would give access to the gym and to the social club; where the fire exits were; and how the cubicles would be arranged.

Vogel explained where adaptations would have to be made to the foundations and to the existing structure and showed where the new plumbing and electricity conduits would come in, and how the roof structure would need to be changed to keep a single profile.

Doyle said, 'So I wasn't mad, then, asking if it was doable. You're saying it is.'

Vogel's eyes behind his glasses darted from Doyle to Storey and back again.

'Perfectly possible, of course, as the plans show. But given that so much work has been done on the build so far, it's likely to be costly. Do you think it's worth the extra cost for what is, in the end, a gym?'

'You don't get it. People go to gyms all the time now,' Doyle said. 'They know what they want. Swimming pools and squash courts and weights rooms and all sorts. Expectations. Well I can't match that, can I? I'm not one of the big franchises, your David Lloyds or whatever. You get somewhere to do weights, somewhere to learn boxing, punch a bag and spar a bit. Then somewhere to shower and get changed, then sit and have a norange juice afterwards. This,' he said, pointing to the plan of the extension, 'is a bit extra. Blokes who don't belong to a golf club and don't fancy an ordinary pub … they can pay a small fee and come and sit with their mates and natter. Wives will be welcome but I don't actually expect them to come. Maybe it's the dads of the kids who are next door punching crap out of each other. Maybe it's people who want to do a little business, make a deal. Deep carpet, nice chairs, good whiskey. Some fancy classical music playing in the background. That's the idea, see? What do you think, Storey?'

Storey had been looking at the plans, trying to make sense of them. Now he said, 'It's not big enough. Not enough space between the cubicles or whatever you call them. They'll feel crammed.'

Doyle looked closer and asked Vogel whether Storey was right. Vogel thought for a minute, then said, 'You wanted to include at least six separate groups, seated in cubicles for privacy. If we knocked that back to four cubicles on these two walls, two on each, then we could have a couple of armchairs here and here for people on their own, or people who don't need to sit in private. Or we extend this wall another six feet to accommodate more cubicles.'

'No, can't do that. We're up against the limits of the site as it is. What's all this going to cost?'

Storey saw Vogel swallow and knew what was coming, the basis for the man's anxiety from the beginning.

'With the spec you wanted, carpeting, finishes, woodwork and so on, and including our fees, we estimate another seventy-five thousand.'

'For a fucking room?'

'We have to put down more footings, change the roof structure, add more heating equipment as well as upgrading the original heating specifications. Plus, there's all the additional labour. We think it's a workable price.'

'Jesus Christ, I'd want it gold-plated for that. Come on, Storey, let's go for a swim in that canal while I've still got air in my lungs.'

He swept up the plans and left the room, Vogel saying to his back, 'We'll need to know soon so we can work out schedules ...'

But Doyle had already left.

———

In the car, Storey knew that Doyle was fuming, staring out of the side window of the Mercedes as though he couldn't bear to look straight ahead.

After a few minutes he said, 'Fucking architects, got you over a barrel.'

Storey thought Doyle was itching for an argument so measured his words. 'Why did you use them in the first place? Rod seems competent—couldn't he have built it for you?'

'I wanted something special. I wanted it to be different, make a mark. Not just a square box with two rooms. Three, as it's turned out.'

Storey glanced at him. 'Using a fancy designer's always going to cost.'

'Much as I like Rod, he's a builder, not an architect.'

'Do you have to go all in straight away?'

'What do you mean?' Turning away from the window now, looking at Storey's profile.

'Why not have Rod just build the extra room but not kit it out? Bare bones.'

'You mean finish it later, when it's made some revenue?' Storey nodded. Doyle was quiet for a while, then said, 'Won't work. The whole thing of it is, the appeal, is to well-off men who want to watch some boxing then sit back and have a drink. I want that private lounge ready from day one so people will sign up for it. They like the idea of being special, a bit separate from the rest of us commoners in the bar.'

'If you get the boys in first, though, the boxers, you can build a reputation for having a good place, a clean place. The men come into the bar, see it's all well-run, then you offer an add-on—membership of the private club.'

'What are you, a fucking construction expert now?'

'It's about respect, isn't it? You've got to earn respect before people will pay attention.'

Doyle went quiet, pushing himself back into his seat.

A couple of minutes later he said, 'Go out to the gym this afternoon. Have a good look around.'

'What am I looking for?'

'Anything. I don't know. Just show up, keep them on track. I don't think anyone respects Darren out there. Maybe you stand a better chance.'

'You don't want to go yourself?'

'I turn up, it's worse. Everyone's on their best behaviour. They don't say nothing, just keep their heads down. You're not as scary as me. You might hear something I wouldn't.'

After parking the Mercedes back in the garage, Storey had a sandwich lunch then climbed into his Volvo and drove out to the building site.

It was the first time he'd seen it in operation and he was surprised how many men were working on it: carpenters were fixing the triangular roof trusses using a small crane that must have arrived that morning. Others were laying bricks or mixing concrete. He also noticed half a dozen pre-formed uPVC windows stacked against the Portakabin in their packaging. He counted eighteen people, not including Rod, who was supervising the lowering of the roof trusses into place.

There was no sign of Darren.

After half an hour they'd fitted two trusses and Rod called a break, walking over to Storey, lighting a cigarette and squinting at him.

He said, 'You seen Darren on your travels?'

'No,' Storey said. 'I thought he might be doing the accounts in the Portakabin.'

Rod grunted a laugh. 'I'd pay good money to see that. Anything in particular I can do for you?'

'Nope. Just thought I'd show my face so everyone knows who to blame when any shit goes down. That's how it works, isn't it?'

'Approximately. You can take over from Darren in that regard.'

Storey looked at him and saw no rancour, just an acceptance that this was how the world worked.

He said, 'Do you have much shrinkage on the site?'

'What, like things going missing?'

'I should think there's a lot of it on this kind of job.'

'What do you mean?' Rod pushing Storey now, forcing him to say it.

'Like, are you having to reorder more than you thought? Getting through the bricks or the wood quicker than you expected?'

Rod was casual. 'Not particularly. Why?'

'No reason. I just thought it was the kind of thing likely to happen on an open site.'

'It's locked up every night, in case you hadn't noticed.'

'I noticed.'

Rod paused and Storey sensed he wanted to say something, but from his perspective Storey was still an unknown quantity so he wasn't going to say too much too soon. Instead he took another drag on his cigarette. 'Darren's in charge of deliveries and ordering. Purse strings and all that. I tell him what we need and he orders it.'

'And you haven't noticed things going missing?'

'Like what?'

'I don't know ... bricks, wood, tiles, whatever.'

'Are you saying my blokes might be stealing stuff?'

'You know Doyle: he wants to make sure he's getting his money's worth.'

'Well if he's suspicious of my men he can fuck off.'

Storey knew the other man was stone-walling because he'd seen Billy Jenkins drive off with half a dozen timbers and a couple of loads of tiles, and Rod wouldn't have failed to see the space where they'd been. So was Rod playing dumb to protect his men? Or to hide the fact he couldn't care less if materials went missing?

He didn't believe he didn't care. Look at the way he'd supervised the fixing of the roof trusses—he paid attention to the last detail so they landed exactly on the brackets they were supposed to. Rod took pride in his work.

Storey turned to face Rod head on. He said, 'He's not really suspicious. He's just asking the questions. In fact, he likes what you're doing here. He trusts you. And there are plans to expand the place.'

'I heard about that.'

'What do you reckon?'

'I reckon he might have to get another foreman.'

He placed his cigarette butt in a sand ash-tray, grinding it out, and walked towards the building, calling the men back to work.

Later, Storey was glad he'd told Rod that Doyle trusted him and liked his work. He probably didn't hear it from anyone else.

CHAPTER SIXTEEN

WHAT THE MAN Storey had said bothered Rod so much he decided to do something he'd never done before — check up on his own men.

That night he clocked off with the rest of them, made sure the last man to leave had seen him closing and locking the gates. Then he drove around the corner and parked in the housing estate, sitting in the cabin and reading last night's edition of the Coventry Evening Telegraph and listening to Radio 2 until he got pissed off with it and changed to somebody talking about politics, which interested him because he had a cousin who was a local councillor. It got so cold he had to run the motor for a while so he could use the heater.

When the news came on at ten o'clock he left the car where it was and walked around to the site, unlocking the chain on the gate and locking it behind him, then moving to the other side of the Portakabin, where he'd left a folding chair earlier. It was even colder in the open air, but now he was wearing the extra fleece he kept in the back of his Jeep. Always be prepared and think ahead, what his first boss had told him years ago, and what he was good at.

Now it was nearly eleven o'clock and he heard a car approaching, the gears changing down as it approached the site. The chain rattled as it was unlocked and the car came in, sounding close. Rod eased himself from the chair and moved further back into the shadow of the Portakabin. From here he could see the club but not the gate or the car. The smell of diesel from the vehicle was strong in the sharp air.

Doors opened and he recognised the voices immediately—Darren and Billy Jenkins, arguing, talking as if they'd been going at it in the car and were angry enough to continue despite the fact they'd arrived.

He kept well back in the shadows until he heard them moving towards the skeleton of the club, boots crunching on the freezing ground, then he came out of the darkness and followed them. There was no moonlight and he could see where he was going only because of the overspill of the streetlamps from the estate. But there was enough light for him to make out Billy Jenkins' white van. Part of him wanted to wade straight in and ask what the fuck were they doing here at this time of night; another part wanted to find out for himself, though he had a good idea already, bearing in mind what Storey had said. How had he known?

He'd never trusted Darren and he didn't have much time for Jenkins, though he was a strong lad who was handy to have around. Well that wasn't going to last long.

Now Darren was saying from inside the building, 'It's too much. I can't keep covering it up, people will notice.'

'What people?' Jenkins said, and Rod recognised the usual sarcastic tone in his voice, as if he never believed anything you said to him.

'The one who nearly broke your arm, for one, Storey. Doyle's set him up to watch me.'

'You're fucking paranoid, mate. From what I've heard, his card's been marked already. Don't worry about him, he'll be taken care of.'

Rod heard them walking over the concrete floor, their boots scuffing on the hard surface, a flashlight on now, moving around inside. He knew there were timbers and bricks lying around, and even some rolls of electrical cable that had been delivered the day before. He was outside the door listening in when they moved from one half of the building into the other, the dark sky visible through the half-dozen roof trusses they'd put in that afternoon. He stepped inside to follow them, knowing he could disturb them when he liked and throw them out on their ear.

He caught up with them in the other half-finished room as Darren was saying, 'Who are you selling them to, anyway? Why doesn't he go off and buy them from the same place we do?'

Rod could hear the grin in Jenkins' voice. 'Wouldn't be as much fun, though, would it? What do they call it, ironic? Taking them from Doyle ...'

Rod was walking through the doorway now, thinking he'd heard enough and he should close them down. Then for some reason he remembered that when Jenkins' van had stopped outside he'd heard another engine stop a moment later and a little further away. He'd noticed it but given it no more thought.

It was the last thing he remembered, or would ever know.

Storey's run had taken him out into country lanes where there was nothing but the occasional barking dog or the lowing of a cow to be heard. He'd realised that if he wanted to run it was better to do it at night, when Doyle had gone to bed, than try to squeeze it in before breakfast.

When he got back to the compound he saw Felicity Doyle climbing from a taxi and leaning into the front window to pay. Then she stood as it drove past Storey on its way out. There was something in the way she stood and looked at him, even at a distance, that suggested she wanted to say something.

He walked across to her, past the raised decking, seeing that she'd turned and was now staring upwards at the sky, the stars more visible here, almost in the country, where there was less light pollution. She was wearing a heavy coat done up to her neck and her red hair was freshly cut so that it hung straight on either side, framing her face.

He said, 'You okay?'

'Just thinking about men, how you can't trust them.'

'No argument from me.'

There was a pause, Storey unsure how to continue the conversation or even whether he should. These days he felt a little awkward around young girls but didn't know why.

Then Felicity said, 'Sorry about last night. I persuaded Kate into it, a bit of girl talk. She was saying she thought you were going to ask her out so I told her where Nicki and I were eating that night. It turned into a bet, whether she could get you to go out with her or not. A bit unfair on you.'

'What if I hadn't asked her? What would she have lost?'

'Nothing. It wasn't serious. We were going out anyway.'

'Why did you want me know about you and your friend? Did you think I'd be shocked? That's pretty puerile.'

She stared at him, and he thought she was working out how much to say, which way to go with her explanation. Finally she said, 'Call it my act of rebellion. I live at home, I work for my dad's company—hell I *am* my dad's company. Me and Nicki. I can't tell him because it would likely kill him, the old fart. Mr Macho.'

'And you think I won't tell him?'

'Why would you? Anyway, to be honest, I'm past caring. Soon as we find somewhere I'm moving out. I don't mind working for him but I can't live here any more. We're all driving each other nuts.'

'So what's—'

'Do you know what the routine is? Darren comes round and picks me up and we make a great show of it, love's young dream. Then he takes me into town, drops me off and goes out with his mates. At the end of the evening he picks me up and drives me home and we make another big show. Isn't that pathetic? Just to protect daddy's feelings.'

She didn't seem happy with the charade despite the fact she was the one who'd created it.

He said, 'What's in it for Darren?'

She turned away. 'God knows. I think he wishes I were straight. Perhaps he's trying to convert me, being around me all the time with his little Spanish waiter's moustache ...'

Storey smiled, then gestured towards the exit where the taxi had left after dropping her. 'So where was he tonight?'

'Good bloody question. He took me out as normal, Nicki and I went to the pictures, then went for a drink. We'd arranged for him to pick me up at eleven but he didn't turn up, did he?'

'I suppose you called him? Texted, whatever you young people do.'

'Of course. No reply, no anything. Not like him, to be honest.'

'Did he say what he was going to do tonight?'

She shook her head. 'He was meeting Billy after he dropped me off in town. That's all I know.'

'Do you know where he lives?'

'Billy? No. Why?'

'I'm supposed to be security, aren't I? Perhaps I should check things are secure.'

He thought of asking Norton where Jenkins lived—he was bound to know or be able to find out. But instead he took a chance and drove the ten minutes to the gym site.

He knew something was wrong as soon as he arrived: the metal gate was swinging open, the chain dangling.

He drove straight in, parked, and looked around. Darren's Mini wasn't there and the site seemed empty … but the gate was swinging open, the chain dangling.

He moved towards the half-built gym, trying to focus his eyes in the darkness, standing a moment and letting them adjust to the deeper darkness inside the gym, arriving now at the doorway and looking inside, picking out shadowy piles of bricks and tiles and bags of concrete. And on the floor, there, what looked in the shadows like the crumpled forms of two bodies …

He started to move towards them, then half-heard himself saying 'Ow!' as something solid connected with the back of his head, and he was just conscious enough to raise his hands against the onrushing concrete floor.

And then he wasn't conscious at all.

He was swimming underwater, making his way to the surface, but he could smell smoke and hear the distinct crackle of something burning. That was odd, he told himself, wondering why he couldn't see anything ... and then realising he would have to open his eyes.

But it was so hard to do, especially as he was comfortable. And warm. Very warm. Perhaps he could just turn over and get another half hour before he had to get up. Get out of bed.

But he wasn't in bed. It was too hard. It didn't give as he moved, as he tried to straighten his legs further down the bed, under the covers.

But there were no covers. He was in pyjamas ... and he was still wearing his shoes, he could feel them, heavy on the end of his legs, scraping against the floor.

What floor? Why was he on the floor?

He should really open his eyes, he thought, try to find out what was going on. Why it was warm. What that noise was ...

He opened his eyes and the world was blurred. And dancing. There was something moving about in the corner, in the dark.

He remembered where he was: in the gym, in the shell of the building, and it was burning. That was the movement, the blur. It was fire, flames flickering in the dark, casting shadows.

He rolled over and felt the pain from the back of his head explode into a thousand drums. Jesus, that really hurt. He raised a hand to it and felt it was sticky and a bruise was rising already.

How long had he been out?

Long enough for someone to set fire to the timbers stacked in the corner. Whoever it was had brought over newspapers and jammed them underneath the pile and set them going, using some brushwood from outside as kindling.

He stood up and was seeing more clearly now.

And saw the two bodies on the floor in front of him, closer to the flames. Motionless.

But as he watched, one started to move, turning. It was Darren, now raising himself to all fours, hanging his head, touching the back of his skull. He'd been laid out too.

Storey looked around, thinking, still clearing his thoughts. On his visit earlier in the day he'd seen fire extinguishers. Where were they?

The answer came to him: next door, in the corner, where the drinks bar would eventually stand.

He staggered through the door frame and looked around, seeing a bright red extinguisher half-hidden by more bricks. It was heavy but he gathered it up and took it back to where the flames were gaining strength. Darren was sitting on the floor now, staring at the fire. He glanced up at Storey, his hair tousled, his shirt collar bent.

He said, 'That fucking Billy,' then went back to staring at the fire.

Storey turned the extinguisher and got it working, directing a stream of foam at the timbers. He saw how they'd been stacked to lean against the breeze-block wall and take the flames upwards, on to the corner truss that Rod had placed earlier in the day. The flames had licked up the stack and were catching on the seasoned wood of the first truss. He raised the hose of the extinguisher and doused the flames.

Rod.

Still aiming the hose at the now-hissing pile of burnt timbers, he turned to Darren.

'Is that Rod?'

Darren glanced over at the body, then back at Storey.

'Yeah. He was listening.'

'Who did it? Billy?'

Darren shook his head. 'I don't know. I had my back turned. I was arguing with Billy. I didn't hear anything until he fell. I turned to see what was going on and Billy must have hit me. I wondered why he was carrying a piece of wood. Now I know. They lined me up, the pair of them. Billy and whoever. I'm going to bite his fucking nose off for that.'

Storey put down the extinguisher, now empty, and went over to the body, rolling Rod over on to his back. There was blood down the front of his coat and pooled on the concrete floor beneath him. Storey felt for a pulse.

He said, 'One problem with your revenge plan.'

'What's that?'

'As of this moment, we're the main suspects in Rod's murder.'

Storey took out his phone and called Norton.

'What do you want?' the other man said. 'Do you know what time it is?'

'If you want to save yourself and Darren a lot of time and trouble, get in your car and drive to the building site. Now.'

'What—'

But Storey had rung off. He knew he should call the Emergency Services but he needed time to think. He was sure Darren hadn't killed Rod, and from what he said neither had Billy Jenkins.

But Jenkins probably knew who had, so either the police should be given that information or Storey would have to track him down himself.

And then there was Jackie West to consider.

He had little doubt a murder would trump whatever crime her people were investigating, so keeping the death secret for the sake of the other investigation wouldn't work. She'd want to know what had happened as soon as possible so she and her bosses could make a decision. What would they do? Give up the surveillance? Put it on hold while the murder was investigated?

Depending on which units were involved there might even be some competition—the murder investigators wanting every piece of information that had come from the surveillance, while Jackie West's people wanting to keep it quiet until they'd squeezed what value they could from it.

It wasn't his call.

He leaned against a wall, watching the timbers smouldering. Darren had got to his feet but still seemed stunned. He was probably realising that whatever favour he was doing Billy Jenkins was being repaid in a way he hadn't expected. Rod was dead, Jenkins had run off and Doyle's gym had nearly burned down.

Storey wanted to be sympathetic but couldn't find it in himself to let the boy off the hook. He was old enough to have known what he was doing.

What worried Storey most was how far he was to blame for Rod's death—perhaps he was old enough to know what he was doing, too.

———

Within fifteen minutes Norton arrived, swinging his dark Vauxhall through the gates and parking it next to Storey's Volvo.

Darren had come forward when the vehicle's lights had swept across the gym but Storey told him to stay where he was, not to move, while he went and talked to his uncle.

'What the hell's going on?' Norton asked, climbing out of his car. 'Smells like a bloody forest fire ...'

Storey took him by the arm and led him away.

He said, 'Keep your voice down. Rod's been murdered. Looks like he's been knifed.'

'What!'

'Darren's here, but I don't think he had anything to do with it. Billy Jenkins cold-cocked him and left him here. I came looking and I was clobbered too. When I woke up the place was on fire and Darren was just waking up.'

'Why was he here with Billy Jenkins?'

'You'll have to ask him that yourself.'

Even in the darkness Storey could tell that Norton's eyes were staring at him as if he couldn't understand the language he was using. He'd always found it best to be direct when breaking unwanted news but even then there were times when people couldn't take it in or make sense of it.

Now Norton had broken away and was heading for the gym, the smoke from the smouldering timbers still lingering in the air. He heard Norton and Darren talking quietly at first, then Norton raised his voice, followed by Darren raising his, so he walked to them and said, 'Shut up, the pair of you. If people in those houses hear anything it's going to cause problems.'

The two men looked at him, then Norton said, 'What do we do? Have you called the police yet?'

'No. I'm going to get myself in real shit now by telling you two to go. I'll say I came here to check security on the site during night-time and found Rod. I was bashed on the back of the head, which they'll see, and someone had already done Rod in. They'll give me a hard time but they won't keep me long. I've got some credit. I just hope nobody in those houses has heard anything, seeing that it's getting on for midnight.'

Darren said, 'What about me? Where do I go? What do I do?'

'If you show up, you're a suspect. They'll say you were jealous of Rod's position, angry with Bran Doyle, bit of a tearaway— they'll find something. If it comes out you were here we'll have to think of something else. We'll say you were knocked on the head, then came to and wandered off. Concussion.'

Norton said, 'This is insane. He should stay here and face the consequences.'

Storey knew he was right, and in his previous role he would have put Darren in handcuffs without thinking twice.

But he wasn't a cop any more and he could do things differently now. Even if it meant making life hard for himself.

He took out his phone, saying to Norton, 'Take him and put him somewhere safe. And you—' turning to Darren '—you stay indoors and you don't talk to anyone except your uncle. Understood?'

'I suppose.'

Storey looked at him for a second, then seized him by the elbow and took him out of the building and into the yard, keeping his voice low. 'I know you and Jenkins were stealing materials from here. So don't give me the victim shit. You got Rod killed, unintentionally or not, and a little bit of solitary confinement won't make up for that. Now get out of my sight.'

Darren remained where he was. 'What do I tell my uncle? He wants to know why Billy hit me.'

'What have you told him so far?'

'I told him I don't know why he hit me. We had an argument and he did it while my back was turned. Now he thinks Billy did Rod.'

'It's your bed, you lie in it. I'm not making up any more lies for you.'

'So why are you doing this? Protecting me from the police. What's in it for you?'

Storey didn't have an answer. He said, 'There's no point you being locked up for something you didn't do.'

'How do you know I didn't do it?'

'Because you don't have the balls.'

Darren said nothing, his eyes moving over Storey's face. Then he turned towards his uncle and said, 'Can we go now?' and Norton came out of the shadows of the gym.

Storey said, 'Wherever your car is, fetch it and put it under cover. And don't go home.'

Norton walked past him but halted, saying, 'I suppose I should say thanks. I hope we're doing the right thing.'

'We're not,' Storey said.

CHAPTER SEVENTEEN

T HE CONVERSATION WITH Jackie West was exactly as hard as he knew it would be. First, she was pissed off because it was close to midnight when he called. Second, when he told her someone had been murdered, she asked whether it was his fault.

'That's not fair,' he said. 'I'm the one telling you. I'm actually giving you a heads-up.'

'What? Haven't you phoned it in yet?'

'I thought you'd like to take credit for it. Your contacts. Your information.'

'Don't be light-hearted, Storey. This is serious shit.'

'I wasn't.'

She asked him who had died and where and he told her and explained what had happened, leaving out Darren and Norton's involvement.

'So you got there and the place was on fire and there's a dead body on the floor?'

'No, I got there and I was going to turn over a body which looked lifeless when I was whacked on the back of the head. When I came to, some timbers were on fire. I put them out then checked the body was actually a body. His name was Rod, the site foreman. I'm sorry I don't know his surname.'

'Jesus, what a star you are. Stay there while I get the services on it. Do you need the fire brigade?'

'Yes, they might want to look for the cause of the fire, look for accelerants or whatever, then check out the place to see if it's safe. I think it's just a few charred timbers.'

'Okay. Don't you bloody move. Do you have any idea who might have killed this man?'

'None,' Storey said. 'Unless he startled some burglars and it got out of hand.'

'Did Frank Ivory have anything to do with it?'

Shit, he'd forgotten she'd seen the photo of Ivory. Thankfully, Billy Jenkins had been out of shot, just his arms showing as he dumped timber in the back of Ivory's lorry.

'I have no idea. Perhaps you should ask him. If that doesn't blow your cover, as they say.'

Jackie went quiet on the other end of the line, thinking it through. Whatever she concluded, she didn't tell him. Instead she asked, 'Where was Doyle when all this was happening?'

'At home, as far as I know.'

'And what the hell were you doing at the building site after dark anyway?'

'I'm supposedly hired as security. I thought I'd have a look around the site at night, see what it was like, whether it was safe. It was my bad luck to find poor Rod. But then I suppose I did stop the place from burning down.'

'You're in the shit, Storey. We've got a nice little operation going and you turn up and suddenly there's thieving and murder all over the place. You've got some explaining to do.'

'Does this screw up your surveillance?'

'What do you think?'

'I think I'm in the shit.'

———

It was after seven o'clock the next morning when he arrived back at the compound, two police Volvos parked in front of the entrance looking incongruous, as they always did in a domestic setting.

He pulled up on the drive of his cottage and went inside. He showered and changed his clothing, which still smelled of smoke, and was drinking a strong coffee in his kitchen when Norton knocked on his back door. Storey let him in. Norton looked pale and had bags under his eyes, his air of slightly superior calm having given way to an intense urgency.

'What happened?' he said. 'Where've you been?'

Storey was tired and was sick of answering questions but knew it was better to reply to Norton than put him off. He was beginning to doubt the other man's stability.

He explained that the police had arrived in full ceremony twenty minutes after Norton and Darren had left. Lots of questions and walking around the site, Storey explaining who he was, showing off his bump, describing the scene when he arrived and what happened to him. All very serious and straightforward.

Then, after his statement had been taken, he'd been driven to the station. They let a paramedic clean up and look at the wound on the back of his head. It didn't need stitches, more of a contusion than a cut. The doctor tested for concussion by asking some simple questions and by shining a light in his eyes to check his pupils. He passed, though he now had a throbbing headache.

Later on, perhaps three o'clock, someone called Greaves had questioned him for a couple of hours. Greaves knew him, having been partly involved in the investigation of the deaths of the Syrian smuggler and his men a few weeks ago. Then they'd left him alone for an hour or so, until Greaves had come back and they'd gone through it all again. He was interested why Storey hadn't called a lawyer—or anyone else for that matter, Storey saying as an ex-copper he knew the ropes and was happy to deal with their questions by himself. Greaves was a big man with blond hair cut short and thinning on top. He'd shaken his head when Storey said that, but after another couple of hours they seemed to accept what he said—especially the evidence on the back of his skull—and let him go.

'Did they ask about Bran?'

'Not much. They knew it was his place but I told them he was at home and anyway, what motive would he have for having his own foreman murdered, someone he relied on to get this job done?'

'Do they know about Darren?'

'Not from me.'

'How did you explain what you were doing there? It must have seemed a hell of a coincidence, you finding the body ...'

'You're forgetting, they know me, they know I was one of them. I told them I was working as security and was checking the site at night, which in a way was true. Plus, I've got an honest face.'

'Bran's furious. There's two of them in there now, questioning him. Of course he knows fuck all, which I think is what's making him mad. He thinks we've been keeping things from him.'

'Well he's right, isn't he? Did you tell him anything last night, or this morning, before the police turned up?'

'This morning. I didn't have much time because the police were waiting downstairs. I told him you went out there and found Rod.' He paused. 'He was upset about Rod and then he asked about Darren. I said I had no idea where he was. I don't know why he jumped to him so quickly. I suppose he really doesn't like the boy. Can we sit down? I need to sit down.'

They moved into the front room and Norton collapsed on to the sofa, staring at the ceiling. Storey took the armchair.

Norton said, 'Bran never really liked Darren, except he's going out with Felicity.'

He paused and his eyes met Storey's, who had a sudden insight. He said, 'You know, don't you?'

Norton blew out air, saying, 'About her? Yes. Darren's not a bad kid really, helping her out. He knows what Bran would think if he knew about Fliss and her girlfriend.'

'He was always going to find out eventually. Where is he now, Darren?'

'I put him in a B & B.'

'The police will be looking for him.'

'I thought you said you didn't mention him?'

'I didn't. But they'll want to talk to everyone working on the site. When they find Darren not turning up for work they'll look harder. He may have to front up.'

'He doesn't know anything.'

'He knows more than you think.'

'You don't think he killed Rod, do you?'

'No. He hasn't got it in him. The anger.'

'Then who?'

Storey hesitated. 'I don't know. Do you have any ideas?'

'He says Billy Jenkins hit him when his back was turned. Maybe he did you as well.'

'Maybe.'

Norton's eyes flicked to the windows. He said, 'The police are leaving. You better talk to Bran.'

'What are you going to do about Darren?'

'I don't know.'

'I'd suggest you don't tell Doyle anything. Say you don't know where he is. It might make Darren look guilty, but Doyle probably won't believe us if we try to convince him Darren's innocent.'

'Do you know what? I don't give a fuck what he believes right now.'

CHAPTER EIGHTEEN

D OYLE STOOD ON his doorstep watching Storey walk towards him, the long, loping steps he had, hands in his jacket pockets against the cold. He wanted to like the man, thought he was straight, but there was something hidden about him, as though he never really told you what he was thinking.

Doyle admired that because he knew he was too open himself, too willing to talk to strangers. But by the same token he liked to know the people who worked for him, and so far Storey was a blank page.

Now Storey was standing there, looking at him, his face neutral if a little pinched in the wind.

Doyle said, 'You're turning into a bit of a liability, aren't you?'

'You can always fire me,' Storey said, and Doyle liked that, liked the spirit, thinking the man knew who he was and what he stood for. Unlike Norton, who was just a soldier — you wound him up and pointed him at a job and he went away and did it. Storey had balls.

Throwing the car keys at him, Doyle said, 'Take me there. I want to see the place.'

Storey looked as though he was about to say something but instead nodded and started walking towards the garages.

When they arrived the forensics team was still working and the site was barricaded, a uniformed officer standing by the metal gate lifting his palm towards them as they drove close.

Storey turned off the engine and they got out, Doyle not liking the fact he couldn't even get close to have a look at his own bloody building. Storey had told him what had happened during the ten-minute drive but now he saw it he felt himself growing angry — who the fuck would set fire to his place and kill Rod? A decent man just doing his job. Who would do that?

He turned to Storey. 'Where's Darren? Have you seen him? He should be around.'

'I don't know where he is. Ask Norton.'

'I have — he didn't know either. Why am I the last one to know anything around here?'

He thought back to Norton waking him up that morning, knocking on his bedroom door, telling him the police wanted to talk to him, giving him a quick run-down while he got dressed, Charlotte turning over in bed and going back to sleep ... and they'd all known about it since midnight. Fair enough, Storey was in a police station somewhere, answering questions. But Norton knew, didn't he? Storey had telephoned him straight after calling the police, apparently. Why did Norton keep it to himself until he had to break the news, and only then because the cops had turned up? What was he doing between midnight and six o'clock?

Now he said to Storey, the pair of them still standing to one side of the policeman, staring through the wire fence at the forensics team in pale blue one-piece coveralls, 'The detective this morning said the club was burned deliberately. Like, they set a fire.'

'Superficial,' Storey said. 'Replace a couple of beams in the roof, nothing much.'

'What the fuck's going on? What was Rod up to?'

'It looks like he disturbed some thieves and came off worse.'

'They wouldn't tell me how he died. Did you see?'

Now Storey glanced across at him, that cool look in his eyes, weighing what he could say, or what he was going to tell you. 'I think he was knifed. Blood on his clothes and on the floor.'

Doyle felt a ripple of fear run through his stomach. He'd been hit lots of times and knew what it felt like, and could deal with it. But he had a fear of knives, the thought of a blade slicing his innards ...

He said, 'Poor bugger. I should talk to his partner.' He felt Storey looking at him again, interested. 'He never married, apparently. Been living with a woman for a while. Friend of a friend of mine. Who won't be talking to me now, after this. Shit.'

'You're going to need another site manager.'

Which reminded Doyle of something. Glancing at his watch, he said, 'Where are all the men? It's half eight, they should have turned up by now.'

'When do they clock on? Eight?' Doyle nodded. 'The coppers will have taken their names and phone numbers and sent them home. They'll talk to them later, they won't want them trampling over all this.' Gesturing through the fence to the muddy and rutted site.

'Why will the cops want to talk to them? Find out where they was last night?'

'Some of that, yes. But also to check if there were any grudges, any ill-feeling. That kind of thing.'

'I doubt it. Rod was a good lad.'

'So I heard. He seemed okay to me.'

Doyle was thinking back, now, to when he first met Rod — when was it, seven or eight years ago? He was just starting out on renovating properties instead of buying them and re-decorating them for a quick turnover. Rod knew exactly what Doyle wanted and was honest and kept the men in line. Tried to keep the same bunch of lads together so they all knew each other and worked well. Got rid of any that were idle or trouble-makers.

Damn, it was a shame.

He said, 'Take me home. Then I want you to come back here and see what you can find out.'

'They won't tell me anything.'

'Do it anyway. I want whoever's done this to know I'm not giving up.'

'What about a new foreman?'

'I know someone. You met him, Alf. Owes me a favour. He'll send a man to take over from where Rod finished. If these bastards think I'm stopping now then they don't know me. If nothing else, I owe it to Rod to get the job done.'

He walked back to the Mercedes knowing that Storey was watching him.

Good.

Doyle wanted him to know his job in 'security' was just beginning.

There was work to be done, finding out who killed Rod, who tried to burn down his gym. Bran Doyle didn't like it when someone laid down a challenge but was too much of a coward to come and stand in his corner like a man.

He was going to find out who it was and punish him.

CHAPTER NINETEEN

S INCE HE GOT involved with Doyle's plan to build a gym and social club, Norton had started to take more notice of places where he drank. What was the decor like? How did they put together a theme? What made a successful one different from others?

He was beginning to learn what worked and what didn't, and by now he was pretty damn sure that Swann and Lethbridge's pub in Binley didn't. The colours were all wrong—the green benches not matching the purple lampshades, for one thing— and the choice of drinks was limited. Lots of different whiskeys, because that's what they liked to drink themselves. But no guest beers and if you wanted a gin and tonic, no slices of lemon or lime to go in the glass. Amateur hour.

Plus, there was a television on the wall pumping out Sky News with the sound turned down, a ticker along the bottom providing a weird transcription of what the talking heads were saying.

He'd suggest to Doyle that they didn't bother with a television … or if they did, they only showed sports events: Wimbledon, Champions League soccer, the Rugby Six Nations. They'd draw a crowd on the big screen, whereas news was just a distraction.

Assuming that the gym got built. After what happened last night he wasn't certain Doyle would be able to carry on. Not because he wouldn't want to, but because the finance might go, pulled by the banks.

The door opened and he watched Swann and Lethbridge come in and nod to the barman, who moved away to start making their drinks.

They came over and sat facing him, neither of them taking off their coats, which told him something. He wondered what they did during the day. Did they travel between their betting shops, counting up their money, tracking down debtors, encouraging the punters to spend more money on increasingly long odds? Did they set the odds themselves these days, or was it all done by computer? He had no idea. He'd never even set foot inside a betting shop and had no desire to. As far as he was concerned, a betting shop was a place desperate people went to waste whatever little spare cash they had.

Swann arranged himself on the wooden chair and leaned forward. 'Two meetings in two days. I hope this is important, Craig. We were rather hoping to keep some distance between us, know what I mean? We don't like being summoned like a couple of naughty schoolboys.'

'Don't blame me,' Norton said, hearing a hoarseness in his voice, as though he'd been talking for hours. 'You heard what happened last night, at Doyle's site?'

Swann and Lethbridge glanced at each other, Norton unable to tell what it meant. Was it knowing, or just curious?

Lethbridge said, 'We're all ears, Craig. Please enlighten us.'

So he laid it out for them, how Paul Storey was over there late at night checking the site's security when he found Rod Spencer's body and was bashed on the back of the head for his trouble.

'Who's Rod Spencer?' Swann asked.

Norton explained he was the man Doyle entrusted all his building work to, a man he'd worked with for several years. Storey had woken up and found some of the timbers on fire and put them out, then rang the police. Not surprisingly, Doyle was livid.

Swann took a deep breath and sat back, nearly colliding with the barman carrying their two drinks. He placed them on the table and retreated.

Lethbridge said, his dark eyes devoid of any warmth, 'So you brought us over here because you thought it was a good idea to tell us in person. Very thoughtful of you, when I could be at home watching the Antiques Roadshow.'

Norton felt himself growing still inside, knowing the question he was about to ask could send the conversation in a variety of directions. Swann must have seen something in his face, saying, 'What do you want to ask us, Craig?'

'Did you have anything to do with Rod's murder? Was this a way of slowing down the build so yours gets finished first?'

'*Ours*, Craig, *ours*. And I'm shocked you could even think that.'

'Because if you're involved, I'm walking away now.'

'We'd be very sorry to hear that, wouldn't we, Eric?' Swann said, glancing at Lethbridge. 'We were just saying on the way over that you've been doing very well for us. We're very happy with the way this relationship has developed.'

'It's not a relationship,' Norton said. 'It's a business transaction.'

Swann spread his hands. 'Every successful business transaction is based on a relationship.'

'You haven't answered the question.'

'Did we have anything to do with your man Rod's death? Of course not. We don't do things like that. We're part of the business community here in Coventry. It'd be more than our reputations were worth if we did anything like that.' Adding with a grin, 'And were found out.'

'You can cut all the bullshit. If I find out you were involved—'

'What?'

Norton turned his gaze on Lethbridge. 'No one will come out of it well.'

There was a silence, then Swann, as always, re-started the conversation. He didn't like silences. He said, 'So this Storey character was there, was he? What did you say he was doing?'

'Doyle hired him as a driver but also to do some other things — like security, and keeping an eye on Darren. So he went to the site to see how secure it was at night.'

'Is he someone we need to be worried about? I assume he doesn't know about our ... arrangement?'

'Of course not. You think I'd tell anyone?'

'No, you wouldn't. You're too ashamed of yourself, aren't you? Despite the monthly addition to your income.'

Norton had no answer to this so turned away, feeling the heat of both their pairs of eyes on him.

Finally he said, 'He's got nothing to do with all this.'

Swann had been sipping his drink. He put it down, smacking his lips with relish.

'That's some fine fucking drinking there. I didn't start drinking whiskey till a couple of years ago, you know? It was my man Eric who turned me on to it. I'll always owe you that debt.'

Lethbridge said nothing, waiting for Swann to ask the next question.

But instead Norton added, 'Storey doesn't know what he's doing most of the time. Doyle asked him to look after Darren, in relation to the site, but he hasn't a clue what he's looking for.'

'And Darren is where?'

'He's out of it. He's got nothing to do with what we're up to.'

'You've got to look at it from our perspective, Craig. You keep telling us that these people, Storey, Darren, will have no impact on our little project. But this is all a distraction for you now. Are you going to be able to keep up with what's happening on the site, especially if this man Storey is all over it?'

'Don't worry about me. I'm on top of it. We're here, aren't we, with me reporting in to my handlers?'

Swann ignored the jibe. 'It's not you we're worried about, Craig. It's this man Storey. Perhaps we should look into him.'

'Don't do anything stupid. I've already had the police talking to me, wanting to know where Doyle was, where I was.'

'Did they ask about Darren?'

'Why should they? He wasn't there.'

'From what you've told us before, he's family, isn't he? Who knows what kind of behaviour they might infer from that?'

'Well he's also a grown man and can look after himself.'

'When was the last time you saw him?'

'Yesterday afternoon.'

'Before the fire?'

'Yes.'

'And not since?'

'I just said no. Why?'

'No reason. It's always good to be certain of your facts, isn't it?'

CHAPTER TWENTY

H E'D NEVER STAYED in a B & B before but he liked it—there was breakfast this morning and he didn't have to wash up or even clear away his table. Then his bed was made up later in the day and now he was lying on the bed watching the first Jason Bourne movie, the one he liked best because of the hand-to-hand fighting using household implements.

What was getting him down was the idea that this might be it for him: he'd seen a man get murdered and said nothing to the police. So now he was officially on the run. Like Bourne, only without the skills to fight back. He wished he could do something, track down Billy Jenkins, find out who he was working for, sort it out so he could have his life back.

Talk to Fliss again.

He knew she was gay but he didn't see much sign of it. She was very girly, wasn't she, not at all hard-faced or butch. He couldn't understand why she fancied other women instead of him. He knew women liked him, some of them, anyway, so why was she so hard to please? He'd thought if he hung around her, being nice, doing her a favour, she'd come to see he was a better option than Nicki-with-an-eye, as she'd introduced herself, who he thought was pleasant but a bit dull.

The thought of not seeing her again gnawed at him, making it hard to concentrate on the film. Matt Damon running across the field now with that funny stiff-legged run, shooting the other assassin then going over to talk to him. Is that what they did? Professionals? Showed a bit of respect. Unlike Billy last night, Christ …

He turned away from that line of thought and focused on the film again, Bourne getting the girl to tell the man who owned the farm to come and take her away, keep her safe.

Perhaps he could do that with Fliss—phone her up and ask her to go away with him … shit, listen to him, making plans like he knew what he was doing. Who was he kidding?

There was a knock at the door and Darren asked who it was. His uncle's voice was muffled on the other side but Darren could tell he was pissed off. He opened up and let him in.

Norton was red-faced with cold and he took his gloves off and blew into his hands. Darren went back to lying on the bed, his eyes drawn to the TV screen standing on the little chest of drawers next to the tea tray.

Norton said, 'You been okay? Had something to eat?'

'The woman give me breakfast this morning and I went out for a burger later. Don't worry, I kept my scarf on over my head like a fucking Muslim or something.'

'I don't think anyone's looking for you yet but you did well to take precautions.'

'There's been nothing on the News about it. Are the police looking for me?'

'I haven't a clue. Storey says they'll talk to everyone working on the site and when you come up missing they'll start looking for you.'

'Great. Perhaps I should just talk to them. Show them my bump.'

'Which reminds me, turn around, let me have a look.'

Darren sat up and turned on the bed so Norton could look at his wound. He prised off the large dressing he'd put on the night before, then looked inside a plastic bag he'd brought with him, pulling out a box of hygienic wipes. He opened the box, took out one of the wipes and touched it to the back of Darren's head, who flinched.

Norton said, 'You're all right. You and Storey must have skulls made of concrete. A bash on the back of the head can lay you out for days. Your eyes been okay, no double vision or blurring?'

'I'm watching TV, aren't I?'

'I should have got you to a doctor, really, but it was all a bit rushed. No headaches?'

'Not what you'd call a headache. Just a throb where he got me. What's Doyle saying?'

'Not much. A lot of swearing. He wants it all to go away.' He reattached the plaster to Darren's head and tested that it would remain stuck. 'Tell me again what happened with you and Billy Jenkins last night.'

Darren turned and laid back on the bed, careful to rest his head on the tee-shirt Norton had placed on it the night before, in case there were blood-stains. He said, 'We were arguing.'

'What about?'

'Stupid stuff.' Feeling nervous now—he didn't like lying to his uncle: he always found out. 'He was angry about some girl he's been trying to get off with. He wanted to talk about it.'

'And so you went to the site? Come off it. Look at it from my position: you don't have a real reason to be there, do you? Can you see what the police would make of it?'

'I know, I know! We went there just because we could. It was Billy's idea. Said he wanted to talk where we wouldn't be interrupted.'

'And Rod found you.'

'He must have done. First thing I knew, I heard something behind me, like someone breathing out, really loud, and when I turned round Rod was on the floor.'

'Who did it?'

'I don't *know*, do I? It was all dark and the bloke must have hit him in the other room, well, where the other room's going to be. It was all in shadow. Rod fell through into the room we were in. I barely had time to see him on the floor when Billy must have hit me. He'd been holding a piece of wood and bloody hell, I remember now, I was wondering why he was holding it when he'd said he'd come to take the bigger pieces, like the joists or whatever you call them. Fuck, they must have had it planned. They didn't know Rod was going to be there but there were two of them—Billy and this other person. They were going to bash me on the head, set the place on fire and leave me there. I suppose Rod just got in the way.'

'Maybe they thought the police would blame you for it.'

Darren was thinking in overdrive now, seeing it all again, Billy standing there in a thick lumberjack shirt and padded jacket, his hair wild as usual, the eerie quiet in the half-built gym, the lights from the houses the other side of the hedge. It made him shudder to think what they might have done to him, or what they thought would happen when the wood caught fire and the roof burned and collapsed on him. He'd woken up in the other room, where the wood was stacked, so they'd dragged him and Rod there to burn.

He said, 'So how did Storey get there? Why did he come?'

Norton told him what Storey had said—he'd met Felicity and she was angry because Darren had failed to pick her up from the cinema. Storey got thinking and wondered whether Darren had gone to the site.

'Yeah, because I do that all the time when I've got an hour to spare,' Darren said. Thinking, shit, he'd forgotten about Fliss. Perhaps she'd been worried …

'You didn't see him?' his uncle asked. 'Why would he think you were there?'

Darren looked away, knowing very well why Storey might think he was on the site: he knew he and Billy had been stealing building materials. He was probably checking whether they were at it again. But he couldn't tell his uncle that, so he said, 'I don't know. Lucky guess. And lucky he wasn't killed, like Rod. Was Rod hit on the head too?'

'He was knifed.'

'Shit.'

'Storey said when he got there the place was deserted. No cars.'

'Yeah, we went in Billy's van so there'd be less noise, you know, disturbing people. He would have driven off in it.'

'But whoever did in Rod must have followed you. Then after he hit you perhaps he hadn't had time to get off the premises through the front gate before Storey rolled up in his car. So Jenkins bashed you and later the other man bashed Storey and then he left the pair of you on the floor and set fire to the place. You're lucky he didn't knife both of you, just Rod — but then there wouldn't have been a, what do they call it, a patsy.'

Darren reached for the remote control and switched off the television. He couldn't concentrate on the film with all this going through his head.

He said, 'So what am I supposed to do now? Hang around until it all goes quiet?'

He saw the look on his uncle's face change to one he didn't understand. Then his uncle leaned down and swiped his feet off the bed, saying, 'Listen, pull yourself together. Don't be such a twat. It's not going to go quiet. It's murder. The police and the press will be on to this because of the circumstances, dead body on a building site, respected man, liked by everyone etcetera. You've got to get out of here.'

'But you were in the army and this Storey was a policeman … can't you vouch for me or something?'

He watched Norton stand up and shake his head, turning away to look around the room — a bed, a small table, the chest of drawers with the television on it and a narrow wardrobe with a mirror on the front. Seeing it through his uncle's eyes he saw how pathetic it was. *He* was. At that moment he hated Billy Jenkins more than he'd hated anyone in his life.

His uncle turned back to him and reached inside his pocket, coming out with an envelope.

He said, 'There's a couple of grand in there. Go to Scotland. Stay in another B & B, move around. Don't use your own name. Pay cash. Buy a cheap phone and text me the number. Break your current simcard in half. Don't contact anyone else, even Felicity. Go to the pictures —' he gestured towards the television '— seeing as you like them so much. Learn Scottish. Wear a kilt. Just stay the fuck away and don't get into trouble. Can you manage that?'

'How long for?'

'I'll let you know when it's safe to come back.'
'When is that likely to be?'
'How the fuck do I know? Next week or next year.'
'What am I supposed to do in the meantime?'
'Grow up.'

CHAPTER TWENTY-ONE

WHAT STRUCK HIM later was the timing: why would someone phone him at midnight? Was it because they knew he'd be home and presumably alone, so would take the call? Or was it the other way around—it was the only time the caller could be alone without being overheard?

The thing was, he'd had a good day and the call pissed him off.

He'd gone back to the site, as Doyle had asked him to, and watched the forensics team do their work. He'd got talking to the uniform on duty, told him he used to be on the force down in London, and eventually the man had let him in, just as forensics were wrapping up. He thought they wouldn't find anything incriminating because the site was too much of a mess. The two weapons used were a knife and a piece of wood, both of which would have been taken away by the culprit, and because the site was open to the air it was doubtful there'd be any fibre or hair samples lying around … and if there were, what would they prove? Darren and Billy Jenkins were both regulars on the site so if their DNA were found on anything it would prove nothing.

Never mind the fact they'd first have to find the pair of them to take comparison samples.

So he'd had a quick look himself, in daylight, while the uniform was talking to someone on his mobile phone.

And saw nothing, as he expected. A concrete floor, piles of wood, bricks and tiles. Nothing much seemed to have changed from his last daytime visit.

So then he'd come back to the house and got the name from Norton of the agency who were providing the manpower for the site. Although they'd all worked for Doyle before—through Rod—they were actually on the books of an agency that provided labour for construction sites. Once he'd got through to someone in a more senior position he'd introduced himself and given the man his name and number as a temporary measure until Doyle's new man came on-site. He'd told the man that if anyone had anything to say, they should call his number and talk to him in confidence.

He didn't expect to hear from anyone.

Now it was almost midnight and his mobile phone rang as he was cleaning his teeth. His first thought was that either Norton or Doyle was ringing to tell him his agenda for the next day.

But he knew within seconds what kind of call it was: the Warning. A man's voice, slightly muffled, said his surname without inflection. It was a statement, not a question.

'Who wants to know?' Storey said.

'Consider this a friendly conversation,' the man said. 'It can get much worse.'

'Did you kill Rod Spencer?'

'I have no idea what you're talking about.'

'I'm recording this conversation on my phone.'

'Good for you. As I said, or maybe I didn't, but I'm saying it now: you'd be much better off if you walked away. Don't get involved in Doyle's gym. Walk away, while you still can.'

'Frank, is that you? Tell Billy I know what he did and so do the police. They have photographs and everything.'

There was a pause and Storey wondered whether his bluff was working. He still hadn't said anything to Jackie West or to the investigating officers about Billy Jenkins. Or Darren. That was the problem. Mention one and you have to bring up the other.

He said, 'Are you still there? Have you finished warning me yet? I have to tell you, I don't feel particularly threatened by an over-the-hill boxer and his half-wit comedy-giant son. You'll have to try harder.'

The phone line went dead. He looked at the call history on his phone but the number had been blocked.

Never mind. He was beginning to put together a theory that connected Billy Jenkins stealing goods and selling them to Frank Ivory, who in turn was acting out some weird grudge he still held from thirty years ago. He knew from the meeting at the golf club that Ivory viewed Doyle as competition of some kind, someone to pick a fight with, physically or verbally.

And from what Doyle and Norton had said so far, there was no one else with a sufficient grudge against Doyle to warrant murder. The thought that it was just a theft gone wrong didn't stand up when you considered what Darren had said— someone had knifed Rod and Billy had clubbed him. Billy and the mystery man had set it up, and given that Ivory was Billy's customer for the stolen goods it wasn't much of a stretch to see him as the instigator of the murder.

So how could he go about proving it?

CHAPTER TWENTY-TWO

T HE CALL FROM Doyle came the next morning, just after seven.

'Have yourself a nice breakfast then pick me up. Eight o'clock, front of the house.'

'Where are—'

'I'll tell you on the way. Wear jeans.'

Doyle directed him north, out of the city, saying, 'Turn right at the next crossroads,' 'Straight on here,' 'Left by that pub,' till eventually they were in the open country south of Birmingham, the roads quiet early on a Thursday morning.

Eventually he said, 'See that gate ahead? Into the field? Pull in there.'

Storey did as he was told and watched as Doyle climbed out of the passenger seat, walking towards the gate and pushing it open. He turned back to Storey and waved him out of the car.

The air was chill but the day was sunny and it was pleasant to be away from the house and the building site, treading on grass and listening to birds. Storey wasn't really a country person but he appreciated it from time to time, in small doses.

Doyle had moved ahead now, keeping to the edge of the field they'd entered, which was bordered by trees whose names Storey couldn't remember, if he ever knew them. Doyle seemed to know where he was heading and Storey moved quickly to catch up, wondering where they were going. Did Doyle own this land? Were they heading for another building site that he'd kept quiet until now?

He realised they were out of sight of the road now and ahead of them was the furthest edge of the field, bordered this time by a hedge of bushes with a stile cutting through them to give access to the next field. Doyle stopped momentarily then turned left and went into the treeline. Storey followed and the ground changed underfoot to dry bracken and crisp leaves. The air was dark and musty. Doyle was a couple of yards ahead, moving purposefully between the trees, his boots crunching heavily. Storey felt disorientated, out of his comfort zone, unsure where they were heading or why.

He was beginning to sweat in his jacket and he was just thinking about taking it off when Doyle spun round and launched a swinging punch into his midriff.

The air whoomped out of him, *shit*, and he doubled over, gasping, staring at the curled leaves and broken branches on the ground. He heard himself coughing and then he drew a huge breath, the air entering his lungs giving him the strength to stand upright, ready to fend off another blow.

But Doyle was standing straight ahead of him, hands on his hips, frowning slightly, watching like a scientist to see how well Storey recovered. He said, 'Tell me what you know about Darren and the gym.'

Storey thinking quickly now, rehearsing what he should say, where he owed loyalties, what would cause the least damage ... and also thinking, Why should I care? Just walk away and let them fight amongst themselves.

Still drawing in deep breaths, his hands on his stomach, his head down again now. Maybe he should give up Darren and Billy Jenkins. What would Doyle do? He wouldn't find Jenkins if he didn't want to be found. Would Doyle tell the cops about

Jenkins? Probably not. Old One Punch would want to deal with it himself. Find the guy and string him up. Or punch him.

Doyle said, 'You was there that night, when Rod was killed. What did you see? What are you not telling me?'

Storey breathing more easily now, standing up, his hands on his hips like Doyle, hearing the birds again, getting the smell of cow dung, too. This was why he didn't like the country.

He said, 'All I saw was Rod on the ground. I was knocked out from behind. You want to see the bruise? I told the police what I saw, over and over again, and that's it.'

'Darren was there, wasn't he?'

'Why d'you say that?'

'Because it's the kind of thing he'd get mixed up in. I know him. It was probably all a lark till Rod showed up then him and his mates panicked and the next thing you know Rod's got a knife sticking in him and everyone else has scarpered.'

'You've got other things to worry about apart from Darren.'

'You forget—he's going out with my little girl. He's a fucking pain in the arse, but if he's making her happy …'

'Well I didn't see him. I was out cold with my nose in the mud. I'm getting pretty pissed off with being hit and punched. Have you finished? Can we go home?'

Doyle looking at him now, weighing him up. Storey felt judged and didn't like it. Doyle said, 'You need to work out where your priorities are. I'm paying you to be on my side and I think you're hedging your bets. Maybe it's because you're an ex-copper and don't want to go all in with a villain like me. You don't trust me or mine. But you better wake up. You're living in my house and driving my car and eating my food. You wanna play games, do it on your own time.'

Storey said nothing, still getting his equilibrium back. So this was what it was like to be an employee again. You give something of yourself away … in return for what? Not being used as a punchbag?

He didn't know whether he could live with that.

If he let Doyle hit him would it mean he was a lesser man than he thought he was? He was weak and didn't stand up for himself. Or would it mean he was actually the stronger man because he took the punishment and didn't let it anger him?

Whichever way he looked at it, being punched by Doyle was not a good feeling. But he wasn't going to give him the satisfaction of seeing that—letting him think he'd made a point.

Then Doyle walked past him towards the car, saying, 'Just sort out the gym. Get it up and running again.' He stopped and turned back, pointing a finger. 'And don't think you can quit because I can find you by snapping my fingers.'

They drove back in silence and when they arrived Doyle climbed out and left without saying anything more.

Storey sat in the Mercedes for a while, staring at the open mouth of the garage, wondering what he was doing. He should just leave. Doyle's threat was meaningless—there was nothing he could do if Storey decided to quit.

But he thought if he quit now it might look suspicious to the detectives investigating Rod's murder. And besides, he wanted to be involved wherever he could in finding the murderer. If he was magnanimous he could understand Doyle's anger. He'd lost a friend and discovered he had an enemy and he probably felt it was all out of his control and in the hands of the police, who would tell him nothing.

As he was sitting there he had a flashback to the moment he was hit on the back of the head, and raised his hand automatically to feel the bruise. It still hurt like a bastard when he touched it through the dressing the paramedic had attached. Like Doyle, he wanted someone to pay for it. Was it as simple as that? He was staying in the job because he wanted revenge?

Not very noble. But why should he be noble? Where did it get him?

After another couple of minutes going back and forth with it he realised he wasn't getting anywhere and parked the car and closed the garage door, then phoned Norton.

'Where are you?'

'The office.'

'I'm coming up.'
'I'm already looking forward to it.'

He entered the wing of the house he hadn't been in before, opening the back door facing the garages and looking around, checking it was empty. He'd walked into some kind of mud-room, with rows of boots standing on a low shelf and an open rack of overcoats above it. There was a scarred wooden table and a wood-burning stove in the fireplace, a single log burning low inside. The decor wasn't as contemporary as the other half of the house, though the walls were white. The floor, though, was made of huge York slabs, worn smooth. He supposed this was the older of the two linked buildings, maybe the original farmhouse.

And now it was the wing where Felicity lived and Norton had a room and an office, both upstairs. He wondered how Felicity felt about Norton roaming around her section of the family home—would it be comforting or weird? He also wondered why Norton was living there. He must have lived somewhere else before the family had moved in three years ago. He wouldn't have been living in the same caravans the Doyles inhabited during the renovations, would he? Perhaps he'd been renting elsewhere and Doyle gave him a good deal on the rent when this place became habitable.

Now he moved from the mud-room into a large open space with high windows that felt like a conservatory, with some bamboo furniture and large plants standing in the light from patio-doors. Bookshelves took up all of the rear wall, facing him, but looking at them now he saw they didn't contain books but DVDs and VHS tapes, hundreds of them, probably going back to the eighties if not before. He supposed they were Doyle's, because of their age and because he'd seen at first hand how the ex-fighter liked to watch drama playing out on a screen.

He found his way upstairs, meeting no one, and then saw Norton standing in a doorway, looking irritable.

'Come in,' he said, retreating into his room.

When he got there Storey saw it was a medium-sized room with a view over the back of the house, towards the garages whose grey-tiled roofs he could see. If he'd wanted to, Norton could have watched Storey sitting in the Mercedes being decisive. Or not.

Norton had sat down at his computer again, a small laptop showing a spreadsheet or bank account listing. He'd taken off his jacket and rolled up his sleeves, revealing a tattoo of a cross on his left forearm. Norton hadn't struck him as religious but you never knew.

Storey said, 'Where's Darren?'

Norton continued to stare at his screen. 'I sent him away. Better if he's not around to screw things up. He didn't know anything anyway.'

'So he says.'

'You know different?'

'I saw him help Billy Jenkins steal building materials from the site. Then Jenkins sold them to Frank Ivory.'

Norton swivelled his chair so he was looking up at Storey. 'You're a fucking liar.'

'I've got photos if you want.'

'Why are you telling me this now? Why did you keep it from me?'

'I didn't think you'd want to hear it. Seems I was right.'

'You think Darren was helping Frank Ivory?'

'Not necessarily on purpose. He might not have known the stuff was going to Ivory. I think he thought he was helping Billy.'

'Why would he do that?'

Storey moved further into the room, seeing cabinets filled with box files, little white squares stuck on their spines, each one labelled neatly, and noting on the wall several photos of a uniformed Norton saluting a series of older men. It was his equivalent to Doyle's photo wall of celebrities in the other wing of the house.

Storey said, 'People keep telling me Darren's the salt of the earth. Maybe he was playing good Samaritan, giving Billy a source of income.'

'I doubt it. He'd know Rod or I would have caught on eventually.'

'He's your nephew. Perhaps he thought you'd look the other way.'

Norton was thinking now, staring at a spot on the floor, showing Storey the perfect parting in his hair. Everything about this man was buttoned-up and neat. Except his nephew.

Norton said, 'What am I supposed to do now?'

'Up to you. You're my boss. You can tell Doyle or not.'

'What good would it do? It's too late for Rod.'

'It would keep him up to speed with what was happening on-site.'

'He'll want to kill Darren. He'll feel let down. He's loyal but if he thinks you're an enemy, you're in trouble.'

'Now you know why I didn't say anything earlier. I was waiting for more evidence.'

'Bullshit. You wanted to take them yourself, be the hero again.'

Storey hadn't thought of that. The idea worried him briefly but he put it out of his mind. He said, 'You should also know I've had a call.'

'What do you mean?'

'Someone telling me to keep my nose out. Threatened me with what happened to Rod.'

'Jesus Christ.'

'Yes.'

'Have you told anyone else?'

'It only happened last night, midnight. You're the first.'

'Then keep it to yourself. Things are complicated enough as they are.'

'Just tough it out, like the tough guy I am?'

Now Norton was getting agitated, Storey saw it in his eyes. 'There's more to take into consideration than you know.'

'Care to tell me?'

'Nothing that you're paid to give a shit about.'

'When my life's threatened I think I've got a right to know what's going on.'

'As you said, I'm your boss. I'll tell you what you've got a right to know.'

'Will you tell Doyle about Darren and Jenkins?'

'I need to think about it.'

'Don't think about it too long. You need to get on the right side of it.'

'Which side is that?'

'I have no idea.'

CHAPTER TWENTY-THREE

S TOREY WAS LEAVING through the front entrance
when Charlotte Doyle called his name. She appeared in
the doorway to the lounge a moment later wearing a peasant
blouse and a patterned dress, her hair pinned up under a band.

Storey said, 'You running away to the circus?'

Now she was walking towards him, unable to keep the sway
from her walk, though her face was grim.

She said, 'Have you seen Fliss?'

'No, why?'

'We haven't seen Darren since Tuesday. She's worried about
him. What with all this ... activity.'

'You mean Rod Spencer's murder.'

'Yes, sorry, that wasn't very correct, was it?'

'No.'

'Have you seen Darren?'

'He's a grown man, he can look after himself.'

'Barely. Listen, can you talk to Felicity?' She was close enough
now to place a hand on his arm.

'About what? We're not exactly best friends.'

'I was hoping you could put her mind at rest. Having been an
upstanding member of our fine police force and so on. Give her
some comforting words.'

'Like what?'

'You know … how these events affect people differently, depression, that kind of thing. Maybe he's off somewhere not wanting to talk to anyone.'

He moved closer to the door and she let her arm drop to her side. He said, 'I'm not a grief counsellor. I don't know the right words. It's not my speciality.'

'I know. It was guns, wasn't it?'

There it was—the fascination again with his role. It always came out eventually, people wanting to know what it was like to aim a rifle at another human being.

To move off the topic he said, 'Does she seem worried, Felicity? Are we talking about her or Darren? I'm confused.'

She smiled thinly. 'I think she's coping okay. She barely knew Rod, just to say hello to. The same as me, really, even though we were parked in a caravan out there for months while he worked in here. The problem is …'

She stopped and looked away and Storey wondered whether her eyes had become liquid.

'The problem is what?'

'She doesn't talk to Bran, or to me. We have no idea what's going on. She's practically living a separate life over there.'

'It's a five yard walk.'

'Don't be cruel to me.'

'It works both ways. She could come over here if she wanted to. Besides, she's what, twenty-six, twenty-seven? Perhaps she wants her own life.'

'As long as we're paying the rent.'

'Ask her to leave if that's how you feel.'

'It's not,' she said, moving away, putting distance between them, he thought, because he wasn't being particularly sympathetic. 'And Bran's very protective of her. I don't think he'd like it if she moved out.'

'Would he stop her?'

'How could he? She's old enough to go if she wants.'

Storey had opened the door to leave the house but now he pushed it closed again. Seeing Charlotte was actually upset by this conversation. Feeling pity for her position between her daughter and her husband.

He softened his voice. 'Do you think she wants to leave?'

'That's the point, isn't it? I have no idea! We've lost touch. You saw what happened the other day, when we came back from shopping. We'd been okay in the car but as soon as we got back she asked Kate if she wanted to go up and see her new clothes. No thought of doing that with me, her mother.'

'They're similar ages ...'

'I know, and I'm an old frump.'

Storey heard a warning go off in his head and decided not to respond to her, changing the subject. 'What does she do for a living? She mentioned something about working for her father.'

She pulled a face, realising he'd switched subject and wasn't going to flatter her, perhaps surprised, too, by the change of direction. 'It's a nothing job. Calls herself a consultant. It just puts her on the payroll, helps her and helps him in some way.'

'Consultant for what?'

He could see she was getting bored, now. She said, 'She looks after his properties, all right? Like an agent, dealing with renters, organising repairs, plumbers, electricians, things like that. All the stuff Craig Norton used to do before this bloody gym business started up. A few hours a week and he gives her and her assistant a decent living wage.'

'Nikki.'

'Yes.'

'You sound like you resent it.'

The fire went out of her eyes. 'God, I do, don't I? Well I don't. She's never really settled down, she went to college but didn't finish her degree. Geography. Wouldn't have been that useful, would it, unless she wanted to be a teacher. Which she didn't. I think she'd like to do what Kate does—interior decor. I'm not sure she's got the eye for it, though.'

'Perhaps she can learn.'

'Perhaps. Listen, can I get her to call you, if she will?'

'I don't know what good it will do but yes, of course.'

Storey watched her as she nodded at him and then turned and went back into the lounge, into whatever internal hell she seemed to be putting herself through on a daily basis.

'Two days in a row, Craig. We'll have to introduce you to the wonders of the telephone and modern communication.'

They'd been waiting for him in the pub this time and it was as though they hadn't moved since he'd met them the previous day. They were in the same seats facing in the same direction. He wondered whether they were trying to make a point, get under his skin.

It was working.

He sat facing them, saying, 'I want to be upfront with you. And I don't like this kind of conversation over the phone. It's too … secretive.'

Swann's hair was still wet from a shower and Norton realised that he was probably older than he'd thought. The slight quiff he'd worn had given him a sprightly air. Now the blond strands were plastered to the top of his head he seemed less suave. Even less dangerous.

When had *that* happened? When had he began to see them as dangerous? He'd always thought Lethbridge with his unswerving owl's stare was creepy, but he realised he'd started to feel intimidated by them. Not just by the lack of conscience in what they were all doing, but by the dark hinterland they both alluded to from time to time and which, if he thought about it, seemed to offer a threat.

He said, 'Look, you need to know Storey is getting more involved. He's walking around with his nose to the ground, sniffing like a bloodhound. He's bothered about the fire, as we all are. And the murder, of course. He met Rod and liked him.'

'We understand.'

'What if he finds out about this, you and me, the new gym?'

'It's a poser.'

'I fired the last man, Monks, because he was getting too nosey. I can't do it again. Besides, it was Doyle who picked Storey so I can't sack him without a good reason.'

'Going back to the events of the other night,' Swann said, 'what bothers you particularly about the fire? Why did you bring that up?'

There it was—an edge in his voice, as if he were homing in on something that interested him. Norton said, 'I need assurances. I need to know there was no involvement from you in what happened.'

'We dealt with this yesterday, Craig.'

'I think it's all part of a strategy to delay Doyle's gym, to give it a bad reputation before it's even open. I might even see it as getting rid of the competition.'

'Now you're being silly,' Swann said.

'Silly,' Lethbridge said.

'Storey says he's had a call.'

'What kind of call?'

'A threatening one. Telling him to keep his nose out. It just seems to have made him worse, and I can't really say I blame him.'

Swann leaned forward over the table, his voice low. 'We're businessmen, Craig. We don't threaten people.'

'No we don't,' Lethbridge said.

'I hope I can believe you. I thought I should mention it.'

'Thanks. But it wasn't us.'

CHAPTER TWENTY-FOUR

W HEN KATE CALLED, Storey was on his way out of the door, having been told by Doyle that the police had released the building site and the new foreman was on-site and he should go talk to him. He was called Gerry and had done work for Alf, one of the men he'd met at the golf club when they'd had lunch. Doyle said he should sound him out, see if he was up to speed yet. Alf said he was a good man.

So he stood next to his car and took the call from Kate, realising the flutter in his chest was a rare event and maybe he should pay attention to it and what it meant. He didn't know exactly what it meant except that it felt good.

'I gather it's been busy over there,' she said. 'I never met Rod but Bran always said he was a good man.'

'He likes competence. He said exactly the same thing about the new guy twenty minutes ago, though he's never met him. I think he believes if he says something is true it will be.'

'What does that say about Rod?'

'No, he was okay. Good at his job from what I could see. You didn't call me to talk about Rod.'

'I might have done.'

'Are you calling to arrange another get-together?'

'Is that what they are? Don't we use the word "date" any more?'

'I think we're supposed to say we're "seeing each other". Or is that too American?'

'I can live with it. Better than "walking out with".'

'Or "courting". My dad used to talk about the time he was "courting" my mum. We're a very old-fashioned family.'

'I could tell that from the way you held the door open for me. And offered to lay your cape down over the puddles.'

'I don't have a cape.'

'Then it must have been someone else.'

There was a pause, then Storey said, 'Is it a good idea for me to keep seeing you?'

'Why wouldn't it be?'

'Well, for one thing you're very forward. I don't think I've ever been propositioned like this before.'

'That's because you're an old-fashioned family.'

'And for another, there's a lot going on here, police and so on.'

'Are you saying it's not safe?' she asked, that ironic tone back in her voice. In his mind's eye he saw her looking at him over her shoulder again, smiling, and liked it.

'I'm pretty sure we're safe,' he said.

'Okay. Then pick me up at my place tonight at seven and we'll see if we can live dangerously for a while.'

'I don't know where you live.'

'I'll text you the address. Or I could send the map co-ordinates if that'll make you feel more at home.'

'I'll track you down through your address.'

'Make sure you do.'

Gerry wore black jeans with a sharp crease and a denim jacket over a thick check shirt. He had a full black beard and a voice that Storey heard before he'd even climbed out of his car. Storey thought there was something outsized and piratical about him.

As he shut the door he watched Gerry walking towards him, his head glancing left and right and checking the workmen were taking him seriously.

They shook hands and Gerry said, 'Mr Doyle said there'd be someone coming out. Is it Mr Storey?'

Storey said it was and asked if there was anything he needed to get started. Gerry said he had everything for the time being, they were still assessing how much damage had been done by the fire. He added, 'Is there anything I need to know about this?'

'Like what? I suppose you know the circumstances.'

'Aye, there was a man murdered. I know that, and I don't like it. But I spoke to a copper who was here this morning, rolling up the tape, and they think your man interrupted a burglary and was unlucky. I'll say he was bloody unlucky.'

'Is that what he told you? It was a burglary?'

'Aye. Isn't it true?'

'I don't know.' He led Gerry further away from the men, most of whom were inside looking at the damage to the wooden beams. 'Look, it was probably a burglary that went wrong. There's next to no chance anything like it'll happen again. Just make sure the site's locked up at the end of the day and there's no one here at night.'

'I was gonna put on a night watchman, to be safe.'

'Did you say that to Doyle?'

'Aye. He said he'd pay.'

'Okay, then make it two men. Better in pairs.'

'Right,' Gerry said. 'Do you want to see what's what?'

They walked over to the site of the fire and Gerry pointed out the charred corner of the truss that had caught fire—however minimally—before Storey had extinguished it. There were two other horizontal beams that were blackened and Gerry suggested it would be best to replace them as well.

'How long?' Storey asked.

'Couple of days. Get the crane back on site, take out the old one, make up and put in a new one.'

'You don't need me, then.'

'Not unless you're handy with a mallet.'

'Not to professional standard.'

His phone rang and he moved back towards his car. He'd noticed that the men were watching Gerry guardedly but without rancour. He seemed to have impressed them already, despite having Rod's shoes to fill.

The phone call was from Doyle again.

'You done there yet?'

'Just finishing up. Gerry knows what he's doing. I've told him to put two men on overnight.'

'I said he could pay for one.'

'Two are safer than one. If anything else happens.'

He let that linger and felt Doyle get his implication.

'You don't think it'll happen again?'

'Who knows?' Storey said, exasperated with Doyle's penny-pinching. 'Maybe burning the building was the point of the exercise, not murdering Rod. Perhaps they'll come back for a second go.'

'Don't say that.'

'You have to be realistic.'

'Never mind … I need you to come back. We're going to see someone in town. It might ease some of the pressure.'

'I'm not feeling any pressure.'

'That's because it's not your bloody money.'

CHAPTER TWENTY-FIVE

D OYLE'S FACE WAS unreadable as he climbed into Storey's Volvo, looking around at the cabin and the back seats. Storey had thought it was easier to use his own rather than park it and fetch the Mercedes from the garage. He expected Doyle to make some remark about the car but he didn't.

Doyle buckled up and told Storey to drive into town and go to the West Orchards car park in the centre of the city.

'Short-term or long-term?'

'It's only short-term. Should be enough for those bastards to let me know the bad news.'

Storey glanced at him as he drove out of the compound but said nothing.

After a few minutes Doyle said, 'Sorry about thumping you yesterday. I realized I was a fucking monster years ago. I get angry, I hit something. I get frustrated, I hit something. Used to be handy as a way of earning a few bob. Now I'm supposedly a businessman and it's a fucking liability. I let meself down yesterday and I've got to stop doing that. Charlotte keeps telling me being violent doesn't help outside of the ring and she's probably right.'

Storey said, 'It wasn't that hard—more like a friendly pat,' and turned to watch Doyle smile almost in spite of himself.

'You wanker,' he said. 'Twenty years ago that punch would've sent you to Germany without a passport.'

'Do you regret it—that life?'

'Do I fuck. Look at where I live, the missus, she's got a heart of gold, that woman … Felicity, the business. I'm doing all right. I could still be down in London ducking and diving with the gangsters down there. But I got out at the right time.'

'Were you ever a proper criminal?'

'What's this, professional interest?'

'Boxing and fighting have always been close to villainy, haven't they? I used to see the photos of Henry Cooper and others cosied up to crooks. They all used to hang around in the same pubs and clubs.'

'Yeah, I don't know what either of them thought they were getting out of it. Who had the most glamour? Course in the sixties it was the Krays—everyone wanted to be next to them. Actors, models, photographers. That'd all died down by the time I was coming up.'

'You didn't answer the question.'

'What, me, a crook? Nah. I tell you what, I didn't have the balls for it. Some of them men had no conscience. They'd put a fork in your eye as soon as look at you. None of that, what do you call it, empathy. Loved their families and said they did everything for them, but they had a really cockeyed view of what they was doing. It was all about "looking after the family", as if nobody else had a family to look after. We didn't all turn into crooks just to put a roof over our head and food in the fridge, did we?'

'Did you know any, then? Real crooks?'

They were close to the car park and Doyle seemed interested in the pedestrians on the streets, his head turned away. Finally he said, 'I knew some of them. Even worked with some. But only legit stuff—working the doors, things like that. Sometimes they asked me to take care of someone, know what I mean? Duff 'em up. But I wouldn't do it. I didn't need that kind of money. Refusing didn't make me popular. But I did lots of things like that—making myself unpopular. One of the reasons we come up to Coventry afterwards. Get away from the stink.'

'It tends to follow you, though, doesn't it?'

Doyle glanced sharply at him. 'You talking from personal experience?'

Storey said nothing, made a big show of watching his driving as he manoeuvred into the narrow opening of the car park and lowered his window to take his parking ticket from the machine.

Doyle led them up the slope of Cross Cheaping, through the pedestrian subway, and past Primark, crossing Broadgate square and heading towards the banks clustered on the road that led down to the council offices.

'Just listen and tell me whether I'm understanding right,' he said, stopping at one of the banks and holding open a door for Storey, who wondered why he was here and not Norton. Wasn't he the one who looked after the money side?

They joined a queue in the middle of the lobby and when a woman approached, Doyle told her he had an appointment. She took his name, pointed them towards some seats and asked them to wait.

Two minutes later a different woman came out from the back and led them to an office that held only a table, three chairs, a laptop and a printer standing on a waist-high cabinet in the corner.

As they sat down, a woman in her mid-thirties with a round face and precise make-up entered and sat facing them. She knew Doyle and shook his hand and he introduced Storey as a friend. Storey hid his surprise at that and tried to look interested and concerned, though he had no idea why they were there. He saw from a badge on her jacket lapel that she was called Jeanette Corby and was an Assistant Manager.

She'd brought papers with her and she pushed the laptop to one side and placed them on the table, spreading them slightly as if laying out her cards. She said, 'Did you get the letter I sent you last week, Mr Doyle? I think I made it clear that unfortunately we won't be able to extend your credit any further. You're already at a maximum, given your situation, and you have to understand we have very strict rules about how much we can lend people these days.'

'I got the letter. I wanted to check there hadn't been a mistake.'

The woman was pleasant enough but there was a hardness behind her smile, perhaps something she'd learned to use to deal with difficult customers. The precision of her make-up gave her features a plastic, unreal air. She said, 'I'm sorry, we can't help.'

'You know why it's more important to me now?'

'I understand you had a problem on the site.'

'So I've got to get more materials and pay more overtime. We might not even make the deadline for opening night.'

'I'm sure it's a very difficult time.'

'But I'm gonna get it all back. Insurance'll pay for the materials and damage. I'll be able to pay you back as soon as I'm paid off.'

'I'm sorry.'

Storey had to turn away from the woman's smile. It was beginning to irritate him.

———

Doyle raged most of the way home. Banks were bloodsuckers who were happy to take your money but wouldn't lend it out if it didn't suit them. What was it coming to when a twenty-year-old with a name badge was making decisions over his career? What right did they have to prevent him finishing off his project when he'd already spent so much of their money on it?

Eventually he was quiet—Storey not feeding him and concentrating on driving—until they were nearly back at the house. Then he shifted his whole body in his seat and looked Storey up and down.

He said, 'How close are you to the coppers up here?'

'Not very. Why?'

'No reason.'

He turned back to the windscreen and Storey felt the need to say more, as if he'd been asked a question he hadn't properly answered. He said, 'I was in London. It's different down there, another world. I didn't get back up here that often.'

'So you don't know anyone in the local nicks?'

'Only the ones I came across the other day. And some who were involved in that thing a couple of months ago.'

'Oh yeah, that. Did it bother you?'

'What?'

'Working with those gangsters. They were stealing stuff, weren't they?'

'Re-stealing it, actually. It'd been stolen from Syria in the first place and smuggled out. They were stealing it again. Why are you asking about all this? I thought I already passed the interview.'

Doyle pointed ahead, to a spot where the road widened before the gate to his house. 'Stop here.' He waited while Storey slowed and then pulled in. He left the engine running, but said, 'Now what?'

'Would it bother you, being involved in something?'

'Like what?'

'I don't want to say right now. No violence involved. No one gets hurt, it's not like that.'

'But it's not legal.'

'Not by the letter of the law, no.'

Storey found himself gently blowing out air through pursed lips.

'Do you want to do that?'

'What?'

'Risk everything. Your reputation. What people think of you, given you're going to want them as customers soon. People don't buy from crooks.'

'You reckon? Did you see that banker woman?'

'Aren't there other places you could get the money from?'

'Everything's in the house. You think me and Norton haven't been racking our brains?'

'So what is it, then, this bit of villainy? Are you going to tell me or not?'

Doyle hesitated. 'Not just yet. What are you waiting for—drive in.'

CHAPTER TWENTY-SIX

I T WAS LATE afternoon when Storey phoned Jackie West. He stood in the front room of the cottage, looking through the windows at the big house, its lights just popping on as it grew dark outside.

She said, 'I can't talk to you right now. We're a little busy.'

'You'd be bored otherwise. I remember what it was like.'

'What do you want, Storey?'

He hesitated, knowing he was about to step on toes. He could tell from the hard tone of her voice that she wasn't about to go easy on him.

He said, 'You know I'm going to ask about Rod. Anything new?'

'No. Next question.'

'They released the building site quickly.'

'Look, I'm not privy to everything going on over there. I expect they did a thorough job. Don't you?'

'It looked like it when I saw them working.'

'Do you know where Darren is? He didn't turn up on site and I know Greaves and his DS haven't found him yet.'

'Is he missing?'

'Don't be coy. Tell him to come in and talk.'

'I don't know where he is.' Thinking, *Well that's true.*

'Doesn't his uncle know?'

'He hasn't mentioned it. Besides, I don't think Darren would have anything to do with murdering Rod.'

'That's not up to you to decide.'

'He's a kid. He didn't strike me as particularly vicious.'

'Neither do you, but you've killed three people that I know of.'

'Thanks for bringing it up.'

There was a pause and Storey thought she was going to hang up. There'd been an edge to the conversation that he didn't like.

Then she said, 'There's more, isn't there? It wasn't just asking about Rod Spencer's case.'

'I need to know why you're looking at Doyle and bugging his place. What's he done?'

'Hold on.' The sound quality on the call changed and he guessed she was moving. When she spoke again the noise in the background had diminished and he presumed she'd walked out of the office. She said, 'Don't do this, Storey. You know I can't tell you. As much as anything, it's to protect Doyle's privacy. It's not because you're an interfering pain in the arse who we want to keep in the dark. Well, not just that.'

'If I knew what you were looking for I might be able to help.'

'Then come in and tell us what you know so far. Starting with Darren.'

'You're not understanding me. If I'd known more beforehand I might have been able to prevent Rod Spencer being killed.'

She was quiet and he didn't know whether he'd upset her or whether she was thinking it through. Then she said, 'It's not up to me to tell you. There are bigger fish swimming here.'

'Well get permission, or ask someone to call me. I'm not an idiot, Jackie, and we're on the same side. I think Doyle's a bit cracked sometimes but I don't see him as a bad man. Tell me what I'm not seeing.'

'Oh, for Christ's sake,' she said quietly. 'You say this to anyone and I'll personally strangle you. It's about people-smuggling.'

'What does that mean? Sex slaves?'

'Worse,' she said. 'Some of that. But there's a lot of people, often girls, who are being brought in to have their kidneys removed.'

'Jesus.'

'It's a market for replacements. You start looking into it, you see how big it is—they reckon over seven thousand kidneys were traded worldwide last year. Just think of the people involved each time that happens: a recruiter, to find the so-called volunteer, a medical professional to do the job, then someone to organise the trade, drivers for transport, nurses and so on … it's a full-time business.'

'I can't see Doyle involved in this.'

'Do you know about his transport company?'

'He hasn't mentioned it.'

'He's co-owner of a company that do international removals. Furniture. If you're moving house from the UK to anywhere in Europe, they'll take your sofas and boxes. Of course then they've got an empty van on the Continent so they try to find business to bring back a full load instead of an empty van. Whether or not they find any kosher customers they still have to come back. So why return with an empty van if there's another option?'

'You think they bring girls back? In a hidden compartment or something?'

'Maybe. Who knows? That's one of the things we're trying to find out. Border Control are watching the ports, where they can. We're looking at several likely people and trying to get the evidence together. Solid police work. Hence the bugs. And you're causing an almighty fuss by getting in the way.'

'Have you stopped any of the vans and looked inside?'

'Of course, on the pretence of random searching. No luck so far. All we've got is hints and tips, anonymous calls from people on the edges who don't want to put their faces up front. We're stopping lots of vans, not just ones from his company. Of course we know this trading goes on and has done for a while. We usually find the culprits in a boat off Calais, or flying in to a small airport somewhere on the South Downs. But we haven't caught one of the vans yet.'

Storey had a flashback to Doyle asking whether he'd object to doing something shady. He hadn't thought it would be seriously criminal, especially when he promised no one would be hurt. He wondered whether he should tell Jackie West what

Doyle had said, but realised the man hadn't done anything except ask a couple of leading questions. It wasn't evidence of anything except verbal diarrhoea.

Jackie West said, 'You know you can't tell anyone I told you this.'

'I thought I might mention it on Twitter.'

'Don't joke,' she said.

'Who's joking?' he said.

That night Storey picked up Kate outside her house in Earlsdon, on a broad pleasant street where nearly everyone had converted their front gardens into parking spaces to keep their cars off the road. When she saw his car she came out of a thirties semi-detached house with bay windows and a porch, turning the light off behind her.

She directed him to where they were going and ten minutes later they pulled into the car park of a sixteenth-century hotel and pub next to a slender stretch of river that glistened in the moonlight.

Inside, Storey liked the old beams and the low ceiling and was happy to be led by Kate to a place by a window where they could look over the river. A girl in a white pinafore brought their drinks on a tin tray.

He asked Kate about her day, now she was released from working for Doyle, at least temporarily, and she talked about the visit she'd made to the client who wanted her to convert the Victorian folly; he liked her ideas but he wanted a more contemporary feel. She'd tried to produce a design that was in keeping with the original, but the owner—a young IT professional working at the Land Rover Engineering Centre— said he wanted to go post-modern, forget the blending-in, make a statement ...

'So did you make one?' Storey asked. 'Or did you accept the brief?'

'It's a challenge,' she said. 'My job isn't to impose myself on what the client wants. It's to interpret him. Do you think I'd have put that awful mural in Bran Doyle's loft if it were my choice? I'd rather stab my eyes out.'

'Charlotte says Felicity wants to be like you, work in interiors, but she doesn't think Felicity's got the eye for it.'

'That might be true but it's not necessarily a problem. You develop a feel. You learn what works, what doesn't. You get to know what's available to use, what's possible to do. Then you experiment, you draw, or you use computer programs to try things out. There are ways.'

'I guess so ... oh, for God's sake ...'

Kate followed his eyes towards the door then turned back to him.

'I'm sorry. That's twice I've done this. You'll never trust me again.'

———

Felicity Doyle was walking towards them between the round dining tables, followed by the blonde woman Storey had seen with her a few nights before. Nicki.

They arrived at the table and Felicity said, 'Is it okay if we sit down?'

Kate had already shuffled around on the curved bench seat and Storey did the same. Felicity said, 'This is Nicki.'

Storey nodded at her across the table. She looked to be a little younger than Felicity but her face was open and her eyes were clear. She smiled at him and he liked her immediately.

Felicity said, 'Have you seen Darren?'

'No, I haven't. People keep asking me that as if I'm his keeper.'

'Sorry, I just thought with him supposedly working at the site you might have come across him.'

'Does it matter, now?'

He saw her frown, then realise he was talking about her relationship with Nicki, grin shyly, then shrug. He thought she seemed more relaxed than the last time he'd spoken to her. She said, 'I just wanted to know he was okay. I haven't seen him for a few days.'

Storey spoke carefully. 'There's no reason he shouldn't be okay, is there?'

'Well, with Rod Spencer's murder and all ...'

'I don't think Rod's murder and Darren's disappearance are connected.' Listening to himself saying those words as if he believed them.

Felicity was sceptical. 'Is that what the police will think, though? If he's run away?'

Storey glanced at Kate, who was watching them closely. He wondered what she was thinking, what she thought about being used by Felicity as a way to get to him. Which led him to another thought.

He said to Felicity, 'Have you spoken to your mother?'

'Not recently, why?'

'She wants me to help you.'

'With what?'

'She thinks you might be struggling with Darren's running away, with Rod's death ... I think she thinks you're a delicate flower in need of care.'

Nicki burst out laughing and she and Felicity shared a look that irritated Storey.

He said, 'Look, I'm not a charity. And I'm no good with soothing platitudes. What is it you want? Why are you here?'

Felicity took a moment to find the right words and he saw the struggle flit across her face. 'I want to move out but I can't do it by myself.'

'Just do it—you're old enough to make your own decisions.'

'My dad won't like it.'

'So what?'

'And he won't like the fact I'm with another girl.'

'So what?'

'You're not very sympathetic.'

'You're a grown woman. I don't see what the difficulty is.'

'You don't know my dad as well as you think you do. You've seen the jolly side, mostly, not the angry side.'

'Not true, but I'll give you the point. I haven't seen him from your perspective.' He looked again at Kate who was watching him steadily. He began to feel trapped. He said to Felicity, 'I don't know what you want me to do.'

'Kate says I can trust you. Can you help me get my stuff out?'

'What, like smuggling you out of Colditz piece by piece?'

'What's Colditz?'

Storey took a sip of his drink. 'Never mind. When you get out, where will you go?'

'Nicki's got a flat.'

Nicki said, 'Problem is, it's a bit small for one, never mind two, and I'm being turfed out soon—the landlord's selling up. We'll have a couple of weeks to find somewhere.'

Storey looked from one young woman's face to the other, feeling old. There was something about the Doyle family that was … what had Charlotte said? Persuasive. They were larger than life and twice as difficult.

Finally he said, 'You can stay at my place, if you want. I won't be using it for a while. And I doubt your dad'll think to look there.'

The young women looked at each other.

Felicity said, 'As long as that weasel Norton doesn't find out.'

'I won't tell him,' Storey said. 'So tell me about Darren.'

'What about him?'

'I'm interested … was that never really a thing? He seemed to think he could charm you in his favour.'

'I know he did. We used to argue about it. But use your eyes. Would I prefer him over Nicki?'

Kate said, 'Careful what you say, Mr Storey.'

CHAPTER TWENTY-SEVEN

T HERE WAS NOTHING Frank Ivory liked less than waiting. He was so impatient he sometimes went out with his shoelaces undone: in a rush to put on his coat he'd forget to bend down and tie the laces. Or, he'd be watching something he recorded on the television, usually a TV crime show like Morse, and he'd fast forward to the end, eager to find out who was the murderer. He thought it was probably why Valerie left him, though the fact he gave her a right-hander now and then might have had something to do with it, too.

He looked up and down the street. Late now, just the street lights on. Bloody cold. He said to Lionel, 'How long's he gonna be in there? Are they at it?'

Lionel looked at the house as if he might see what was going on in the bedroom. He was never the brightest bulb on the Christmas tree. A disappointment, Frank thought, waiting for whatever gem Lionel would come up with. Eventually he said, 'I followed them, didn't I?'

'I didn't ask whether he was *in* there. I asked how long is he gonna be?'

'The fuck do I know? He could be giving her one.'

'Which was my second question. Don't you ever bloody listen?'

'I heard you. That's his car. I followed him here. Called you. That was twenty minutes ago.'

'Spent a bloody fortune on a cab to get here.'

'I could've fetched you.'

'Then we run the risk of losing him, don't we?' Jesus Christ, it was like dealing with a trainee adult. '*And* I've been freezing my nuts off since I got here.'

'That's him.'

Frank stood more upright as the woman's door opened and Storey came out, giving her a short wave as he came down the path and turned at the gate.

Touching.

Of course he saw them before he reached his car. Why wouldn't he, with Lionel being six feet six inches of solid muscle? Frank thought it would be nice, just the once, not to be walking around with a bloody great signpost beside him. But these days he couldn't take chances, could he? Not with things working out the way they were.

The man Storey was gutsy, though, saying, 'Evening, Frank. Off the paintwork, Lionel, if you don't mind.'

And shit, Lionel stood up straight as if Storey was his boss … something in his manner, the hardness in his eyes that said don't fuck with me. Frank said to himself, *This is going to be interesting*.

He said to Storey, 'You remember us, then.'

'Bran Doyle gave me a history lesson. He didn't tell me anything about Lionel, though.'

'My boy. Does the same things for me you do for Bran.'

'Well I don't wipe Doyle's backside, so maybe that's where we differ.'

Frank smiled—yes, he had guts. He'd done his research and knew Storey was an ex-cop so maybe he thought he was protected in some way. Frank knew it didn't work like that, though. He'd been around policemen one way or another most of his life and knew they looked after themselves but forgot you when you left the station. He said, 'I remember you had a mouth on you in the golf club.'

Storey was jiggling his car keys, standing there staring at Lionel, then back to Frank, looking as though he was ready for anything. He said, 'So what can I do for you, Handsome Frank? Incidentally, how do you live with a name like that? Bit of a responsibility.'

'Not my choice, was it? But it was nice to have. Set a tone, especially in mixed company. That's how I met Lionel's mum — she wanted to see whether I was handsome all over, so to speak.'

'Yeah, well,' Storey said, 'Charlie Kray was a ladies' man too, wasn't he? No accounting for women's taste. So what is it you want?'

Getting down to it now, Frank thought, the banter over. 'I understand you've taken over as foreman at Bran's site.'

He liked the idea of surprising Storey, letting him know Doyle's building wasn't a secret, but the man was cool, didn't show any surprise, saying, 'What's it to you?'

'And you were the one who found poor Rod Spencer.'

'You knew Rod?'

'Only by name.'

Storey took half a step closer and Lionel stirred but didn't intervene. Storey said in a quiet voice, 'Were you there too?'

'You've got a vivid imagination. Why would I be there?'

'I'm working up a theory.'

'What would that be?'

'You've been buying materials from Billy Jenkins off Bran Doyle's site. You're disrupting his gym-building project for reasons I haven't worked out yet. It might be pure spite or maybe jealousy. Or you're still angry because he knocked you on your backside a couple of times and you haven't got over it.'

'So what did I do? Break into his building site and stab his foreman in the back? What does that get me?'

'How do you know he was stabbed?'

'It was in the newspaper.'

'Are you sure about that? The papers don't release that kind of detail.'

'I'll find a clipping and send it to you.'

180

Storey was walking around to the driver's door now, pressing the key fob to unlock the car. He stood by the door, saying, 'So you're here to … what? Mark my card? Tell me to keep my nose clean?'

'I was close by. Thought I recognised the car. Just wanted to pass on my condolences about Rod. It goes to show, doesn't it?'

'What?'

'It's what happens when you go looking for trouble. You generally find it.'

'Very deep. Is that what passes for a threat in your neck of the woods?'

'More of a greeting, I'd say. Welcome to the world of construction.'

'Did you call me the other night?'

'How do I call someone when I don't have their number?'

Storey opened the door to climb in but straightened before he did, looking over the top of the Volvo at him. 'One more thing.'

'What?'

'You're not as good-looking as I thought you'd be.'

Frank smiled again but Storey hadn't waited to see his reaction, had ducked inside the car and now it started up. Frank and Lionel stepped back and the car moved off quietly.

Lionel said, 'Nice car.'

Frank glanced at him. 'You in love?'

'I just—'

'If you hadn't noticed, that bloody car was parked down the road when Billy brought us that load Sunday morning. Tell him I want to see him tomorrow. He's got some explaining to do.'

CHAPTER TWENTY-EIGHT

SATURDAY MORNING CHARLOTTE rang Storey early and asked if he'd take her and Felicity shopping. It wasn't just they wanted a driver, they needed someone to carry bags, she said, but he also thought she might be looking for a little adventure, having a younger man around. He wanted to say no but couldn't think of a valid excuse.

He also wondered if she was trying to provide an opportunity for him to talk to Felicity—she wouldn't know yet that he'd already seen her and talked about Darren.

He drove them into town and parked in the same car park he'd used when taking Doyle to see the banker.

Then he followed the two women around as they window-shopped for a while before getting serious and buying a handbag each and finally, in Debenhams, Charlotte bought a bolero jacket that was a tight but attractive fit. Hearing himself think this, he realised he'd been spending too much time with them …

'Let's go for coffee while we're here,' she said, taking the jacket, folding it, and stuffing it carelessly into one of the bags that Storey was already carrying. 'My feet need a rest.'

He followed them to a small coffee bar and found himself enjoying their company. Both women were more relaxed than when he saw them separately, though he was conscious of the renting agreement he'd made with Felicity and didn't like keeping Charlotte in the dark. He found himself avoiding Felicity's eyes in case anything passed between them that her mother might see.

Charlotte told a story about touring with a New Romantic group in America, which ended with her and the lead singer walking five miles along an Arizona black-top because the tour bus had left a truck stop without them.

'Imagine what I was wearing,' she said. 'Nineteen-eighty-three, remember, so tight blue jeans, orange ankle socks over the bottom of the jeans, white flat-heeled shoes, short denim jacket a bit like the one I've just bought … and my hair up in one of those curly bouffant jobs so I looked like a cauliflower. No wonder nobody offered us a lift. Though I suppose the fact Damon was wearing skinny striped trousers, a purple shirt ripped down the front and had hair like he'd just plugged himself into an electric socket didn't help.'

'Oh, mum!'

'Fortunately the bus realised we were missing and turned around. We were about to flake out through dehydration.'

'Couldn't you have phoned?'

'Phoned who? Nobody had phones in those days. The best we could hope for was to hitch a ride and catch up with the bus.'

Storey watched as Felicity's face grew serious and she turned away. Charlotte said, 'What's the matter, darling?'

'Nothing,' Felicity said. 'There's a lot I don't know about you and dad, that's all.'

'Plenty of time to catch up,' Charlotte said, but Storey wondered how true that was.

———

That night, just after Storey finished eating, there was a knock on his door. Doyle stood there, the Mercedes parked on the drive, its motor still running. Norton was sitting in the back seat, his pale face turned towards the house. Doyle said, 'Can I have a look inside?'

Storey stood back with his hand still on the door and Doyle came past him, Storey seeing in close up the damage to his ear and the marks on his left eyebrow caused by many years of fighting.

Doyle went into the front room and stood with his hands on his hips, looking around, as though he were interested to see what Storey had done with the place after a week's habitation.

Storey said, 'Was it anything in particular? Or are you just slumming?'

'Get your coat. We're going out. You're driving. Don't dress up. Not that I suppose you can on what I'm paying you.'

He walked out of the room and Storey took his jacket from a hook on the kitchen door and followed.

———

'It's not far,' Doyle said, directing Storey towards the city centre, then telling him to turn right along the Allesley Old Road then right again, eventually turning off past a health and beauty spa, empty at this time of night. It was a short road that came to a dead end with a row of lock-up garages that Storey thought probably served the houses they backed up to. They had roll-up metal doors, most of which were covered with graffiti.

When he killed the engine Storey said, 'Frank Ivory had a word with me last night.'

Doyle turned in the passenger seat to look at him. 'Oh yes? What did he have to say?'

'He and Lionel were waiting by my car and he said he wanted to pass on commiserations about Rod.'

'How did he know your car?'

'He must have had Lionel follow me from your place. I take it he knows where you live.'

'So ... commiserations. Anything else?'

'I think he thought he was leaning on me. Giving me a warning. It was weird.'

'Why's he picking on you? What did you ever do to him, apart from show him up at the golf club?'

Storey noticed Norton's eyes in his rear-view mirror. Doyle still didn't know about Billy Jenkins selling his building materials to Ivory, and Norton was giving Storey a reminder to stay quiet.

He said, 'I don't know, you'd have to ask him.'

'I'm asking you. Did he talk about me?'

'Not that I remember. It was my charms that interested him.'

'Well we all know you're a tart, that's true,' Doyle said, and opened his door.

Norton climbed out of the back and opened Storey's door. 'Take note of where you are,' he said quietly. 'You're in deep now.' Storey wondering what all the secrecy was about and whether the next ten minutes were going to change his opinion of Doyle.

Doyle had been fiddling with some keys and now found one, unlocking a padlock on a bar attached to one of the garage doors that prevented it from sliding up. He took out the padlock, pulled a lever and stepped back to pull up the door and slide it overhead. It ratcheted loudly in the quiet air. He went inside and turned on a light and Norton touched Storey on the arm and they both followed him inside.

Doyle closed the door behind them.

Storey looked around. A single yellow bulb in the ceiling showed that the garage was piled high on both sides and at the far end with cardboard boxes, most of them sagging as though the weight inside was too much to bear. The cardboard smelled fusty and he recognised the odour of damp cardboard.

He glanced at Doyle, who nodded him to go investigate. He pulled open the flaps of the nearest box and peered in.

Piles of DVDs were stacked neatly inside. Dozens of copies of the same film—a recent Star Wars movie. Each one was shrink-wrapped and had a round price label stuck on the front: £2

He moved on to the next box and found the same thing, the same movie, each with a familiar cover and, on the back, an authentic-looking bar-code.

He turned back to Doyle, 'How are you getting them in?'

'Man in Hong Kong had thousands of them to get rid of. He was about to be prosecuted and wanted to get rid of some evidence. None of them legal but they look legit, don't they?'

'What are you going to do with them?'

Norton said, 'Local shops, clubs, bars, car-boot sales.'

'But it's peanuts, isn't it? Everyone's downloading now.'

'I only need ten or fifteen grand to keep going,' Doyle said. 'Short-term gain.'

'Why are you showing me this?'

'Call it a loyalty test. You're in it now, you know where I'm coming from, what we have to do.'

'And what do you expect *me* to do? Set up a stall at the market?'

'I don't expect you to do anything. It's all in hand. But you won't be surprised now. Anything comes up, you're in the loop.'

'Nothing you do surprises me any more.' He looked around at the boxes again. 'How many here?'

'A few thousand.'

'How long have you had them?'

'Took delivery a few days ago. We can't hang on to them too long, they're costing me money here.'

Storey realised something. He said, 'This is where you were when you told Charlotte you were out seeing your mates, the night before we went to the golf club. You were unloading these.'

He'd seen the guilt that day on Doyle's face, on the way into the club-house, when Storey had commented that Doyle had seen his friends two days running. Evidently not.

Doyle said, 'You don't say anything to Charlotte about this, get it? This is on me.'

'And is this why you asked me whether I'd do anything illegal?'

'You haven't done anything yet.'

'I've touched them and know what they are. I'm a hair's breadth away from being guilty.'

'Don't be such a dick. We're not asking you to do anything. They'll be gone in a few days. I just thought you ought to know what was going on, where the money's coming from. The new money.'

'You had all this set up before the bank turned you down.'

'I had to have back-up, didn't I? I knew that bitch wasn't going to extend my credit.'

'Who else knows about this lot?'

'Us three, the lorry driver who transported them, the guy in Hong Kong and maybe a couple of others.'

'You're probably wrong.'

'What do you mean? We was dead quiet with it.'

'There's always more people know than you think. The Customs people might even be tracking them. If I were you I'd take them to a landfill and dump them. Sell them and you're in a hell of a mess.'

Doyle was staring at him. 'I didn't bring you here to get your fucking advice on how to run a business.'

'Well you need it. And you'—turning to Norton—'what the hell are you doing letting him get involved with this?'

Doyle said, 'He didn't know anything about it till the other night. It's my own business, my own contacts, people I used to know.'

'Burn them, bury them, for your own good. You won't flog them. The world's moved on and you're ten years behind. You don't need this aggravation.'

'I need something.' Sounding unnerved now, less confident. 'If I don't get hold of some money quick the gym will go down the drain. And I tell you now, that's not going to happen.'

'Then get another idea,' Storey said, and walked back to the car.

When Storey arrived home he dropped off Doyle and Norton in front of the house, neither of them saying anything to him, then put the Mercedes in the garage and locked it. He glanced through the windows as he walked past on his way to the cottage but it was dark, everyone gone to bed.

Inside his living room he sat on the sofa and stared at the television for a while. He thought about what Jackie West would say if she heard the major criminal was engaged in smuggling a few DVDs. A crime, but not perhaps the same urgency as people-smuggling or kidney-harvesting.

He didn't know whether he was relieved he hadn't misjudged Doyle completely or frustrated because Doyle had proved, in fact, to be involved in some proper crime. He wondered where Jackie had got her information from and how far they trusted it—though to get permission for the bugs they must have made a good case on good intelligence.

How could he tell her it was wrong? Or was he missing something?

He also thought about Frank Ivory and the meeting the night before, outside Kate's house. Ivory was one of those men who were confident they could dominate you because they were big or had resources you didn't. Storey had met them in the police force and amongst the criminals he'd known. Their confidence was often built on shaky ground but usually they were too stupid to see it.

So why did Ivory make the effort to talk to him? What was he trying to prove? Storey knew he'd belittled the man in the golf club—so was that it? Ivory just trying to reassert himself, show he wasn't fazed or suffering from wounded pride?

Perhaps. Or perhaps he was checking him out, assessing him to see how much of a threat he was, given he'd been a police officer. Measuring himself against someone who stood up to him.

Bullies never liked that.

Eventually he took out his phone and called Jackie West. He knew it was late but he also knew she'd been keeping late hours.

'Have you seen Darren?' she asked, without even a greeting.

'No, I haven't,' he said, then went on to describe where he'd been with Doyle and Norton. Explaining the boxes of DVDs and how they were Doyle's plan to earn the money to finish the gym.

Jackie listened in silence and when he'd finished, said, 'And you believed all that? It's just DVDs?'

'Why not? He's got no reason to pretend to me.'

'For an ex-cop you're very naive. They're pulling the wool over your eyes.'

'Why bother? Why even tell me in the first place?'

'They're preventing you from looking any further. Or trying to implicate you so you won't be tempted to ask more questions about what they're up to.'

'You still think it's about kidney-harvesting?'

'That's the information we have.'

'And you've got a lot invested in it now.'

'It took a lot of effort to set it up, true.'

'Are you going to pull him in and talk to him? That could fuck me up here.'

'If we do we'll keep you out of it. We'll try to let you keep your job.'

'You're sure about that?'

'We'll do the best we can.'

Storey took the phone from his ear and held it against his chest, then raised it again, saying, 'That's not exactly comforting.'

'I told you at the beginning not to get involved. There's the bed, lie in it.'

'You don't know these people. It's a family. They're not rational when it comes to looking out for each other.'

'I don't know what you're trying to say. He's not squeaky-clean and never has been. We're not interested in his wife or daughter.'

'Well that's the difference between you and me,' Storey said. 'I am.'

CHAPTER TWENTY-NINE

H E LIKED A leisurely breakfast, not too early, two cups of tea and maybe a piece of fruit to finish with.

So he was pissed off when the phone rang halfway through his toast and egg and Charlotte didn't seem to be around, so he had to walk nearly the full length of the kitchen to answer the phone plugged in at the far end.

He was even more irritated when he heard a voice identifying himself as a police officer and asking him to come in for a conversation about what had happened at the building site, and that he could bring a lawyer if he wanted.

Well he didn't want, because he'd done nothing wrong, and if they were going to talk about Rod Spencer then the business with the DVDs was safe and if he took a brief with him it might look suspicious. At least that's what all the TV shows and films said. Despite the edginess of the life he'd led, he hadn't suffered too many dealings with the police in their official capacity, though he'd known a couple when he was working the doors in London, years ago. He'd kept his nose clean, hadn't he, so they had nothing to hang over him except driving when drunk, which was always marginal from his perspective. A pint of beer and two scotches were hardly drunken revelry.

He called Charlotte into the room and told her, and as he was talking to her, Norton wandered in from the other half of the house. Doyle wondered why he always dressed as if he were going to a gentleman's club, the tweed jacket and tie done tightly at the neck, even at nine o'clock in the morning.

He said, 'I've got to go to the nick, talk about Rod Spencer. You hold the fort.'

'You want me to come with you? Contact Selhurst?'

Selhurst was the lawyer Doyle didn't want to bring for fear they thought he was hiding something.

He said, 'Just stick around here. Don't call Selhurst, I don't want him getting all worked up. I'll take Storey.'

'Why him?'

'Yes, why him?' Charlotte asked.

'He was a copper, wasn't he? He'll know the ropes.'

'Assuming he tells you what's what. He might jump ship, go back to being a cop.'

'So what? I've got nothing to hide when it comes to the site.'

He caught Norton's eye and nodded imperceptibly. They were both thinking about the smuggled DVDs. If Charlotte caught the gesture she didn't say anything. It was one of the ways she had of keeping out. Fifteen years ago she might have demanded to know what was going on. These days she looked in the other direction.

He understood why she'd lost interest. But it made him sad anyway.

He called Storey, who picked him up ten minutes later and drove towards the town centre. He didn't ask any questions but Doyle explained where they were going and why and Storey nodded, that calmness he had, never getting excited, taking it all in and thinking.

Doyle said, 'I want you to come with me.'

'What for?'

'You're a face down there, aren't you? Perhaps they'll go easy on me if you're holding my hand.'

'If they question you I can't come in.'

'I thought as much but I want you there anyway.'

'I won't do you any good.'

'Just fucking *be* there, will you?' Regretting his anger immediately—perhaps he was more wound up or worried than he thought.

He reported to a desk sergeant and was told to sit and wait, so he and Storey took two plastic chairs and looked at posters on the walls for ten minutes. Eventually a big man with thin blond hair and wearing a dark blue sports coat came out and introduced himself. He seemed to know Storey, nodding at him but not saying his name or shaking his hand.

He asked Doyle to follow him and they went along a corridor and turned into a room with a table and a box on it that he took to be a recorder, seeing as there was a microphone on the table too.

Another younger policeman came in and they all sat down and the big detective said that he wasn't being cautioned or arrested, he was just helping with inquiries. He could have legal representation if he wanted it.

Doyle said, 'Can we just get on with it? I'm supposed to be running a business.'

Then they started asking him all the same questions the first two men had asked, at his house, the morning after they found Rod's body. Where was he, who was he with, could anybody corroborate it, what did he know about Mr Spencer, when was the last time he'd seen him ...

It went on and on, with new questions thrown in occasionally: did he know anyone who might wish Rod harm? Did *he* have any arguments with him? Were there any problems on the site, any financial irregularities?

The big detective, who'd introduced himself as Greaves, had left most of the questioning to his younger colleague. They'd made a few notes but hadn't recorded anything.

Finally Greaves looked up from his notes and said the words that turned Doyle inside out.

Ten minutes later they'd given him a phone and he called Charlotte.

'They've fucking arrested me,' he said. 'It all started out lovey-dovey and then they got all official and read me my rights and that was that.'

'What for? What did they say?'

'It's bullshit—a little caper I had going on the side.'

'Oh for Christ's sake … Shall I call Selhurst now?'

'Yes. Tell him where I am and what's happened. Perhaps he can get me out.'

He hung up and someone brought him a cup of tea, and the next time Greaves walked in Doyle asked if he could talk to Storey. Just to tell him what had happened. Greaves shrugged, not seeming too bothered one way or the other.

Storey came to the door and Doyle told him he'd been arrested and he should go home and talk to Charlotte, see if she wanted anything. He'd spoken to her and she was going to sort out the solicitor.

Storey said, 'Arrested for what?'

'Some bullshit about DVDs. Do you know anything about that? About who would tell such lies about me?'

Storey glanced to one side, a muscle working in his cheek. 'No, should I?'

'I thought you might.'

'Well keep your thoughts to yourself.'

Like Greaves, Storey didn't look particularly worked up about what had happened to him. Perhaps cops just saw it as bureaucracy, not the fucking liberty it was—taking away his freedom because they needed more time to dig into his business.

Storey said, 'Don't get aggravated by it. I'm sure it can be made to go away.'

'But why's it come up now? Bit of a coincidence, ain't it?'

Storey's face gave nothing away. 'Somebody's said something. Someone with a grudge. Wonder who that could be?'

'It doesn't look good, though, does it, with Rod getting knifed last week. They're going to think it's all connected.'

'How do we know it's not?' Storey said. 'They may be thinking if they hold on to you long enough you'll blow a fuse and give something away. I recommend you don't do that.'

'Look at me—sweetness and light.' He rotated his neck, feeling a stiffness settling in already. 'Take the car home and look after the missus. I know her—she'll get more worked up than me and start throwing stones at things. Tell her it's all in hand. Use some cop talk. See if she believes it any more than I do.'

Storey nodded and moved away.

Doyle watched him go, realising that he couldn't follow. That was an odd feeling.

And he didn't like it.

CHAPTER THIRTY

S WANN AND LETHBRIDGE picked him up at the Macdonalds on the Gallagher Retail Park, off the Stoney Stanton Road. They sat in the front and Lethbridge turned from the passenger seat to stare at him.

'How's Doyle doing?' he said. 'We hear he's in a bit of bother.'

'I haven't seen him since first thing this morning.'

'How did you do it?'

'Do what?'

'Get him in trouble. We thought that was a good move. Shows you're thinking of your future.'

Norton felt uncomfortable. As far as he could tell there were a limited number of options for who'd informed on Doyle—himself, Storey, the driver of the truck who'd brought the load and the man in Hong Kong who'd sold the DVDs in the first place. None of them made sense as an informer except possibly Storey, but why would he do it? What would he gain?

Lethbridge was still staring at him, unblinking. Norton said, 'I didn't do anything. I'm in as much trouble as he is if they follow through. Anyway, how did you hear about it?'

Lethbridge reached up and touched the side of his nose. 'Contacts. In our business you need friends.'

Norton looked away, disgusted. He thought back to his time in uniform, when he had respect from people and gave respect to others. There was structure and discipline in his life then, and now there was day-to-day contingency. Making it up as you went along. Dealing with moral stains like these two just because his own ego had asked for a bit more satisfaction than it was currently getting. Ridiculous.

It was properly dark now so he lost track of the last couple of turns. He knew they were up near Alderman's Green somewhere, on a trading estate, because they were passing lots of grey-sided warehouses. If you'd have asked him he wouldn't have thought it was a good location, but what did he know? He presumed they had to go with what they could afford.

But then they came to a roundabout he recognised and they were suddenly driving along a tree-lined lane heading out of the city. This was better, more suburban, he thought.

Swann pulled through a gate and they'd arrived. He saw the place through the windscreen and was immediately impressed: bigger than Doyle's and with a larger footprint, meaning more room for a decent car-park and space for expansion.

He climbed out and followed the pair of bookies to the front door. The place looked almost finished, except for some work in the grounds and, of course, concreting the car-park.

So when he went inside it was a shock. Swann turned on a torch and handed it to him and he saw straight away the place was empty. The rooms were defined but the doors weren't in and there was no furniture and, from what he could see, no facilities—the bar was up but walking around he saw there was no sink, no refrigerator, no cupboards for glasses and bottles. There weren't even any pump handles for beer.

It was the same story in the other rooms. Swann said, 'This is where the ring's going to be, with changing rooms and showers and stuff through there.' Pointing through another doorway into darkness on the other side.

The floor was concrete and the walls were plastered, with holes poking through where further light fixtures would go.

But it was almost a shell—an attractive shell from the outside, but still a long way from being finished.

'You should feel proud,' Swann said, looking up at him. 'This is just the first. What do you think?'

'When will it be finished?'

'Good question,' Swann said, and Norton noticed that the question had attracted the attention of Lethbridge, who'd been checking the fit of the double-glazed windows by prodding them with a bony finger. Now he stood up and moved towards them, saying, 'We need to talk to you about that.'

Norton felt his heart beat a little faster and told himself to calm down.

'Don't worry,' Swann said. 'We're not going to ask you for a few thousand out of your pension. My esteemed colleague is right—we needed to talk to you about funding. Which is why we've brought you out here, to see the fruits of your efforts. But all we have to say to you is that you should be aware we've brought someone else on board to help with the extra money we need.'

'Who?'

'A local businessman.'

'Look, I've had something to tell you, too. I've got to scale back on my involvement. With Doyle under arrest and Darren missing, I'm under a lot more pressure. I've got to cut back how much time I can devote to this project.'

'Oh really?' Swann said. 'It's disappointing to hear that. Especially when we thought it might be a good time for you to step up your involvement. Help the transition.'

'What transition?'

'Well obviously with a new backer involved there'll be a period of adjustment. Some new guidelines, perhaps a new contract. Of course the lawyers will see to all that, but it'll be good to get your input. After all, you are the Chief Finance Officer.'

'I don't like that title. It's too grand for what I do.'

Lethbridge grinned. 'Makes your involvement more obvious, you mean.'

Norton swung the torch around again and looked at the concrete floor and the pale plaster walls. You make a few wrong decisions, he thought, and two months later they grab you by the throat. He said, 'Last time I looked there was plenty in the account. What happened to it?'

Swann and Lethbridge looked at each other as though they'd been waiting for this, Lethbridge putting his hands in his pockets to show he didn't care what Norton thought, saying, 'Expenses.'

'Yeah, expenses,' Swann agreed. Both of their faces were shadowed and it made Norton feel odd, as if he were suddenly dealing with people who were barely human. He turned away, not wanting them to see the look of repulsion he knew was on his own face. He knew his lips were thin and he tasted bile in the back of his throat.

'Expenses,' he repeated. 'Of course. You can't have a company with all this money sloshing around and not take some expenses.'

'Hey, it's our money!'

'And now it's tax-efficient. I get it. You should have made this a laundry, not a gym.'

He went outside and waited for Swann to lock the door. The air was cold, the sound of the nearby motorway grated on his ears.

He said, 'So who's this local businessman you've asked to join the project?'

The same look passed between Swann and Lethbridge, the one that was really beginning to piss him off.

Swann said, 'You'll find out soon enough. Eagerness is good but don't be too hurried. That never ends well.'

CHAPTER THIRTY-ONE

S TOREY THOUGHT IT was because he'd been woken so early in the morning that he was seeing things in more detail.

Felicity was standing in his doorway in jeans, a thick jumper and a furry fleece zipped halfway up, and he could see how red with cold the tips of her ears were, and how her eyelashes seemed touched with moisture and how her breath came in little clouds when she spoke.

He said, 'What time is it?'

She stopped in the middle of a sentence, which he hadn't been following, and said, 'I dunno. Just gone seven, perhaps.'

'Tell me again what you want.'

'Can I at least come in? It's freezing out here.'

Storey stepped back and she came past him, bringing the cold with her. She went straight from the tiny entrance hall into his front room. When he followed her in she was pulling open the curtains. He went to the hearth and switched on the gas fire and they both stood in front of it.

She said, 'I've never been in the cottages. The idea was to put up mum and dad's relatives but they never come, do they? They always expect us to go down to London, centre of the universe. I wish Dad would get over his obsession with white walls. Poor Kate can't do much with them. I'd probably have that one—' pointing to the wall behind the sofa '—in chocolate brown, maybe put some mirror tiles on it to make the room seem wider. And a coloured carpet, this oatmeal is bland.'

Storey stood with his hands under the arms of his tee-shirt, warming them, and said, 'Say again what you said on the doorstep. I wasn't awake.'

'I want to move out today, while Dad's not here.'

'That's not very fair on him.'

'It's perfectly fair. I'm not doing anything to help and I just get in the way. So I'll go to work and look after his houses and I'll come over from time to time to see them both.'

'Have you told your mother?'

'Why do you think I'm here so early? We were at it till three o'clock in the morning and I couldn't get to sleep afterwards.'

'Does she know about Nicki, about where you're going?'

'No and no. At least I don't think so.'

'It'll hit your dad hard.'

'No, it won't. He won't care with all this other stuff going on.'

'I think you're wrong but I'm not going to argue. What do you want me to do?'

She told him there were some boxes she needed help with and if the offer of his place was still open, she'd like to go there straight away.

So he went upstairs and dressed and then they walked over to the house where Charlotte, wrapped in a thick dressing-gown, watched them bring down suitcases and cardboard boxes filled with CDs and books and put them in the back of Felicity's car, a Fiat Punto. There were too many boxes so Storey fetched his Volvo and they put the overspill on his back seat.

Half an hour later they'd finished and were drinking tea made by Charlotte, who sat in the enormous kitchen and watched them drink.

Storey didn't know what to say to her. He could tell she and Felicity had argued out everything by the way they acted civilly towards each other but didn't say much else. He wondered whether Charlotte knew her daughter was gay. He didn't think she'd care but was unsure Felicity would tell her outright.

He didn't say anything to her about where Felicity was going to live. He assumed she would think Felicity had rented a flat somewhere. How long would it be, he wondered, before she'd want to visit ...

They were still in the kitchen when Norton appeared, taking in Felicity's and Storey's outdoor clothing and presumably having heard some of the noise as they manoeuvred boxes and suitcases downstairs.

He said, 'You're going, then.'

'You can break it to Dad next time you see him.'

'You'll still be at work, in the office?'

She told him she would and they could use her mobile number for any other contacts. Where she was going didn't have a landline. Storey kept his face straight, said nothing.

Charlotte left the kitchen, almost as though with another adult in the room it was all right for her to get dressed.

Norton made himself a drink and stood leaning against the kitchen island.

Felicity glanced at the door through which her mother had left, then said quietly, 'If you see Darren, say thanks.'

'What for? Oh ... '

And then Storey remembered that Norton had known Darren's relationship with Felicity was fake but had said nothing to Doyle.

Felicity said, 'I haven't been able to get through to him. Is he all right? His phone goes straight to messages.'

'Last time I spoke to him he was okay. I think he was having trouble with his phone.'

Felicity said, 'Okay. Tell him I'll be in touch.'

'If I see him.'

Storey looked down at his drink.

They went outside and Storey climbed into his car. He'd parked it behind Felicity's to give a show of following her to her destination, as if he didn't know where it was. As soon as they left the compound he would have to overtake her so he could lead her to his house. He turned on the heating and stared through the windscreen, wondering what he'd say to Doyle if he asked difficult questions. He would plead ignorance as far as he could but it could get tricky if he asked where she'd moved to: how could he refuse to tell him? And if he did, what would Doyle do? He'd certainly sack Storey, and although that wasn't really a problem he felt there was still a lot to do and at the moment he felt like he was the only one with a grasp of the bigger picture.

Which seemed to be turning into some weird abstract blotch rather than a nice, understandable landscape.

He wondered why Felicity was taking so long to come out of the house, then saw her in the entrance and realised she was waiting for her mother to reappear.

Which she did, eventually, dressed in tight pants and a pale green jumper. She came to the doorway with Felicity and looked out at the cars, their exhausts running cloudy in the cold air. Storey couldn't hear what was being said but saw that the body-language wasn't as chilly as before. There was a final hug and it looked as though Charlotte gave her daughter an envelope—no doubt money to get her started in her new place.

Felicity climbed into the Punto and Charlotte stayed on the doorstep. She looked directly at Storey and nodded at him but he had no idea what the gesture meant, her eyes clear but empty, as though she'd decided she wasn't going to show any emotion to the help. Storey noticed that Norton had disappeared.

———

Arriving at his house he showed her how the heating system worked and where there were towels and sheets. Then he carried in the final boxes and took the suitcases upstairs for her. He'd emptied a lot of the drawers already by taking things to his cottage on the compound. Now he sorted the remainder of his underwear and socks into one drawer and took his jackets, trousers and coats from the built-in wardrobe in his bedroom and put them in the free-standing one in the second room. There still wouldn't be enough space for all Felicity and Nicki's stuff, he thought, but they were supposedly there on a temporary basis, until they found a place of their own.

When he went downstairs he found her still wearing her overcoat and staring out of the front window.

He said, 'I grew up in this house. Strange to see someone else moving in.'

She turned to him and smiled. 'We'll look after it. I appreciate what you're doing. I don't know why I didn't do it before. Move, I mean. Now I'm doing it, it seems easier than I thought.'

'Well, it's two decisions, isn't it? Not just the one.'

'How do you mean?'

'You're not just moving out. You're moving in with someone else—you're telling your parents something.'

'It's pathetic, isn't it? I'm a modern girl, aren't I? Why have I had such difficulty with it? With my Dad in particular?'

'He's a strong character. People want to be liked by strong characters.'

'It doesn't seem to bother you. Wanting to be liked by him. Or anyone.'

'I have my moments. But I found out early it's a mug's game.'

'You think I should have said something earlier, don't you? Told him and damn the consequences.'

'It's not my place to tell you what to do.'

She turned back to the window, saying nothing.

CHAPTER THIRTY-TWO

H E SAW THE station through her eyes, guessing she'd never been inside one before: the odd mix of formality and its opposite; men and women in uniform but acting casually, as though they were wearing jeans and tee-shirts; the deference to authority that you didn't see outside of a uniformed hierarchy.

They were told to wait and then a female officer came and took them down a corridor and into a sparsely-furnished room: a table and half a dozen black plastic chairs; a water dispenser in the corner and a pile of old magazines.

Charlotte said to Storey, 'Is it all right not having the solicitor here? Bran didn't want him but I don't know if it's right or not.'

'He's seen the solicitor,' Storey said. 'He'll be trying to find out what the police are up to, if anything. Don't worry, he'll be out soon.'

'You sound confident.'

'Don't let it fool you. I can sound confident on the slightest evidence.'

She smiled at him grimly.

The door opened and Bran walked in, looking no different to when Storey had seen him the day before. Someone had even lent him a razor for a shave.

A young officer came in behind Doyle and stood in the corner. Bran glanced at him, then pulled out a chair at the table and sat on it. Storey and Charlotte sat facing him. Storey had noticed that the couple hadn't embraced, though now they were holding hands across the table.

Charlotte asked how he was bearing up and Doyle said it was all right but he was bored. Nobody was telling him anything and there was nothing to do but read and re-read newspapers.

They talked about the situation for a while and then Doyle asked if anyone had seen Darren yet.

'No,' Charlotte said. Storey thought she might add something about Felicity being worried but she caught herself. Doyle was too self-involved to notice she was holding something back. He said, 'What does Norton think? Doesn't he have any ideas? This doesn't look good for Darren, whether he did it or not.'

Storey said, 'He hasn't seen him.'

'They were close. I doubt he's vanished completely — keep an eye on Norton for me, in case he's trying to be sly by keeping Darren hidden.'

'I've got plenty on my plate.'

'Now you've got more. Are you talking to Gerry? How's he doing?'

'He seems to be on top of it.'

'I'll need you to talk to the employment agency, tell them I'm sorting out payment. Those buggers will walk off the site if they're not paid on time. And I don't blame them, I would.'

'How are you getting their pay to them?'

Before Doyle could reply, Charlotte said, 'Bran, Fliss has moved out.'

He turned to her. 'What?'

'She said she wanted to get away.'

'Hold on, hold on. What do you mean, "moved out"?'

'What does it sound like? She's packed her bags and gone.'

'Where? Where's she gone?'

'Calm down.'

'Don't tell me to fucking calm down! Get her to come back. Talk to her.'

'I can't bully her into coming back. She's twenty-seven. She's got every right to go find a place for herself. She's not leaving her job, or us.'

Storey saw that Doyle was struggling to keep himself in check. He bowed his head, unable to look at his visitors. He said, 'I don't need this shit right now. What's she playing at? She's never lived anywhere else, she won't know how to do it.'

'She'll survive. You can't keep hold of her forever.'

'You don't know what you're talking about.'

'What do you mean?'

Doyle looked at Storey as though asking for help, his eyes pleading. He said, 'It's a rough world out there.'

'It's no different to when we were growing up,' Charlotte said. 'The crowd your family knew. The things we did. She's the same age now as when I had her. And what I'd done before that ... well, you know what I was like.'

She used a light tone of voice as if trying to persuade him out of his mood, but it didn't work and Storey wondered if there was something deeper going on between them.

Doyle said quietly, 'I don't mind her wanting to leave. Not if I'm sensible about it. I knew it was coming. But the timing's not right, not now.'

'She didn't want to be there when you came back. She thought she'd make a clean break and when it had all died down she'd come and visit.'

Doyle lowered his head again and closed his eyes. 'It's not that straightforward.'

Storey caught something in his tone, said, 'What's happened?'

Doyle looked up. 'They showed me a picture this morning,' he said. 'They found Billy Jenkins face down in the canal.'

CHAPTER THIRTY-THREE

W HEN EVERYONE WAS out of the house Norton felt comfortable. Living with the Doyles was a daily trial and he was sure his health was suffering. It wasn't just that he felt like a butler, supposedly ready to fulfil every request—it was the tension caused by Doyle's suspicious nature. Of course he had every right to be suspicious, given what was happening, but Norton wished he would just relax.

Yes, he thought, then I could betray his trust with a quiet mind.

When had it happened? When had he made the decision to shift his allegiance away from Doyle and to those bastards Swann and Lethbridge?

He knew he kept pestering himself with the same question but he couldn't believe he'd shown such a lack of ... constancy, his mother would have called it. Ever the romantic, she wound up hating her husband, his father, because of his lack of constancy. He'd betrayed her, the same as Norton was now betraying Doyle, only not in a romantic way. It was business, he told himself. And self-preservation. Someone had made a better offer and he'd accepted the terms.

Only he didn't want to accept the terms now.

He stared again at his laptop screen. He'd accessed the company accounts online—the company whose directors were Swann and Lethbridge, and whose accounts he kept tidy before they were signed off at year's end by their tame accountants.

There had been a deposit from another company, one whose name he didn't recognise. 'F.I.Delity'. The deposit was a large amount and was evidently the sum promised from the new investor. A further £20,000. This gave them enough to start kitting the gym out and getting the next electrical fix started.

He opened another tab on his browser and navigated to the Companies House website, then entered F.I.Delity in the search bar. One direct hit. He clicked on it and then clicked on the People tab on the next page.

Two current officers of the company were listed: Frank Ivory as Director, and Lionel Ivory as Secretary.

If he'd been honest with himself he'd known before he'd started the search. There was only one 'F.I.' with any business in Coventry and any possible interest in supporting a club to rival Bran Doyle's.

Still, he felt manoeuvred and outsmarted. Disloyalty and dereliction of duty. They were racking up.

———

He picked up his mobile phone and called Swann, whose condescending voice answered after two rings.

Norton said, 'Why didn't you tell me it was Frank Ivory?'

There was only a slight hesitation before Swann said, 'I said you'd find out sooner rather than later, didn't I? I take it his cheque's gone in.'

'You're making me look a complete idiot. And a dishonest one at that.'

Swann said nothing and Norton realised he was silent because he was agreeing, making a point. Eventually Swann said, 'What's the problem? Frank likes to invest his money. He's always looking for opportunities.'

'You know very well he hates Doyle and will see this as a perfect opportunity to ruin him. Make a brighter, shinier gym and use his business contacts to turn it into a winner.'

Swann's voice turned hard, a tone that Norton had never heard before. He said, 'Norton, you'd better grow up quick. I appreciate you had to retrain when you came out of the army and business finance might not be what you had in mind. But here we are. You've got to toughen up. The bit of book-keeping you did in Afghanistan buying fruit and veg from the locals isn't the same as being Chief Finance Officer of a large company.'

'No, the Afghans were less crooked.'

Swann laughed but Norton thought it sounded like a gesture, he didn't mean it. Despite what Swann had just said he *had* toughened up and was reading him and Lethbridge more easily now.

Swann said, his voice changing again, 'You have to see yourself in the job, Craig. Imagine yourself in charge of the finance for many franchises, all over the country. Imagine the money you'll be making. Then suck it up and get on with what we're paying you for.'

'What if Doyle finds out?'

'So what? Don't you have plans to leave him anyway?'

'Per my own decision and timing, not because I've been forced into it. He'll crucify me. And to be honest he'd have every right, given the way I've treated him.'

'Don't start talking like that. You'll be feeling sorry for yourself next, instead of thinking about the you that you can turn out to be. The best you.'

'Do you read this claptrap in books?'

'Big reader of self-improvement literature, me. None of us knows so much that we can't learn something, Craig. Keep your mind open. Learn from the setbacks, make yourself stronger. When the time is right you can leave Doyle and tell him what you think of him.'

'I can't … not yet. Don't ask me to.'

'Then stop moaning and carry on. This is the new world. You can't afford loyalty when you're talking about business. And you won't find that quotation in a book, I made it up.'

'How did Frank Ivory get involved? Did you talk to him?'

'You'll find this hard to believe, Craig, but we talked to lots of people. About finance, I mean. Frank was one of the first. He liked the idea but wanted to see something concrete happening, so to speak. More than just plans. He's not one much for using his imagination, is Frank. He wanted to see what we came up with. Then he decided to come along for the ride.'

'He didn't say anything about getting back at Bran, making a rival gym and so forth?'

'It may have come into the conversation. Coventry's a small place. Everyone knows what everyone else is doing.'

Norton found he was shaking his head. 'So the bastard let you put up all the risk, then comes in at the last minute so he can act as the saviour, and no doubt come across as someone who cares about the kids of the City. He's despicable.'

'That may be right,' Swann said. 'But he's our despicable. You don't have to deal with him.'

'Can I talk about this, face to face?'

He heard Swann sigh and knew he was being a nuisance. But right now he didn't care.

Swann said, 'Come tomorrow night. You know the drill.'

CHAPTER THIRTY-FOUR

HAVING DROPPED CHARLOTTE at the house, Storey drove out to the building site. He didn't know what he expected to see, but it wasn't the sight of the new foreman, Gerry, laying bricks.

He parked and walked over to the other man, who had straightened and taken his hard hat off. Storey noticed that the scorched beams still hadn't been replaced.

He said, 'What happened? Where is everyone?'

'No one turned up. I rang the agency and they said they'd heard Doyle had been arrested, so they pulled everyone off. And he owed them money. They weren't going to take any more risks until they knew what the situation was. I tried to phone you but you didn't answer. I left two messages.'

Shit, Storey thought. He'd left his phone in the house when he went to help Felicity pack, first thing that morning. Then when he'd returned from helping her into his house he'd picked it up quickly before driving Charlotte to the police station. He hadn't checked it because he'd been too busy. And anyway, no one ever phoned him.

He said, 'Sorry about that. Busy day with the Doyles. He mentioned the agency this morning. I'm supposed to call them. I should have their number somewhere.'

'Are you always this efficient?'

'This is a good day.'

'I can see why Doyle left you in charge.'

He found the number in his phone's history and walked away to make the call. He went through two layers of management before someone with responsibility came on the line—not the same person he'd spoken to before. He sounded like someone from Accounts, with a dry, uninterested tone and a precise way of speaking. Being in Accounts, his customer-service skills lacked refinement, Storey thought, wandering around the site listening to the man describe how it was part of the contract that if the hiring body—Doyle—was found to be in breach of regulations or any other pertinent legislation, then the contracted workers would be asked to cease work while an investigation was undertaken.

Storey argued that no regulations had been breached and that he couldn't see how Doyle's arrest could be said to contravene any pertinent legislation because it wasn't at all related to construction.

'And besides,' he asked, 'how did you find out about the arrest? It's not been reported in the press as far as I know.'

The man from Accounts said, 'I'm not at liberty to divulge that information.'

'Was it one of the people from the site? Did they find out and let you know?'

'I'm sorry, I can't say.'

'It was a private call, wasn't it? Someone rang you and asked if you knew, and you didn't. So you rang the police station but they wouldn't tell you anything. But they wouldn't deny it either.'

The Accounts man said nothing.

Storey said, 'Look, Mr Doyle is organising payment of the debt he owes. It'll be with you in a couple of days. Does he have a due date for payment of the last invoice?'

'Three days' time.'

'Well there you go. I saw him earlier today and he's going to be released shortly. When he is, the money will be with you soon afterwards.'

'Our regulations are very clear—'

'I understand. But I'm sure you'd rather have the men working on this contract than waiting at home for a call, wouldn't you?'

'Of course.'

'In case you're wondering who I am, I'm working for Mr Doyle as the site manager at the moment, but I used to be a police officer. I know how these things work—you can take my word for it that he'll be out soon, probably within twenty-four hours.'

There was a long pause.

'We have your guarantee for that, Mr ... ?'

'Storey. Paul Storey.'

'All right, I'll release the block on the account and the men will be with you again tomorrow. But the latest invoice must be paid off within forty-eight hours.'

'Thank you, we appreciate it.'

He hung up and turned to find Gerry close behind, listening. He said, 'Was any of that true?'

'Which bits?'

'Any of it?'

Storey grinned. 'Are you questioning the word of an ex-police officer?'

———

It was getting dark when she saw Storey's car pull in through the gate and turn into the parking space beside his cottage.

She went to the front entrance and was on the point of walking towards him when she saw that he hadn't gone inside but was striding towards her, head down, as if thinking about something. She liked the fact he was pragmatic and got things done. Monks, the previous driver, was passive, sitting around the place and asking questions all the time. And whenever you answered one, there was always another, as if he never learned anything. It go so irritating Bran had to fire him in the end. That and the fact he was supplying her with dope. Bran never liked her smoking.

Still, Monks was no great loss.

Storey had almost reached her door when he looked up and saw her. She thought he had a good face, a strong nose and very direct eyes, though she also knew it could turn hard and unforgiving. She wanted to talk to him about Felicity—as she'd thought more about it that afternoon, going over her daughter's moving out earlier in the day, it seemed to her that Storey and Felicity had shared some private knowledge. He was polite to her, the boss's daughter, but she'd also deferred to him on occasion, as though his opinion or knowledge was more valuable than her own. She'd never seen that before in Fliss and it made her think that Storey knew something, something important. Something that gave him a hold over her, reined in her stroppiness.

But now he'd stopped on the driveway and looked up at the house, as though wondering whether to come any closer. He said, 'Get your coat. Let's have a look at the pond.'

Not understanding why, she reached behind the door and unhooked a padded jacket and put it on, then joined him as he walked towards the decking. A thin winter sun was setting beyond the trees, not having risen much above them all day, and glinted through the tallest branches as they approached the pond. It was overgrown with algae and, like the tennis court and swimming pool behind the house, needed some professional care.

He stood next to her with his hands in his pockets, saying, 'What do you do with this in the summer? Fish?'

'Bran sometimes brings a gas barbecue out and we eat steak and sausage and burnt chicken. Baked potatoes wrapped in silver foil. He likes it. Makes him feel like a real man again. I swear the little fishes' heads pop up out of the water begging for scraps.'

Storey nodded. He was always very self-contained, she thought. Never told you anything about himself.

Now he said, 'There was a bit of trouble at the site today. The men didn't turn up because their agency hadn't been paid.'

'Bran's sorting that out.'

'That's what I told them. It's all square.'

'Why have you told me? What could I do?'

'Nothing. I just thought you should know.'

'Was that it?'

'Isn't it enough?'

She stared over the water, which was slowly turning orange in the sun's last rays.

She said, 'You're very good at keeping us all happy, aren't you? Bran, Felicity, me. It's like you're doing that thing with plates spinning on sticks. What do you do for Norton?'

'I ease his burdens.'

She glanced at him, but he was looking over the water, too, the pair of them leaning on the thin wooden rail that Bran had nailed to the dock as a last-minute safety feature. Though she thought she could push it with her little finger and it would drop into the water.

She said, 'Craig has lots of burdens. The biggest one being Bran and his crazy ideas.'

Storey opened his mouth and then closed it again. She said, 'What? What were you going to say?'

'I was going to say, and Darren.'

'Does anyone know where he is yet? I never particularly liked him but I wouldn't want him to come to harm. Or to think he murdered Rod.'

'I'm sure he's all right,' Storey said.

She was quiet for a moment, then said, 'I want to know about Felicity.'

He shifted his position. 'Know what about her?'

'You were hiding something from me this morning. The pair of you.'

'Has she rung you?'

'Not yet. She's probably straightening the pictures on her walls and lining up the edges of the blankets on the bed. She's very … precise. Where is she?'

'I'm not supposed to tell anyone.'

'Is she going to be safe?'

Now Storey turned to her and he must have seen something in her face because he sighed and said, 'She's at my place. It's safe. Don't tell her I told you.'

'Is she ... alone?'

Now he turned away again. 'Not exactly.'

'Is she with ... with a woman?'

He didn't move but something changed in his posture, perhaps a slight stiffening of his shoulders. He turned his face to look at her. 'You knew, didn't you?'

'I wasn't sure. But she never went with boys, all through her adolescence. Even Darren—well, she never talked about him. She never seemed particularly interested, to be honest. They didn't do that much together—went to the pictures or for a meal once or twice a week. Or they'd go out together and she'd come back separately.'

'She doesn't want her father to know. Not yet.'

'I won't tell him. It's her decision. Besides ...'

'What?'

She turned to face him directly. 'Stress isn't good for him right now.'

She said it as though laying down something for him to pick up. He said, 'Why's that?'

'A couple of years ago he had a bit of a heart thing ... nothing serious. They fitted a pace-maker and he's been okay since. But they told him to avoid stress. Imagine saying that to Bran Doyle.'

'Contradiction in terms.'

'Exactly.'

'So is it a real problem? Do I have to watch out for him keeling over?'

'I shouldn't think so. But over-exertion, stress ... none of it's good for him. Being active is one thing, killing yourself's another.'

'Okay. I'll be mother hen.'

'That I doubt.'

They were quiet again until she said, 'You weren't really coming to tell me about the men on the site, were you?'

'I thought you should know.'

'You were checking that I was okay, with my husband in jail and my daughter flown the coop.'

'Whatever gave you that idea?'

'I'm getting to understand you. You're not as tough as you'd like us to think. Do you think Bran will be back tomorrow?'

'They can't hold him any longer without an extension. Which I don't think they'll get.'

She felt a sudden curiosity. She said, 'Why are you doing this?'

'What do you mean? It's my job.'

'You don't need this job. You're not the kind of man who needs a job to know who he is. What do you want from us?'

Storey didn't look at her and took a long time before he spoke. 'When my mum died I was young and I didn't really understand what was going on. With her illness. It all went over my head. Then my dad died a couple of months ago and I knew what was going on but I couldn't do anything for him anyway. It was out of my control. I felt useless.'

'But you left the police force, didn't you? Weren't you doing something useful there?'

'In the great scheme of things, perhaps. But it didn't feel like it on a day-to-day basis.'

'So what are we, then—a project to make you feel good about yourself?'

'It didn't start like that.'

'And then you found out how fucked-up we all were and thought you could help.'

'I've got certain skills that might come in handy.'

'You said you'd never rent out your place. What changed? Did Fliss persuade you?'

'I changed my mind,' Storey said. 'I realised I wasn't using it and Felicity needed somewhere, so why not? I was just being stupid and I should have known better. I've spent too long living by other people's rules to start making them for myself.'

'You're spending too much time with Bran. He's never met a rule he didn't want to break.'

'It doesn't always get you what you want, though, does it?'

'No? You seem to be managing.'

'Am I?' He laughed bleakly. '-I wonder sometimes. I'd like to think I'm learning through experience.'

'My experience is telling me it's cold now,' she said. 'Can I go back inside?'

'You're the boss.'

'Look where it got me.'

CHAPTER THIRTY-FIVE

S TOREY HAD THE sense that things were moving towards some kind of ending. When he'd started with the Doyles everything seemed settled and relatively calm. Since then two men had been murdered, a building set on fire, Felicity had left home and Bran Doyle had been arrested.

Plus, he'd started a relationship with a woman who didn't work for the police force—a novelty for him.

Having walked Charlotte back to the house he'd returned to the cottage and had a shower. Now he fried a couple of sausages, threw in some mushrooms and tomatoes and toasted some bread while they cooked.

He ate on his knees in front of the television, watching the news and weather. There was nothing about Rod Spencer or Billy Jenkins, but he hadn't expected there to be. Too small, too local. There were bigger things going on in the world.

He thought for a while about Billy Jenkins. A bad way to end up, face down in a canal, your head bashed in. He wondered whether he saw it coming or whether the man who'd killed Rod had caught him by surprise in the same way.

Storey touched the back of his head. The bruise was still tender but going down. He must have been lucky or the man had held back. Perhaps he'd reached his quota for that night.

He supposed Billy Jenkins had done something to earn his early death—perhaps he'd mouthed off to the wrong person, or he was being punished for knowing too much. Another witness got rid of.

Storey saw Frank Ivory and Lionel in his mind's eye, the night they'd waited for him outside Kate's house. They were watching him as he walked towards his car, Lionel saying nothing but looking as if his hands were itching to grab him by the throat. Frank smiling a slightly lop-sided smile, trying to be ironic, letting you know he knew it was all a game, everyone was trying to fool everyone else with bravado and posturing. Like boxers walking through the crowds to the ring, their capes flowing behind them as if they were superheroes. When in fact their hearts were thumping with adrenaline and anticipation and someone back in the dressing-room was swilling their vomit down the sink.

———

When the phone rang he knew who it would be because he'd thought about her earlier. That was the way it worked.

He said, 'I knew it was you.'

'Can you meet me tonight?' Kate asked. 'I've got to tell you something.'

'Tell me now, if it's urgent.'

'Meet me where we went last time, by the river. An hour.'

They hung up and Storey sat and thought about her for a while. He didn't like the sound of her voice but he couldn't imagine what the problem was.

———

He arrived early and saw her come in. She stopped to order a red wine at the bar and then came through the tables carrying it. He liked the way her hips moved.

Now she was pulling out a chair to sit facing him, saying, 'Thanks for coming.'

'I had no choice. You sounded keen.'

She drank some wine and licked her lips, then opened her handbag and took out a tissue and blew her nose. Then she put the tissue back in the bag and closed it and re-settled herself in the chair and finally looked directly at him.

She said, 'I've been acting under false pretences with you.'

'So you don't really like me at all and you've just been leading me on?'

'This is serious. I'm not who you think I am. God, this is hard.'

'Go on. Take your time.'

'A long time ago Bran Doyle boxed against a man he should never have fought. The man was young and inexperienced and was lighter and smaller than Doyle. But someone put up the money and they fought and the younger man didn't come out of it well. He was in a coma for six months and when he surfaced his speech was slurred, he couldn't use his left arm properly and he had difficulty concentrating.'

Storey watched her telling the tale with the same distance he'd used when working as a beat policeman many years ago. You take in the facts, the details, and you try not to be affected by the personal circumstances of the people involved—you don't empathize, you don't imagine what it must be like to go through that experience, to feel that pain. You keep it clean by focusing on the facts.

He said, 'When was this?'

'Just under thirty years ago. Doyle was in his early thirties. The man, my dad, was twenty-three. I was five. Just old enough to remember what he was like before the fight.'

Storey leaned back in his seat, thinking over what she'd told him.

'That's why you were in Coventry. You came up here to do something.'

'My mum had to look after the two of us while trying to earn a living at the same time. Dad stayed at home and watched TV, flicking channels all the time because he got bored quickly. He'd shout at me and then burst into tears. He'd try to make a sandwich but couldn't hold the bread in place with his left hand while he buttered it. He drank.'

'Is he still alive?'

'He lives with my mother. In Camden. They get help now, but he's a relatively young man. My mum aged but she's got spirit. She still loves him.'

'You told me Doyle came into your shop and asked you to do work for him. Was that a coincidence? Were you just waiting for that to happen?'

She took another sip from her drink and placed it down carefully. He saw the tension in her body then. She said, 'I came to Coventry because I knew he was here. That was the first lie. I didn't go to college here. I moved to get a job. I did get my own shop, though, more of an office actually. And I put an advert in the Telegraph and put flyers through doors. To get work, make a start. I found out where he lived and made sure I put one through his door. I also changed my name, not that he would have guessed.'

'What did you want to happen? Were you going to stick a kitchen knife in his back? Or just find a way to make him feel guilty?'

'I didn't know. I thought something would come up. I thought I'd find something that would incriminate him in some way, bring him down to earth.' She pulled a wry face. 'I didn't count on Felicity. We weren't that far apart in age. Interested in some of the same things, design, clothes. And I quite liked Charlotte, too, though she's a bit more touchy.'

'And Doyle himself?'

'That's the tragic part, isn't it? Because I was determined I wasn't going to forgive him, but it turned out I liked him. What happened to Dad wasn't his fault. It was the people who set it up, the fight. They were just out to make money. They took a young, promising scrapper and put him up against Bran Doyle. If my dad won, it was a great story of youth beating the old dog. If Doyle won, it was a story about his career still flourishing, even though he was getting older. They couldn't lose.'

'Who were the promoters, then? Have you got any sort of action you could take against them?'

'You don't mess with these guys. London gangsters. And that's what they are. They dress themselves up as property developers and businessmen but they'll beat you to death with a cricket bat as soon as look at you.'

'Does Doyle have anything to do with them now?'

'I don't think so. He never talks about them. That was their first promotion. I know they've been after some land he owns in London for years. But he won't sell. He's keeping it to sell to the highest bidder later, whenever Felicity needs money. The rumour is they're obsessed with it.'

'Doyle's mentioned it, the land.'

'They used to work for Bran, you know, in the ring. Until they set up for themselves and promoted this fight and started making money of their own. Charlie and Bert Tate.'

'I've seen them,' Storey said, surprising her. 'In a film Doyle showed me, working his corner. Evil-looking bastards.'

'That's them,' Kate said. 'But they don't just look evil—they are.'

'They're in London. What can they do?'

'Anything they possibly can to fuck him up.'

It was awkward in the car park, as though neither of them knew what the problem was. Storey walked her to her car and they stood by the driver's door.

'Well,' she said. 'Here we are.'

'We have to be somewhere. Am I going to see you again?'

'I don't know. Are you?'

'I've got your number. Perhaps when things cool down with the Doyles.'

'Perhaps.'

They each hesitated, then he bent down and kissed her on the cheek. It was the first kiss he'd given her, of any sort, and wondered why that was. What made him so reticent? A question he'd never been able to answer.

He turned and walked back to his Volvo, looking over his shoulder and seeing her staring at him. He raised a hand then felt embarrassed and lowered it and climbed inside the car thinking it was a relief. Now he wouldn't have to worry about her.

He'd think about her later. After he'd stopped thinking about the Tate cousins. Charlie and Bert.

They'd just risen out of the swamp like monsters in a fifties film and he didn't know what it meant.

CHAPTER THIRTY-SIX

NOW HE WAS out he didn't feel as good as he thought he would. A couple of days away from home had tied him in knots, inside. He wasn't there when Felicity left. He wasn't there to look after Charlotte ... not that she needed much looking after, but he thought it was his responsibility.

His whole reason for doing things was for his family. They take that away, they make him a lesser man. Then he caught himself—he was thinking exactly like the mobsters he'd told Storey about: it was all about family. Was that true? Did he do what he did so he could look after Charlotte and Fliss better? Or was it about him, his ego, his pride? Maybe it was both. Or maybe he should stop fooling himself and start thinking about other people for a change. What he did affected them, made them feel scared or unhappy, and it was usually because he'd been offended in some way. He spent his life taking offence and converting it into a to-do list. What kind of person did that?

Then he remembered the gym. That was different. Yes, it would have his name on it, but it wasn't to glorify himself. It was to attract people to join up, to believe they were getting a benefit. And in the end it would do good if it kept only one kid on the straight and narrow.

The cops had confiscated all the DVDs and told him he'd be facing charges later. Don't go anywhere. Do not pass go. Do not collect two hundred quid, or anything else. That Greaves thought he was a funny bastard. About as funny as the Black Death.

He still didn't know who'd told them. His first thought was Storey, because he'd just been let into the secret, that night in the garage. But why would he do that and carry on coming into work? It'd be obvious that he'd be under suspicion, and Doyle had already shown him how he asked questions—at the end of a fist. No, it must have come out some other way. Not Norton, obviously, and Charlotte didn't even know about it.

So who knew, and who would do the dirty like that? He glanced sideways at Storey now, driving smoothly as usual, taking the job seriously. He liked the fact the ex-copper didn't have any hang-ups about his position. He was paid to drive— and do whatever else Bran wanted—and he never argued or resented being a dogsbody. Well, perhaps he argued a bit. But it was more for show than anything else. He seemed loyal and he could handle himself. He didn't regret bringing him in on the DVD thing, though he wasn't much help in the end. They'd be taken out and smashed up somewhere and his investment, such as it was, would turn to crackly pieces of plastic.

He said, 'I feel like shit. I could do with a bath and a lie-down.'

Storey kept his eyes on the road. 'They say anything else to you about Billy Jenkins?'

'What could they say? I was in their nick when he was done so I was hardly a suspect.'

'If they didn't ask you any more questions they didn't have anything to tie you in. No connections.'

'Then why did they show me the photo of him in the canal?'

'To watch how you reacted. Listen to what you said. He worked on your site, after all, and Rod Spencer was murdered there. It'd be criminal if they didn't ask, wouldn't it? You're the common denominator. It might be random, a coincidence, but cops don't really believe in coincidence. Especially not when murders are involved.'

'Well I am some kind of fucking mastermind, aren't I? Killing off my own foreman then arranging the murder of someone else while banged up inside. You've got to hand it to me.'

Charlotte was waiting for him when he got inside, looking good in jeans and a plain jumper. She always seemed to know what went with what, what the good combinations were. He felt dirty and somehow soiled but he wanted to talk to her before he had a bath.

'Has Fliss been in touch?'

'She phoned this morning. She's fine. She's gone to work. How are *you*?'

'Tired but pissed off. I need a bath. Where's Craig?'

'He's around.'

He turned as the front door opened and a moment later Storey appeared in the room. Doyle said, 'Stay here while I have a bath. Get Norton down for when I get out.'

Before he went upstairs he crossed to the other side of the house and looked in on Felicity's room, annoyed with himself for knocking before opening the door even though he knew she wasn't there, then walking in tentatively. Finding the place stripped bare. Her fitted wardrobe doors still open, the bed without its duvet, her chest of drawers empty of perfumes and make-up.

He came out and closed the door, finding that the corners of his eyes were pricking with moisture.

Then he went downstairs again, crossed the entrance hall and went upstairs to the big white bathroom.

Now he was stretched out in the bath staring straight ahead, looking at the blank white tiles, feeling tension being released, his slight headache easing off. He was even beginning to feel hungry again.

It was time to do something.

Downstairs again, dressed in fresh clothes and smelling of some French deodorant Charlotte had bought him years ago, he found Storey and Norton sitting watching television with Charlotte, the three of them leaning with their heads back on the sofa while some man on the screen talked about economic indicators and the Bank of England. Apparently things were bad. He knew that—he didn't need to watch television to find that out.

When he caught Storey's eye he flicked his head and the man got up from the sofa and walked around it. Norton joined him and all three walked into the entrance hall.

Doyle said, 'I didn't want to talk in there with Charlotte.'

'What are we doing?' Norton asked. 'I mean, about funding.'

'That's why I've called this brains trust together, isn't it? See what fucking ideas we can come up with between the three of us.'

Storey said, 'Have you tried other places for bank loans? You must have your money in more than just the one.'

Doyle jerked his head towards Norton. 'Blame him. His idea to—what was the word?—consolidate all my cash into one place. I haven't got anywhere else to go for a loan.'

'What about friends? All those people who were here at the party—would any of them spring for a few thousand, for a friend?'

Doyle shook his head. 'They see me as the cash cow. They come to me for money, not the other way around.'

'Not even those at the golf club—Alf and the others?'

'Forget it. They either haven't got it or they wouldn't lend it. Alf's already lent me Gerry so I can't really ask him again. Besides, him and me own another business together so I don't want him getting more involved financially.'

'What business?'

'Don't worry about it. I give him some money to start up, I don't have anything to do with it except I'm a director. Furniture removals to Europe and back.'

There was a pause, then Storey said, 'You're not making this easy.'

'It's not supposed to be easy.'

He looked from Norton to Storey and back again, then said, 'Oh, fuck it, take me to the gym. Maybe I'll be inspired.'

Norton said, 'What do I do?'

'Keep biting your nails and hoping for the best.'

He liked the look of Gerry straight away, seemed like a no-nononsense man who'd get on with the job. Like Rod. He came up and shook Doyle's hand, then Storey's, saying, 'Sorry about Mr Spencer. They've been telling me he was a good man.'

Doyle looked around the site. Storey had told him they'd gone missing for a day but he'd straightened out the agency in return for a cheque. Doyle told himself he'd have to fix that when he got home. They had a few thousand left in the bank. He'd sell the bloody Mercedes if he had to. Or Charlotte's sports car.

He said, 'Show me the damage, will you? Bloody police wouldn't let me get near last time I was here.'

They walked over to the shell of the building and Gerry pointed out the scorched beams that hadn't yet been replaced. A couple of men were working on them, undoing the bolts on the trusses that held them in place.

'How will you get them down?' he asked. 'We had a crane to get them up.'

'Gravity,' Gerry said. Manoeuvre them out and let 'em drop. We've got a crane coming tomorrow to put the replacements in. Just the morning.'

He let Gerry take him around the rest of the site, showing progress and proving to Doyle that he knew what he was doing. The men glanced up at him and then looked away. He wondered what they thought of him now — he had no doubt his troubles with the police had got out. Hard to keep something like that quiet. Even if they got it wrong, there'd be rumours.

He said, 'Have the police come around? Any more questions?'

'A couple came yesterday. Asking about someone called Billy …? A couple of the lads talked to them. I've never met him so I couldn't say anything. What's he done?'

'He was a bit of a tearaway. Got himself killed.'

'Bloody hell. I might have to ask for danger money.'

'You can ask but you'll have to get in the queue.'

Gerry let that settle, then shrugged. 'No one ever said life was easy. Then the police asked about someone called Darren. I couldn't help them with him, either, so they talked to the men again about him. I don't know what they were told but they didn't look happy when they left.'

Doyle changed the subject. He didn't like thinking about what those two young idiots had done. He said, 'What's your best guess for finishing?'

Gerry took the time to consider the question and Doyle could see the calculations going on in his head—the roof and the walls, putting in the plumbing and electrics, then furnishing ...

'If the weather holds out, ten to twelve weeks. There's Christmas in there and the weather might be shit, though, so that's a guess.'

'No way to speed it up?'

'Not really. We can't put in plumbing or electrics till the walls and roof are up. Maybe double the electricians, but that doesn't gain you much time in the end.'

'All right. Thanks for coming in on short notice. Tell Alf I owe him one.'

'He told me to tell you it's on the house. He pays my wages.'

Doyle nodded, wondering why he couldn't find anything to say in reply. Then realised he wasn't used to people doing nice things for him. He didn't know how to respond.

Eventually he said, 'You talk to Storey if you want anything, okay? If he can't get it he'll talk to me. Do what you need to do.'

Storey had walked away, giving them some privacy. Having heard his name he took a step closer. Doyle said, 'You look after Gerry. Make sure he gets what he needs.'

He expected Storey to come back with a snappy remark, as usual, but he just nodded and glanced at Gerry, then went back to looking around the site as if scanning for danger.

Doyle realised suddenly what he had to do. It had been staring him in the face but he hadn't wanted to see it. He said, 'Let's go. I'm getting hungry,' then crossed the muddy site to the Mercedes and got in.

Back at the house they found a note from Charlotte saying she'd gone out to meet a friend.

'Fucking friend,' Doyle said. 'Wife of her doctor. Nosy bitch always wanting to know what's going on. I hope Charley keeps her mouth shut. Where's Norton?'

'Shall I call him?'

'Nah. You want a samwich?'

They went into the kitchen and Doyle buttered bread and made two ham sandwiches.

'Can't go into the living room,' he said, pointing Storey to sit at the kitchen table. 'She'll have a bloody fit if there's crumbs on the floor.'

They sat facing each other across the table. Doyle watched Storey eat, his long face chewing regularly, his attention focused entirely on what he was doing whenever he was doing it—driving, eating, it seemed to make no difference. Total focus. He wished he had that. Wished he could just think about one thing at a time without a dozen other thoughts rushing into his head at the same time.

Made life difficult. Especially making decisions.

He said, 'I've got some land in London. I'm thinking of selling it, get some readies. Solve all my problems in one go. What do you think?'

Storey stopped chewing, swallowed, thought. 'It's your land. How much would it fetch?'

'Prime territory in Fulham. I dunno, haven't had it valued in a few years. Probably half a million. There was an old pub there but there was a gas explosion some time in the sixties and the site became derelict. A mate of mine bought it, tidied it up and sold it to me. Lots of people wanted to buy it over the years but I didn't need the cash and I liked having the money in the property, know what I mean?'

'You have to advertise it, wait for offers, negotiate ... could be months before you see any cash.'

'Watch this.'

He fetched the cordless phone from its cradle near the door and picked up the telephone contact book next to it, bringing them both back to the table. He sat down again and leafed through the book until he found the page. It was where he thought it was, written down nearly thirty years ago, a bit faded now. It was going to be the same number because those boys never moved house. That's why they wanted his land — so they could build an extension on what they already had.

He dialled and waited, winking at Storey while the phone rang. He felt good, as though a weight were lifting off his shoulders. He wondered why he hadn't done it before ...

The phone was answered. 'Charlie? Bran Doyle.'

The voice was exactly as he remembered. Perhaps a bit gruffer, now he was older. They talked for a while and then he hung up.

He said to Storey, 'Tomorrow evening. You'll be picking them up from the station. Wear your best shirt.'

CHAPTER THIRTY-SEVEN

I T WASN'T YET eight o'clock, so Storey phoned Felicity Doyle and asked whether he could come over. She told him it was his house so of course he could. The drive took him fifteen minutes.

She opened the door before he pressed the button and looked past him into the darkness as he came in.

He said, 'What's up?'

'Come into the front room,' she said. 'We've got a bottle of wine open.'

He went through and he accepted a glass of red and he and Felicity and Nicki sat on the furniture his father had bought twenty years ago.

Nicki looked different to the times he'd seen her before—more informal, less make-up, her hair pulled back and echoing Felicity's short red pony-tail. They both wore jeans and tee-shirts. They looked like students.

He said, 'Any problems? With the house?'

Nicki said, 'It's great, thanks for letting us stay. My lease runs out this weekend so it's come at just the right time.'

'You didn't have anything else lined up? Or couldn't you extend it?'

The women glanced at each other.

'We always planned to get somewhere together,' Nikki said. 'But it was turning out harder than we thought. My place was too small for two of us, really, with all our gear, but I don't think we knew what we were going to do. Fliss just wanted to get out.'

Everyone drank from their glasses. Storey thought there was something unsaid in the air—more than a strained politeness because he was effectively their landlord. Felicity's face seemed worn and stressed.

He said, 'Have you spoken to your parents?'

Felicity nodded. 'I talked to my dad. It was okay. He's got other things on his mind. Does he know you're here?'

'I didn't tell him.'

She nodded again, then said, 'I think I'm being followed.'

So there it was, now, a feeling or a fact, something to be looked at and discussed by all of them. At last he was in on the secret.

She went on to describe the sense she had when she was driving to work, arriving in the car park—a multi-storey in the city centre—and when she was walking to and from her workplace, an office two minutes away.

'What does it feel like?' Storey said.

'It's like an echo in the air. I don't exactly hear footsteps behind me, but I sense somebody's walking close by. When I turn around there's no one there. When I'm driving I look in the rear-view mirror and there's nothing at first, but a couple of miles later there's a vehicle with big lights quite close. I've never seen any one but I'm sure I'm not making it up.'

Storey wanted to believe it was paranoia but with everything that had happened recently he didn't want to jump to a wrong conclusion either. He said, 'When did it start?'

'Since the beginning of the week, when I came out of the office Monday night. I thought moving house would make life easier but it's not been like that. I've been driving Nicki mad, haven't I?'

'If I see her look through the front curtains one more time I'll scream,' Nicki said.

Storey looked at them in turn. He thought he should do something, if only to calm their nerves. He said, 'All right, stay here. I'm going out the back.'

He stood up and went through the small kitchen to the back door, the wooden one with a pane of frosted glass in its top half. He pulled his jacket together, opened the door and slipped out.

The air had grown colder quickly. He zipped up his jacket and pushed his hands in his pockets, then walked down the paving slabs to the high fence at the rear of the property. He slipped the lock on the gate and went into the alley behind, a rough area of stone and patches of concrete with the graffiti-painted doors of half a dozen garages just visible in the fading light.

He turned left, moving between the high fences of the gardens that bordered the alley as it led out to the main street, its orange sodium lamps casting dark shadows.

He paused before exiting the alley and hitting the street, then took a tentative step forward. He doubted he'd been in this spot since he was a child, playing with friends. Opposite was the old church whose grounds they used to run through. It hadn't changed in nearly thirty years, and why should it? It had lasted centuries. Not too long ago it was a country church, perhaps in a village on the edge of town, and was still bordered by a field to its left. Now it was incorporated into the city, the houses facing it—where he was standing—no more than seventy years old, if that. All around there had been fields, farms and barns. The canal was no more than half a mile away. What was country was now town.

He turned his collar up and moved along the street, pausing briefly at the corner to survey the half-dozen or so cars parked along the curb. The houses on the far side of the road had parking spaces created beneath their bay windows, the brick walls that once divided their front gardens from the pavement having been knocked down to make access; the cars on this side were parked against the curb.

He began to walk along the road towards the front door of his father's house, having circled the block, his footsteps clean and hard on the pavement. The sky was clear and a bright segment of moon threw light on the path.

He'd walked past his own car, parked in a space this side of the house, when a white car fifteen yards ahead moved away from the curb, turning silently into the road and accelerating away. It was so silent he thought it must be an electric vehicle, showing no sign of gearing up or getting louder as it increased speed.

He stood and watched it, unable to see the driver from behind and in the dark, and by now it was too far to read the licence plate.

Back at the house he was let in again and stood to get warm in front of the gas fire.

'Nothing there,' he said, deciding to keep the information about the quiet car to himself. 'But it doesn't mean you're wrong. I can't do anything unless we have absolute proof, so you'll just have to be careful about what you do and who you talk to.'

'I'll try,' she said.

Later, Storey wished he'd been more insistent.

CHAPTER THIRTY-EIGHT

THIS TIME THEY arrived at the same time, Swann holding the door open for him with elaborate grace, then Lethbridge leading the way to their usual seat in a far corner, barely-lit, away from the music speakers set high in the wall.

They hustled chairs around a table and said nothing until the barman had brought over their drinks. The privilege of being the owner, Norton thought: the barman comes to you.

When he'd left, Norton said, 'You didn't tell me it was Frank Ivory buying in to your place.'

'We talked about this yesterday,' Swann said. 'Do we have to do it all again? He's a local businessman, which I said. He can afford it. He wants to invest in local businesses. You can't dispute we're local.'

'If his money comes in, I go out.'

Lethbridge had been drinking from his glass. Now he smacked his lips and put it down carefully on the table. 'That's a daring statement, coming from you. Who do you think you are to dictate to us where the money comes from?'

'I'm not dictating,' he said, feeling his heart rate speeding up slightly, the usual sense of discomfort rising in his chest. 'Despite the fact I'm sitting here with you, I actually do have some loyalty to Bran Doyle. I won't deny I'm uncomfortable working for you while I've been doing the same for him. It hasn't sat right with me for a while. That's the truth, the actual fact of the matter.'

'No, the facts are these,' Swann said. 'We're the majority owners of this club, and you're an employee. If we choose to invite Mr Ivory on to the board because he can help us out, that's no concern of yours. And I'm sure I don't have to remind you that you really wouldn't want Bran Doyle to find out you've been working with us.' His eyes held Norton's and then he relaxed and smiled. 'I don't want to be having this kind of conversation with you, Craig. You're our head man for finance and we want you to stay in place until this job is done and then we can talk about the franchise opportunities. Besides, it's impossible for you to leave, now. You're on too much of the paperwork. Your experience and background have given us a lot of weight with our other sponsors and with the banks. We'd be mad to let you just walk away without putting up some kind of fight, wouldn't we?'

Norton stared at the space between Swann and Lethbridge, his gaze focusing on the far side of the bar where a couple of old men were playing dominoes, rapping their pieces hard against the table. If he'd felt bad before, he felt worse now. They were like a pair of boa constrictors wrapping themselves around his throat and squeezing. He'd let pride and ego get the better of him and he couldn't see a way out.

Please god he wouldn't have to deal with Ivory directly, man to man.

Then the door to the bar opened and Frank Ivory and Lionel walked in.

———

Ivory was wearing a pale suit over a black shirt and white tie. He looked like a gangster from the thirties. Perhaps he was trying to attach the 'Handsome' label to his clothing style and move it away from his features as he got older. Lionel wore black jeans, a black polo neck sweater and a thin zipped jacket. Norton wondered if he was making a statement against his father's flashy style.

They saw the trio in the corner and walked over, Frank saying, 'So this is the famous Mr Norton. Craig, is it? That's a name you don't hear too often these days. All the Craigs must be dying out, eh? Joining the Arthurs and Dereks and Colins. I'm Frank Ivory, by the way, and this is my son, Lionel. Also a name you don't hear often, named after my father. He doesn't talk much. He prefers to stand around looking moody, don't you, son?'

Lionel looked away, suddenly interested in the hunting pictures on the wall. Frank picked up a chair from another table and brought it close then sat down. Lionel sat on one of the torn green benches that lined the wall. Ivory was next to Norton, who could smell a mixture of animal musk and aftershave rising from him like a mist.

Norton felt he was the centre of attention and thought he'd better say something. But he found his mouth was dry, so he swallowed, then said, 'I was just telling Swann and Lethbridge I'm resigning from my position here. I can't work for them and Doyle at the same time. It doesn't feel right.'

Ivory looked at him, his eyes unblinking and thoughtful, then glanced at Swann and Lethbridge, who had muttered greetings when he entered but nothing since and now seemed to be waiting expectantly for a show to begin.

Ivory leaned back in his chair and called over his shoulder to Lionel. 'Lionel, get whatever these chaps have and the usual for you and me.' Lionel stood up slowly, as if he needed time to find his balance, then lumbered towards the bar. Frank turned back to Norton. 'You're probably wondering why I'm involved in this, aren't you? A piddly little gym club in the middle of nowhere, aimed at kids without any money so it's not going to be raking in the cash. You must have thought, Oh, I'll get involved and take the money and not worry too much about it. You must have thought it would be an easy gig for someone of your experience.' He placed his hands on the table and Norton noticed they were like Doyle's—large fingers and big knuckles, used to hard work or perhaps just punching walls in frustration. 'But it ain't that easy, my friend, to walk away. You're in this now. You're going to see it through.'

He paused while Lionel came back with a tray of drinks. He deposited them on the table, then picked up his own dark pint and stepped back. Norton sensed the strength of the man just in the way he leaned over, his arms and stomach close to Norton's face.

Frank continued. 'What you don't understand is that when Doyle put me down in that last fight, he cost a lot of people a lot of money. It wasn't just me, my pride, if you like. I had some, let's say, sponsors ... people who weren't too happy when Bran knocked me over. And worse, they weren't too happy with me. I'd made all sorts of promises to them because of that first fight. I'd learned a lot. I thought I knew what to do to get one over on him. But it didn't work. He was too smart for me.'

'So it's taken you all these years to get your own back. That's petty, isn't it?'

'Perspective, mate, perspective. And it's not all about money — just so you know.'

'What do you mean?'

'My lips are sealed,' Frank said, grinning. 'Give my regards to Darren when you see him, won't you?'

CHAPTER THIRTY-NINE

J ACKIE WEST ALWAYS seemed to know when he was alone. Perhaps it was because the house was bugged so she knew when Doyle was there and not being driven somewhere by his chauffeur. These thoughts went through his head because he was in his living-room watching the lunch-time news when his phone rang and he saw her name on its screen.

She said, 'Anything you want to tell me?'

'They landed a man on the moon but some people don't believe it.'

'How's Doyle doing? He must be pissed off about the DVDs.'

'He wants to blame me for giving him up but doesn't believe I'd be that stupid. He obviously doesn't know me that well.'

'Sorry about that.'

'Did arresting him do any good?'

'It's put the frighteners on him. He's going down for that and he knows it. Perhaps he'll come clean about the other stuff to make a deal.'

Storey stood up and walked around the room, trying to clear his head.

'I don't believe it,' he said. 'He's not acting like someone with a big secret. The DVDs were it, the whole deal. He's still looking for money for his gym and as far as I know he hasn't met Alf Chamberlain or phoned him.'

'Ever heard of email?'

He thought about the meeting Doyle was going to have with the Tates later on, but told himself Jackie probably knew about it already and he was damned if he was going to bring it up. Let them do the police work.

Perhaps he was going native after all.

He said, 'I've got to go. Chores to do.'

She said, 'Yeah, must be hard toting that bale.'

'It's a living.'

'Is that what you call it?'

He hung up on her then, feeling angrier than he'd been in a long while.

Frank ivory had never been nervous in his life, but this meeting was doing something to his head.

Maybe it was because it was important, money-wise. Or maybe it was because the people he was meeting had a lot of power. All kinds of power. They even boasted about it, saying they were coming with two other men, muscle to smooth the path. If it needed smoothing. If it needed digging up and foundations laying and concreting over. That kind of smooth.

It wasn't even that he didn't know them. In fact he'd known them a long time. A very long time. Maybe thirty years. The Tates, Charlie and Bert. He'd used them as his ring-men when they were just starting out and they'd given him advice, too. Toughened him up. Made him a better fighter. Well, dirtier.

Where other London mobsters had gradually gone out of fashion, they were still there, like cockroaches who never died or got trodden on, just worked away in the dark building their empire.

After they'd worked in his corner they moved on, became little grafters, doing work for the big firms in London, weaselling their way into people's good books. Knock over a newsagents here; bash in the head of someone who owes money there. They'd carried on promoting fights as a way of earning cash until their own firm started making money. One-armed bandits. A bit of protection money. Then putting together teams to do their own jobs, like all the big boys did.

Now they were older and the firm was still heavyweight. It wasn't like the glory days of the 60s, or even the 70s—the police were more honest now and the competition was coming in from overseas, the Russians, of course, but also the Romanians, the Turks ... it was harder for the home-grown lads to mark out a claim for themselves. So to keep a business together like the Tates had done had taken some balls.

Maybe that was why he was nervous, he told himself. He didn't know what to expect. The one thing about the Tates, the thing that everyone said, was that they were unpredictable. They didn't travel on the same route every day when going into their office. They didn't eat in the same places, or frequent the same clubs night after night. They mixed things up, made it difficult to know where they were going or what they were doing.

He knew he should have learned from that. He tended to be habitual in what he did and where he went. Dragging Lionel behind him like a tent-pole.

He said, 'Where the fuck are they, then?'

He and Lionel were sitting in his front room, a fake Georgian mansion he'd bought from a builder who needed the money to stay in business but went under anyway. It had a redbrick tiled driveway and a fountain in the front garden and two garages next to each other, both of them white with black beams painted on as if King George had had two cars he needed to park up at the end of a hard day's ruling.

Lionel was standing by the windows, blocking the light, watching the front gateway. He didn't give much away but Frank thought he was excited. He was going to be meeting some genuine bad guys, not the men with big egos but small ambitions he tended to come across in Coventry. He said, 'I'll say something when they arrive, won't I?'

'I don't know,' Frank said. 'You're so fucking terse you might forget to mention the fact they're knocking on the door.'

Lionel turned towards him, his square face giving nothing away. He said, 'They're here. See, I mentioned it.'

The four men came through the front door and looked around, taking in Frank's decor and making him see it through their eyes. He needed to repaint and liven it up. Get some bookshelves in, give it a bit of class.

The Tates were cousins and were physically similar—slightly below average height, straight black hair combed over round faces, thick eyebrows. They seemed to be round in the limbs, too, shrugging off their winter coats and looking like a couple of not-fully-grown bears when they'd finished, their jackets pulling tight across their chests, their shoulders rounded. They must have been in their fifties now. Frank remembered that Charlie was the taller and the older one and consequently did most of the talking.

The two 'bodyguards' that had come with them were bigger and younger, both with fair hair and pale, pock-marked skin, apprentices learning how to do business and how to project power and strength. He saw Lionel eyeing them up to see whether he had anything to learn from them. Apparently not— he turned and went back into the front room.

Charlie undid the buttons of his jacket and looked at Frank, saying, 'Your missus fucked off a few years ago, didn't she? You on your own here?'

'Me and Lionel. Hello to you, too, Charlie.'

'They call me Charles now. More proper, you know what I mean?'

Frank indicated the younger men. 'Who are these?'

'Who gives a shit? Call 'em Ant and Dec.'

The tall blond men nodded briefly then set their jaws. Frank wondered if he saw disappointment in their eyes.

'And are you still Bert?' he said to Charlie's cousin, who'd been reading texts on his phone.

Bert didn't look at him. He said, 'Is it through there?', glancing up and walking towards the front room, having seen Lionel go through the same door moments before.

Jesus, Frank thought, *whose house* is *this*?

He walked them through to the front room. He asked if anyone wanted a drink but they were all business. The two cousins sat on the comfortable chairs and the muscle took up positions around the room, standing awkwardly with their hands crossed in front of them like FBI agents.

'Good trip?' Frank asked.

'Fuck that,' Charlie said. 'I hope we're not up here on a wild goose chase. I'm only here because Bran Doyle is on the point of selling his land. He called yesterday, like I told you on the phone. Will he do it, or will he chicken out, like he's done before?'

'How the hell do I know?' Frank said. 'This was all your doing, wasn't it? Soon as you found out he was building a sports club you were on the blower.'

'Don't complain. You're getting some business out of it, ain't you?'

'I hope so, eventually.'

'The fucker will squirm. So have you been making life hard for him, like we said?'

'One or two bits and pieces. We've had some stuff from his site and he's suffered a couple of personnel losses.'

'Tragic. He won't know where to turn. Does he know about this Swann and Lethbridge pair yet, and their little venture?'

'If he doesn't, he will soon. Coventry's a small town but he doesn't have a lot of contacts in construction so he might not have heard the rumours. I hope he has a bleeding heart attack when he does.'

'We've not come all the way up to this shit-hole for him to flake out before he signs the contract.'

'I know that.'

'So perhaps you should be thinking of more ways of making it obvious to him he's got no choice in the matter. He's led us on before but pulled out at the last minute, like a bloody Catholic priest on a whore. He won't give us the satisfaction. This time I'm not taking any fucking chances. I want some arm-twisting to make it clear we're not fucking about.'

'What time are you meeting him?'

Bert said, 'Six o'clock tonight. He thinks we're arriving later this afternoon. He's sending his driver to pick us up from a notel.'

'Storey.'

'What?'

'His driver, he's called Storey. Watch what you say in front of him. Ex-copper. Probably still has friends, if you know what I mean.'

'Jesus,' Charles said. 'You know how to run a project up here, don't you? You're mixing in the wrong circles. What about Swann and Lethbridge? They married to coppers or something?'

'They're not as hard as they think. They're just bookies who want to expand. They'll do what we say. They've been twisting Doyle's money-man round their finger, he's been feeding us info about what Doyle's been up to, where he gets his materials and so on. So we've been screwing with him and with Doyle. Like I said, I had a man nicking stuff from the site.'

Lionel said suddenly, 'He was giving us some problems so we looked after him.' His voice coming from a corner of the room where they'd forgotten him.

Everyone in the room turned to look at the big man. Frank wished he'd kept quiet—he'd given the Tates some power now.

Charlie said, 'But that's all squared away, right? Nothing can come back on anyone?'

'He's not talking anymore,' Lionel said. 'He'd been doing too much talking.'

Charlie frowned and turned back to Frank. 'You've got between now and six o'clock tonight to force Doyle's hand. Five hours. Make him see it's now or never. Call it insurance.'

'Don't worry,' Frank said. 'We've got a plan.'

CHAPTER FORTY

ALTHOUGH HIS DAD was often rude to him, Lionel knew he had a lot of responsibility.

Frank would sometimes put his arm around his shoulders, reaching up a few inches, and talk to him as if they were equals. Lionel appreciated that. He knew it was easy to see him as just a big lump who did what his dad said and had nothing to contribute. But if his dad was willing to talk to him and ask his advice, which he did occasionally, then that was all right with him.

He shifted position in the car. If he sat too long with his legs stretched out he got cramp in his backside and had to shift to the other arse-cheek. People had no idea how difficult it was being tall—always on show, always visible, always the one with his head above the crowd, easy to see if he fucked up.

But he wasn't going to fuck up. His dad had laid out the plan and told him what to do and he could see no way it could go wrong.

———

From where he sat he could see the blue door that was the exit from the car park's staircase on to this level. He'd followed her to work that morning again and she parked as usual on Level 4 of the multi-storey, as close to the staircase as she could get.

It was now 5.30 and people were starting to arrive at their cars to go home after work. He'd have to time it absolutely perfectly otherwise there'd be an incident. Fortunately it was fully dark outside and the lights in the car park were feeble.

There she was. And she was alone. A couple of times she'd been with the other woman who'd walked to her own car and then they'd driven back separately to the same house. The new place she'd moved to a couple of days ago. Which was very handy because it made it easier to watch her, follow the plan his dad had worked out.

Though he didn't like it when Storey had turned up on the street last night. What the fuck had he been doing there? He had to admit it unnerved him, which is why he'd started up and driven off before the man had seen him.

Anyway, he didn't understand why the women used separate cars when they were living in the same house now and working in the same office. It wasn't very green and Lionel didn't like that—he was looking forward to having children later and he wanted his kids to grow up in a world it was safe to live in. After all, he was the one, wasn't he, who persuaded his dad to buy this hybrid Citroen? He wanted to save the planet and didn't understand when people didn't want the same thing.

He made a note to ask the woman why they did it, travelled in two cars. It didn't make sense to him.

He'd had the engine running and now he eased out of his bay and went the long way around the central rows, knowing she wouldn't hear his approach.

He rolled to a halt, blocking her car in its bay, and he saw the look of surprise on her face and then watched as it turned to fear. Which was because he'd unfolded himself out of the driver's seat and had already taken a couple of steps towards her.

He said, 'You've got to come with me.'

'I'll scream if you take another step.'

'Do it. I'll knock your block off. I'll be out of here before anyone sees me.'

'What do you want?'

He noticed she had her keys out and had pressed the button to unlock the doors. The indicator lights flashed and the car made the unlocking sound.

He said, 'You come with me and you won't get hurt. We're not going to hurt you.'

'Then what the hell do you want?'

'Just get in the car.'

'I'm expected somewhere.'

'I know where you're expected, and who's expecting you. That girl with the blonde hair. Just get in the car.'

'If my dad finds out about this he'll kill you.'

'That's the point. We want him to find out.'

She was staring at him now. He could hear voices at the far end of the level, a couple of people having used the staircase at the far end.

He said, 'If you don't come and sit in the car I'll just take you and put you in the boot. You know I can do it.'

He saw her eyes moving towards the voices, perhaps hoping they were going to arrive before he made his move. He took another step and she raised her hands.

'Okay, okay ... don't touch me.'

He walked her around to the passenger seat and opened the door for her. She got in and he said, 'Give me your keys.'

She handed them over and he leaned over the bonnet and pressed the button to lock her car. Then he gave the keys back.

'See, I'm not a bad man.'

He climbed in and put the car in gear, then moved off slowly.

He didn't know whether it was bad luck or not that the other woman, the one Felicity lived in the house with, came out of the entrance door just as they passed. They went by so close that she looked into the car and saw Felicity in the front seat.

Lionel kept his head turned away and didn't see what Felicity might have mouthed, or signed, as they drove past.

He didn't want to know. If he didn't know then he couldn't lie to his dad or to those other men if things went wrong.

CHAPTER FORTY-ONE

DOYLE HAD TOLD him to use the big Mercedes SUV to fetch the men from the hotel, Storey taking five minutes to understand the controls before reversing it out of the third garage and heading towards the city. It was huge inside, with seven seats and three-colour ambient lighting, like being in a futuristic cocktail lounge, he thought. Doyle said he hardly ever used it but had got a good deal by buying it and the other Merc at the same time.

Now he was pulling up just as they were coming out of the doors—two big blond men and two squat dark ones. The tall ones were younger and probably the muscle so he ignored them. Doyle had told him to remember he was meeting men who could make his money problems go away, so it was up to all of them to play it cool and not piss them off. He didn't like doing business with them but it seemed he had little choice.

Storey recognised them easily from the video Doyle had played of his fight against Frank Ivory. Funny how it was all coming together, Doyle's past and these men from murky videos made several decades ago.

'I'm not going with you,' Doyle had said. 'They're coming like visiting fucking kings so I've got to up my game a bit. Put on a show. You're part of it, so mind your P's and fucking Q's.'

'Yes, bwana.'

'That's exactly what I'm talking about. Keep your lip to yourself. Pretend they're wrapped in cotton-wool and you've got to deliver them without a scratch.'

He pressed buttons to open the electronically-powered sliding doors, then climbed out, leaving the engine running, and walked towards them. The two dark-haired men looked at him and looked at the car and then looked at him again.

The taller of the two said, 'You're Storey. Go on, tell us one.'

He grinned at his cousin and dug him with his elbow. The shorter man said nothing but walked towards the car. The bodyguards were carrying two roll-bags each, one for each member of the group. A change of underwear, shirt, a wet-bag and maybe a Glock or something else, just for show.

Storey said, 'Is this everything?'

'What d'you expect, a couple of violin cases?'

Storey kept his face straight and stared him in the eye, saying, 'A civil question usually gets a civil reply. Sorry if it was too difficult.'

The taller one said, staring right back at him, 'I'm Charlie Tate. I don't have to be civil with no-one if I don't want to. Especially not fucking chauffeurs.' Then moving away, towards the vehicle, 'What's this then, a bloody school bus? We going to be singing songs on the way to the seaside? I'll get in front. Bert, you get in back with the boys and lead the singing.'

Storey manoeuvred the rear seats so the big bodyguards could climb into the back two seats and Bert could sit in the middle row by himself. Charlie was already familiarising himself with the cabin controls.

'I like this rear television. You can watch while you reverse up and squish someone against a wall!'

Storey put the car in gear and pulled away, trying not to catch anyone's eye in the rear-view mirror. He had the sense the bodyguards were laughing at him.

It didn't take him long to have them worked out—Charlie was the motormouth and Bert was the quiet one, spending most of his time looking at his phone and occasionally texting.

After a few minutes Charlie said, 'Have you always been a driver? Is this, like, what you do? Drive people around for a living? Or did you have a career, something more interesting?'

'What does it matter? I'm a driver now, aren't I?'

'Touchy fucker, aren't you? My point is, most people your age, when they're doing something boring like driving, they've had a career beforehand. This is like, what do you call it, an interim job. Temporary. You'll be moving on to something else soon.'

Storey glanced at him. 'Do you know something I don't?'

Charlie's face was florid, a little shiny, his eyes bright with amusement. 'Everybody moves on eventually, don't they? These days. My point is I bet you're more interesting than you let on. Me and Bert here, we're the same. I don't know what Doyle's told you about us, but we've come a long way since we knew him.'

'You towelled down Frank Ivory and gave him a bucket to spit in until Doyle knocked him out. I've seen the film.'

Charlie sat back in his seat, the laughter leaving his eyes. 'Doyle showed you that, did he? I thought he had film. He told me he had film. Fuck, it's probably on YouTube now, ain't it?'

From the seat behind, Bert said, 'Leave it alone, Charlie. Long gone.'

Charlie half-turned in his seat to talk to his cousin. 'I know you want everything to just go away so we can carry on as if nothing's the matter. But I can't do that, Bert. Things stay with me. The idea Bran Doyle's got film of you and me wiping Frank's arse makes me feel poorly.'

Storey was beginning to feel more comfortable now, the two men acting like others he'd known in London—petulant, self-righteous, concerned with the image they gave to the world while still acting like idiots. As if by talking about something on a personal level they could own it. From what he knew of Bran Doyle, he'd wipe the floor with these two. They'd come a long way in terms of their influence and standing, but at heart they were still the young men who'd given Ivory water and rubbed him down with a towel: they'd react to Doyle instead of taking the lead.

They'd even come up to Coventry as soon as Doyle had blown his whistle, hadn't they?

Now Charlie was arguing his way into feeling better about himself and their job today, saying, 'I knew he'd come round eventually. Couldn't sit on that land for ever.' Turning to Storey. 'You know the 'istory of this little caper?'

'Not really.'

'Me and Bert here, we was brought up in Fulham. My dad buggered off to the Merchant Navy so me and him was dragged up by his mum, my Auntie Ethel, my mum having to go to work and so on most of the time. My point is, we lived in the one house all together until I got us out. Then I'd put together enough scratch for us to buy a place of our own. But I never forgot what Auntie Ethel had done for me, so I wanted to buy her house and let her other kids have it. Like, giving something back.'

'Very noble.'

'Well it would have been fucking noble but the land next to her house was an eyesore. It'd been a pub but blew up because of a gas-leak in the sixties. Remember them, gas leaks? Places were always blowing up. Nah, you're too young. Anyway, the house we wanted to buy was condemned by the council because when the pub blew up it damaged the house too. So we had to buy it on a promise of knocking it down. How's that for mad? So we did, thinking we were gonna build another house there for Auntie Ethel. And then we thought it'd be a good idea if we bought the land next door, levelled it all out, and built some nice houses on there. We could make a few bob with housing what it is at the moment.'

'But Doyle wouldn't sell.'

'No, he fucking wouldn't. He wouldn't let the word "sold" pass his bloody lips. So we've been hanging on for twenty-five years, waiting for him to make his bloody mind up.'

'And now he has.'

'He's finally seen sense after all these years and I don't know whether to laugh or cry. But I promise you, if I end up crying, someone's going to pay. I've had enough. So 'as Bert, haven't you, Bert?'

'More than enough,' Bert said, in a voice that made Storey believe he meant it.

Storey turned into the compound and saw Doyle standing there, hands on hips, wearing a black sports jacket over a black tee-shirt and with his cargo pants beneath. Still the man of action. Craig Norton was standing just behind him looking pale.

'There he is,' Charlie said. 'King of his bloody castle. Where's that juicy wife of his? I'd like to have a look at her now—I bet she turned out nice.'

Storey drew up a couple of yards from Doyle and opened the doors electronically. Charlie got out and stood looking around, taking in the house, the decking, the pond and the distant trees. He said, 'Fuck me, Bran, you've done well for yourself. This'd cost twenty million down in the Smoke. What's it cost here, threepence?'

'I don't talk about money, Charlie,' Doyle said, 'unless I've got legal representation sitting at the table. How are you?'

'Fan-fucking-tastic, Bran. Brilliant. Glad to get out of the big city and sample country life. Didn't think there'd be this much country, though.' He nodded towards Norton. 'Who's this?'

Doyle introduced him, adding, 'Craig's the one looks after my money. Ex-Army, so watch your step. Though he did retrain as an accountant so maybe all the vinegar's gone from him. What do you say, Craig?'

'I'll be glad when this is over.'

'I bet you will. Your cheery personality can't take all this fun, can it?'

The other men had climbed out by now and retrieved the bags from the space behind the seats that passed as a boot. Seven men standing around awkwardly, Storey thought. Like a dance class before the women turned up.

Doyle turned to him, saying, 'Park the car round the side then come back. I don't trust these buggers further than I can throw them.'

'Shall I make tea as well?'

'I'll let you know, you cheeky git.'

He turned and led everyone else inside.

CHAPTER FORTY-TWO

IT BEGAN TO unwind after Storey had parked the big Mercedes next to the garages.

He was on his way back to the house when his phone chirped. The screen didn't give a name for the caller and he didn't recognise the number.

He answered and it was a female voice talking very quickly.

'Hold on, hold on,' he said. 'Who's this?'

'It's Nicki, Felicity's friend. She gave me your number if there was a problem with the house.'

'Is there a problem?'

'No! Not with the house. It's Fliss. I saw her been driven away in a car in the car park.'

She went on to explain that she'd arrived at the car park next to where they worked, Doyle's office, ready to drive home. Felicity had left a few minutes earlier. She hadn't waited for Nicki because she was on the phone to a tenant and besides, they had their own cars, so she didn't have to wait ...

Storey interrupted her. 'Tell me again what you saw.'

'I'd just got through the door and this big white car went past me. It was so quiet I didn't hear it till it was nearly on top of me. And Fliss was in the front seat next to the driver.'

'Did you recognise him?'

'No, but he was very big. I could tell because of what I saw through the window. His head must have been touching the top of the cabin. She wasn't supposed to be going anywhere except home. So can you do something?'

'Hold on … did she look as though she was hurt?'

'No, but she turned towards me as they went past and she said something with her mouth, you know, like miming.'

'What did she say?'

'I don't know. I couldn't make it out. But she didn't look happy. She didn't give me a wave or a smile. Do you know who the man was?'

'I've got an idea, yes.'

'Who?'

'It's best if you don't know.'

'Fuck that, he's got my girlfriend! What are you going to do about it?'

Storey was already thinking hard—thinking about what he could do, who he should tell, what his limits were in a case like this.

He said, 'Where are you?'

'Still in the car park. Her car's still here and I thought she might come back. I've tried her mobile but she's not answering and she's not home either.'

'Have you told anyone else?'

'I haven't phoned the police yet, if that's what you mean. I didn't know what to do, whether she was really being kidnapped or what. I don't understand her family. But I tried to ring her dad's house but no one picked up. I didn't leave a message because I didn't want to cause a panic.'

'Good. Stay there. Someone will come and talk to you. Tell them whatever you can. Try to remember details, any letters from the vehicle registration, stuff like that.'

'What are you going to do?'

'I'm going to mobilize the forces of light, aren't I?'

He finished the call and found the number for Jackie West. She answered on the second ring.

'What's up?'

He explained quickly what Nicki had told him.

Jackie said, 'Do you know who the man was?'

'I think it was Lionel. She said he was a big man and he's the biggest man I know.'

'I'll get someone there. How can I contact this Nicki?'

Storey read off the number from his phone's history and then told her he'd said Nicki should stay where she was and someone would come to her.

'She doesn't know it'll be the police but she won't have a problem with that. She's sensible.'

'Okay. Now listen to this. You do *not* get involved. Do you understand? This sounds like kidnapping at the very least. We'll take it from here. Don't go leaping around trying to find Lionel or the girl. Stay out of it. Where are you?'

'At the Doyle place. You should be hearing some very interesting things on your bugs about now.'

'Don't get your hopes up,' Jackie West said. 'They closed the unit down two days ago. No one's listening, no one's recording.'

When he entered the house he heard the men's voices coming from the lounge. He went through into the kitchen and saw Charlotte leaning against a counter, smoking. From the smell he knew it wasn't tobacco. She looked at him coolly, like she wasn't going to take any shit.

She said, 'Does he have any idea what he's doing?'

'Bran? Very little.'

'That's what I thought.'

'Have they had any drinks yet?'

'No. Though the taller one looks like he's sweating through his shirt. He'll need liquids soon.'

Storey hesitated, then said, 'Can you take them a pitcher of water and some glasses, and tell Norton you'd like a word?

Her eyes gleamed. 'What's this, a plot?'

'I need to have a conversation with him, that's all. If I go in and ask it might look suspicious and I don't want Bran distracted or worrying. You ask and it'll seem like something domestic.'

She stubbed the joint in the sink, then threw the butt in the waste-bin attached to the inside of the cabinet door.

'This is turning into a really shitty day, do you know that?'

'I'm sorry.'

'Waits till this morning to tell me the Tates are coming. Then tells me he's selling his plot in London—the one we were keeping for Felicity. Then asks me to leave the room while he talks to those fucking munchkins in there. You're not exactly making it any better.'

Storey had been counting in his head how long it had been since he'd taken the call from Nicki. With the conversation with Jackie West included, he'd wasted nearly ten minutes.

He said, 'Charlotte, do me this favour, all right? I need Norton.'

She seemed to recognise something in his voice and looked at him more keenly.

'What is it? What's the matter?'

'It's something on the site, that's all. I need him to help me sort something out. Contractors. You know.'

She wasn't convinced ... but she didn't argue. She drew a sigh and opened one of the head-height cabinets and took out six matching tumblers, then reached further in and found a carafe. She filled it with tap-water then put it and the glasses on a round tray that was propped up on the counter against the wall.

She made sure everything was balanced, then walked the tray through into the living room. Appreciative noises, raised voices, and a minute later she came back in.

'He's coming.'

'Thank you. I'll take him outside, out of your hair.'

'You do that,' she said. 'I'm very disappointed in you. I thought you were going to be fun but it's not turned out that way, has it?'

———

When Norton came out of the living room Storey gestured to him to follow him outside and then stood with him by the front door.

'I think Felicity's been kidnapped by Lionel Ivory.'

'What the fuck—'

Storey told him about Nicki's call and her description of the man driving the car and the car itself. He said, 'Do you know what's going on? Billy Jenkins sells building materials to Frank Ivory, he warns me to watch my step, then they kidnap Doyle's daughter. Do you have any idea what's happening? Is it connected to the Tates?'

'Why should it be connected to the Tates? They're down in London, he's up here.'

Storey looked at him, saying nothing. Norton had come out of the house looking taut, as though he might shatter if he stubbed his toe. When Storey had told him about Felicity you could almost see him winding up tighter inside.

He said, 'Do you know where the Ivorys live?'

'No,' Norton said, his face setting hard. 'But I know where Lionel might be.'

'Give me the address and I'll go check it out.'

'I'm coming with you.'

'Not necessary.'

'Oh yes,' Norton said. 'It is.'

———

He turned to go back inside and Storey caught his arm. 'Where are you going?'

'Wait here. I'll be a minute.'

Storey let him go and then followed him inside. Norton turned right, towards his rooms. Storey went to the kitchen and found Charlotte still there, now seated at the table and leafing through a recipe book.

'What do you think? *Coq au vin* or fish and chips? What are the boys likely to prefer?'

260

Storey leaned over the table. 'Norton and I are going out. I'm not telling you where or why. If your husband asks, tell him we'll be back and he's not to do anything stupid.'

'What are you talking about?'

'I can't tell you.'

'What's going on? Is it that thing you said, something happening on the site? Haven't they all gone home by now?'

'Just tell Bran we'll be back and he's not to do anything stupid.'

He saw her eyes flick past him and turned. Norton was standing in the doorway wearing a green Barbour jacket and carrying a plastic bag. He said, 'Let's go.'

Storey followed him out and when they were outside with the door closed behind them, he opened the plastic bag, showing the contents to Storey.

Inside two dull black pistols lay together, Storey recognising Glock 17s.

Norton said, 'We might not need them but I'm not taking chances with Lionel Ivory. He's too big to mess around with.'

Storey nodded, saying, 'We'll take my car.'

It had been twenty minutes since he'd taken Nicki's call.

CHAPTER FORTY-THREE

D OYLE WONDERED WHERE this was leading.
For one thing, he wanted to know where the fuck Norton and Storey had gone.

He'd come out of the living room to tell Charlotte he was going out with the Tates, and he wanted Storey to drive, and she'd told him he wasn't there. Then he remembered her talking to Norton when she'd brought in the water and he'd got up and left. It seemed Storey had spoken to him and they'd buggered off somewhere, not telling her where or why they were leaving. That was forty minutes ago and they hadn't come back.

He'd said to her, 'Why didn't you tell me?' and she'd replied that apparently he didn't want her in there while they were discussing 'important men's matters' and besides, what was she supposed to do? Tie them to the table?

So he'd walked back and forth in the kitchen for a couple of minutes, half-listening to Charlie and Bert rumbling on in the living room, while he tried to think it through. He didn't want to drive because he was only a few weeks away from finishing his year's sentence. If he was caught driving now it'd be a disaster. And although Charlotte had volunteered, he didn't want her anywhere near those rough-arsed villains. It was bad enough he was having to deal with them without her getting in arm's reach of them.

In the end he had no choice unless they sent for taxis, which the Tates didn't want to do because they didn't want anyone to know who they were or what they were doing.

He'd fetched the big Mercedes from round the back, where Storey had left it with the keys inside, and they'd all piled in, Bert getting in the front passenger seat and putting an address into the GPS system without even asking permission.

Now the little chequered flag on the GPS was just ahead and he slowed down, ready to turn through the gate. Nearly seven o'clock on a Thursday night and out here, on the edge of the city, everything was quiet.

What the hell was going on?

He knew at once what the building was. Seeing the size of the place, its unfinished condition, and the fact that he'd been taken there by the Tates ... everything came together in his head very quickly. *Fuck*, he said to himself, *what a stupid bastard I've been*.

When Frank Ivory stepped out of the front door he realised he was in even deeper shit than he thought. The Tates and Ivory; a building that looked like an over-sized version of his own gym; the death of Rod Spencer and Billy Jenkins; the fire ... they'd been filleting him from the beginning, making it hard for him to get ahead and make his idea work.

And what about Norton? Where was he in all this? Did he have any clue what was happening? Was he involved, too?

He turned off the engine and realised it was quiet in the vehicle, everyone watching for his reaction.

Sod that. He was Bran Doyle. He wasn't going to give them any satisfaction.

As he climbed out of the car, Frank Ivory came towards him. He was wearing his usual pale suit and black shirt. All he needed was a cane and a fedora hat and he'd look like a song-and-dance man.

Ivory called over to him, 'Bran, glad you could make it. I was beginning to worry. Thought my friends had let me down.'

'So this is yours, is it?' Doyle asked, nodding towards the building. 'Thought you'd nick my idea, did you, you wanker? Never had an original idea that was your own.'

'You've got it wrong, Bran boy. I'm just a sleeping partner. An investor. You've got your two friends here as the real money men. These and a couple of grubby bookies who you'll be meeting in due course.'

Doyle stood with his hands on his hips and looked at the structure. It was roofed and the windows and doors were all in place and sealed, but he could tell it was still incomplete. There was an unfinished feeling to it. He said, 'How long before it's up and running?'

'I'm told just a couple or more weeks. Fixtures and fittings. Bit of furniture. How about yours? Got everything you need?'

Doyle ignored this and turned back to the Tates, now standing next to each other with the bodyguards behind them. Charlie was grinning at him, Bert still engrossed in his phone. Doyle said, 'So this was your big fucking idea, was it? What you wanted to show me? You've teamed up with the biggest wanker in Coventry and you're nicking my idea. Well if you've haven't got me involved, you won't have any clout in this city. No one knows you two. And I expect no one knows these bookies, whoever they are. Without Bran Doyle's name over the door, nobody's interested.'

'You might be right,' Charlie said. 'But hey, they keep telling us competition's good, don't they? So let's compete.'

Bert looked up briefly from his screen, saying, 'The signing.'

Charlie said, 'Let's go inside. Might be a bit warmer. And then you can sign the bit of paper and get your money and we all go away happy.'

Doyle said nothing. Too many things were going through his head. And the first thing was, he didn't want to sign anything that gave the Tates or Frank Ivory any power over him or his future.

Ivory had a key and he unlocked the front door and went in first. He turned in the doorway and said, 'Electric's not connected yet so we've set up a couple of lights. Watch you don't trip over, Bran.'

He went further inside, then through another open doorway, and a moment later Doyle saw a dim illumination light up the space, throwing a dark shadow of Ivory on the wall as he moved around. Doyle passed through the door and followed him, his senses acute now, smelling paraffin or some kind of fuel that was being used to supply the lights. He saw the lamp in the far corner. Ivory was just lighting a second one, an old-fashioned lantern with a bell-shaped glass surround, and standing it back on the floor.

Behind him, he heard the Tates and the two bodyguards come in so he moved further forward.

The room he entered was a large space with an oblong white garden table in the centre. There were no chairs to go with the table, but piles of cardboard boxes were stacked in one corner. They looked to Doyle like kitchen fitments and stores for the bar—boxes of new glasses, cutlery, a sink and draining board wrapped in plastic, a microwave in a box, a couple of taps, several packs of toilet roll and kitchen paper and cleaning cloths. Ivory was walking to the table and now he lit a third lantern that stood in its centre, saying, 'Come out of my back garden, this table. Didn't bring the chairs though, 'cos you won't be sitting long. Boys, have you got the papers?'

Doyle said, 'Don't bother. I ain't signing.'

Ivory looked at him, a slow smile lifting the corners of his mouth. Then Charlie Tate appeared, moving round from behind him and standing between him and Ivory, his round face turning red already.

'What're you saying, Doyle? Did I hear you right?'

'I ain't signing. I don't want nothing to do with you if you're dealing with Frank Ivory. I don't care if it's a separate deal. I'm not too happy about selling my land to you two couple of tossers, but Frank's the last straw.'

'You fucker, you got us up 'ere on false pretences, didn't you? You were never gonna sign. You're just gonna hold on to that piece of fucking land until you drop dead in your socks.'

'If that's what it takes, yeah, I will.'

'Don't think you're gonna get money anywhere else. The banks won't give it, will they, because you're not a good investment. And you haven't got any friends up here. Even your pal Alf Chamberlain's not so keen on you ... nah, you didn't know that, did you? Well him and us have done a bit of business lately and you should hear him talk about you.'

'What business?'

'Never you mind. Nothing to do with you. Moving some things around. Importing, you might say. Live cattle, sort of thing. He give you his foreman, didn't he, to keep you sweet, keep you busy, make you think you're back on track. Meanwhile he's been using your lorries to do a bit of importing. Didn't know that, did you?'

Bert Tate said, 'Charlie, that's enough.'

Charlie turned on him. 'No, it's fucking not enough. He's got us all the way up here thinking he's God's gift, lord of his fucking manor, and it's about time he heard some home truths. It's not all rosy in the garden. He's being fucked over left and right and he didn't even know it. Well now he knows.'

Doyle felt his anger building but swallowed it. He said, 'You always were an evil little shit, weren't you, Charlie? You should have heard him talk about you, Bert, when you weren't in the room. Short-arsed dimwit was the nicest thing I heard him say.'

Frank Ivory stepped forward, then, his arm outstretched. 'Boys, boys, let's not fight. Bran, I think yet again you're over-estimating your position. You see, we had an idea you might back out when you knew I was involved with the lads here. I couldn't help myself, I had to come and witness it even though it's nothing to do with me. But we thought you might ... what's the word? Baulk. Like a norse at a fence that's too high. Charlie especially was worried. So we took a few precautions.'

Doyle didn't like the sound of this. 'Like what?'

Ivory took a couple of steps away, giving himself a safety zone, then said, 'You might have been wondering where my son Lionel was. He comes with me everywhere, doesn't he? Well today he's been otherwise engaged. About an hour ago he persuaded your daughter—Felicity, is it?—to take a trip with him in his car. As we speak he's looking after her at an undisclosed location. It'll take a phone call from me to make sure he doesn't do anything foolish. As he did with Mr Spencer— Rod. And the unfortunate Billy Jenkins.'

Doyle took a couple of steps forward towards Ivory but was immediately seized from behind. The two blond bodyguards had stepped up next to him, almost as though they'd anticipated his reaction, and they'd each grabbed one of his arms.

Ivory said, 'So you see, you don't hold any cards in this game right now. Do you?'

CHAPTER FORTY-FOUR

N ORTON DIRECTED STOREY south and east and he drove as fast as he could without drawing attention to his speed. It was dark but the rush hour was over and Storey found himself thinking through scenarios. Was this going to end in a conversation? Or a fight? Or should he just tell the police and have done with it?

Norton was saying, 'This is all my fault. I should have seen it coming. Once Frank Ivory gets involved in something it all goes downhill.'

Storey threw him a glance. 'What are you talking about? What's this got to do with you?'

Norton was quiet for a while. When he spoke his voice was calm, measured, almost as though he were giving a prepared speech.

He said, 'I've been acting as a consultant for a couple of people who are building a sports club, like Bran's.'

Storey was surprised he had no reaction to this. It was as though some part of him knew before being told. It made sense of so much. He said, 'When you say consultant ...'

'I've given them bits of information about where to buy materials. Lately I've also being doing their books, keeping track of expenditure. The usual project management stuff.'

'And of course Doyle doesn't know because he'd twist your head off if he did.'

'Yes.' He paused. 'There's more.'

'Of course there is. There's always more.'

'I found out a couple of days ago that Frank Ivory's putting money into the new gym. To get back at Bran. I think it's his revenge for what Bran did to him thirty years ago.'

'These guys have got long memories.' He looked sideways at Norton. 'So where are we going now?'

'The men I was working with are a couple of bookies, but they own a pub. It's where we meet.'

'Why would Lionel take Felicity there?'

'Because Frank's a sick bastard and he'll want to rub it in with me. He could have taken her to their building site, where their gym is, but the building's in no better condition than Bran's. Well, not much better. They couldn't keep a woman there. And I'm assuming Frank won't want to take her to his own house. So this is a guess.'

'If she's not there I'm calling the police. I'll probably call them anyway.'

'Turn left here and slow down. That's the place over there.'

There were no lights on in the building and a sandwich board at the entrance read, 'Closed for repairs.'

Storey idled the car into the small car park quietly. There were four cars nestled together in one corner, including the white car he'd seen driving silently away from his house. He said, 'Give me one of the guns.'

Norton unfolded the plastic bag in his lap and gave Storey the first pistol that came out.

'Where did you get these?' Storey asked.

Norton shrugged. 'Here and there. I didn't do a lot of shooting in Afghanistan but I've always liked gear.'

They climbed out either side of the Volvo and closed the doors quietly. Storey kept his hands in his pockets, one of them holding the gun in place.

Norton led the way to the wooden front door and peered through the large plate-glass window to its left, his hand over his eyes. Storey realised he was dealing with a more street-wise version of the man he knew. It gave him more confidence in what they were doing. Looking up at the building, he sensed there were people inside despite the fact there were no lights showing. The cars behind him suggested as much anyway.

He indicated with his hand that they should circle around, so they moved silently away together and did a complete tour of the building. The rear was a wall of plain brickwork to the height of the first floor, with only louvred vents and various grey pipes emerging from it, plus another door, this one heavier than the front. A small brick building stood to one side—it might have held extra beer barrels or the heating system, Storey had no way of knowing.

When he looked up the upper storey was completely dark. If there was anyone here, where were they?

Now they'd arrived at the front door again, Norton leaning towards him, saying, 'No choice. I've got to knock, check it out.'

Storey nodded and stood back.

Norton banged on the heavy wooden door of the pub with the butt of his pistol. He said, 'Swann? Lethbridge? It's me, Norton. Are you there?'

Then banged on the door again.

Storey had his back to the wall, looking at Norton, encouraging him, and when the door opened he saw Norton relax his stance, putting both hands behind his back and smiling pleasantly. Saying, 'You're in! I thought I recognised the car.'

And then stepping forward, whipping his hand up and crashing it down on the side of the man's head, who now fell forward into Storey's sight—a squat man with fair hair, well-dressed in a pale grey suit.

Norton and Storey caught the man before he hit the ground and Storey saw he wasn't unconscious, his eyelids fluttering.

He said, 'Take his tie off,' and saw Norton nod, understanding what they were going to do.

They bound the man's hands behind his back with his tie, then lowered him so that he was sitting on the outside step, his legs sprawled out before him, his head sagging on his chest. A bruise was forming on his temple already but Storey checked his breathing and it was regular.

'Name's Swann,' Norton said. 'He's the talkative one. Bit soft. Lethbridge will be in here as well. He might be harder to crack.'

'And if Felicity's here, Lionel will be, too. That'll be fun.'

They went through the door and were in the main lounge of the pub, lit only by the street lamps outside. Shadows moved across the room as traffic passed on the road. It smelled of stale beer and old furnishings, a musty combination. Storey watched Norton head immediately to a door behind the bar, knowing his route, it seemed, though perhaps it was just educated guesswork, having been here before.

Norton pushed through the door, Storey close behind. Now they were in a narrow passageway with another door opposite and a corridor heading right and leading to the back door they'd seen on their tour around the building. To their left, a flight of stairs led upwards. Norton leaned forward and tried the handle on the door facing them but it was locked.

Storey was thinking if the man Swann had heard the banging on the front door and had come to answer it, Lionel and the other man probably heard it too ... meaning they were waiting—either for Swann to return, or for Norton to come upstairs.

Norton started up the staircase but Storey caught his arm and took the lead. He'd checked the magazine of the Glock when he got in the car so he knew it was ready. Its weight and its grip had both been familiar. More familiar than he'd liked. Now it nestled in the pocket of his leather jacket, not easy to fire accidentally, in the heat of the moment. Until he pulled the trigger the safety stayed on thanks to Glock's patented Safe action system. He noticed that Norton had also put his gun away.

At the top of the stairs was a door. Storey twisted the handle and opened it, then went through, stepping to his right. Norton was behind him and followed him in and moved to the left.

———

It was a large games room. In the middle of the floor were two pool tables, slender cues lying diagonally across them. To their right was a dartboard with a plastic carpet leading from the wall to a line on the floor marking the oche, where players stood when throwing. There were three video game units to the left, including one with a steering wheel, and an Elvis Presley pinball machine, its lights extinguished, Elvis in repose.

Also in the room were two men. Storey knew Lionel and he supposed the other man was Lethbridge.

They were both standing. Lethbridge was drinking what looked like whiskey from a tumbler and leaning with his hip against the left-hand pool table. Storey saw he was slim and relatively athletic compared to Swann, and there was a gleam in his eye he didn't like. He'd seen it before in men who took physical risks and didn't think of the consequences, having a belief in their own ability.

Lethbridge looked at Norton and said, 'Where's Swannie? Is he all right?'

'He's all right,' Norton said. 'Indisposed. Where's the girl?'

Lionel had been standing behind Lethbridge. He wore a black shirt undone at the collar but tight across his chest and arms. He walked forward, looking at Storey. He said, 'We didn't think you'd take the warning. You're the kind who never listen, aren't you? Why don't you just turn around and fuck off, this isn't anything to do with you.'

'I'm past the fucking-off stage, Lionel. Now don't be an idiot. Let Felicity go and we'll all walk out and we'll see what happens afterwards.'

'That can't happen, can it? I've got instructions. If you know me, you know I follow instructions. Unlike you.'

'Was it you who phoned me the other night? Giving me a warning?'

'I don't know what you're talking about.'

'Just put a bag over your head and talk into your phone—I bet I recognise your voice.'

'My dad said he thought you were funny. I had to disagree with him.'

Both Lethbridge and Lionel had slowly edged around the pool table, acting casually, trying to make it appear they were coming closer for the sake of the conversation, making it more natural.

Storey glanced at Norton and saw that he had tensed, his hands by his sides like a Western gunslinger, perhaps wondering whether he should pull out the Glock and send this confrontation on to a different level.

Storey said to Lionel, 'It doesn't have to come to this.'

'You've got a reputation, though, haven't you? For killing people. You won't do me because it's not long since you did the last one. You'll wind up in the clink.'

'Or they'll give him a medal,' Lethbridge said across the pool table. He turned back to Norton and Storey realised that the two men had chosen their point of attack—Lethbridge for Norton, Lionel for himself. He didn't think he could take Lionel, even with the bits of unarmed combat training he remembered from his time in the force. He was just too big.

He called across to Lethbridge, 'Do you think you can take Norton? Is that what you're working on?'

Lethbridge didn't look at him, his dark eyes focused entirely on Norton's face, as if trying to mesmerise him. Storey wondered whether Norton had his hand on his weapon.

And was still wondering about it when Norton pulled out the Glock and fired.

Lethbridge staggered and Storey saw the shot had hit and damaged his left arm. He grunted and took a step back but found the strength to draw a knife from his belt and was already lunging towards Norton, a guttural sound coming from his mouth.

Norton fired again as Lethbridge fell on him, his knife arcing downwards, heading for Norton's chest.

But now Storey was distracted by a shift in the air and the knowledge that Lionel in his turn had launched himself.

Storey pushed his hand in his pocket but it was too late to draw the Glock. Still turning, he saw Lionel's arms and hands outstretched towards him, as if aiming for his throat, a fierce expression on his face.

Storey moved to the side and stumbled slightly, giving Lionel time to adjust and bring a huge arm around Storey's neck. Which gave him more time to bring his other arm around Storey's back, hugging him closer, pinning his arms, squeezing him close to his chest.

Storey found himself looking up at Lionel's face, the distortion of effort pulling back the lips from his teeth, bulging his eyes and reminding Storey of the medieval paintings of demons he'd seen in encyclopedias, their eyes and teeth rabid and ready to gorge on human flesh.

Lionel was grunting rhythmically as he found purchase on Storey's lower back, almost raising him from the ground, squeezing and pulling him closer to his shirt.

Storey found himself being crushed, his arms impossibly imprisoned, feeling almost violated by the strength of the man. His eyes were on the same level as Lionel's chin and he saw the pores, the unshaven hairs, the tears of spittle that came from his mouth as Lionel tried to squeeze the life from him.

So Storey reared back and brought his forehead down on the bridge of Lionel's nose, putting all the strength he could muster into his neck-muscles to crack down hard at the point of impact.

The effect was immediate. Lionel let go and raised his hands to his nose. 'You bastard!'

Storey now held the Glock in his pocket, his finger inside the trigger guard, and was bringing it out when Lionel, enraged by the pain, reached forward and grabbed Storey again with both hands, pulling hard, blood starting to trickle from his nose.

And by doing that he forced Storey's fist to squeeze around the trigger of his gun and it went off, the round searing through Storey's jacket, then through Lionel's black shirt and passing through his kidney before exiting out of his back and shooting Elvis and his pinball machine squarely in the heart.

Lionel frowned, the pain not registering at first. Then he raised his hands to his lower chest and looked down, seeing the blood starting to arrive. He breathed deeply, then his legs gave way and he collapsed to the floor. His long body seemed to go down in stages until he was laid on his back, eyes open, his hands still cradling his chest. His lips moved but said nothing. Then he shuddered and died and the room was suddenly quiet.

Storey looked down at him, then glanced across at Norton, standing over Lethbridge, who was on one knee, holding his left arm with his right hand, the fight gone from him.

Storey said, 'Firearms specialist, me. Deadly at two inches.'

CHAPTER FORTY-FIVE

T HEY FOUND FELICITY tied to a chair in a store room, a gag in her mouth, her eyes huge when Storey opened the door.

Then she became talkative when he ungagged her and worked on untying her wrists.

'What happened? What were the loud bangs? Did you shoot him? That big bastard ... he told me what he did, he was the one who killed Rod and hit you on the head. He wanted the police to think you did it.'

'Then I bashed myself on the back of the head and threw away the murder weapon?'

'He didn't go into details. Anyway, it was all his idea, he said, not his dad's. He was proud of it.'

'Very few people are proud of being dickheads.'

'Did I hear Craig out there? What's he doing?'

'Seeing to one of the other bad guys who got shot.'

'I hope it was the thin one with the mean face. I didn't like him. He kept looking at me funny.'

Storey was undoing the cord they'd used to tie one of her legs to the chair while she untied the other. He said, 'Do you know why they grabbed you in the first place? Did the dickhead tell you that?'

'No, no idea. He seemed more interested in talking about his dad.'

Storey helped her stand up and held her arms for a moment until she got her balance. He said, 'You all have very weird relationships with your fathers. I'm going to have to call someone about all this, then we'll take you back. You should call Nicki, too, she was the one who saw you and let us know.'

'I saw her. I knew she'd work it out.'

They went back into the main room, where Norton was now holding his arm having turned Lethbridge on his back, breathing shallowly but still alive.

'I've called for the police and an ambulance,' Norton said. 'Hi Felicity. How are you doing?'

She said nothing but went over and looked down at Lethbridge's pale face, his eyes shifting to watch her move. He said quietly, 'Don't hit me. Look in the other room.'

Storey turned around and noticed another door in the far corner labelled 'Toilet'. He walked around the pool tables and opened it.

Next to the urinal, on the floor, Darren was bound and gagged, his legs drawn up and tied with thick cord to his wrists. His eyes were terrified.

Storey began to untie him, and when he'd finished he pulled out his phone and called Jackie West.

Jesus, she was angry. Calling him all kinds of names, asking him what the hell he thought he was doing, was he completely nuts. Then telling him to stay where he was.

'I can't,' he said. 'I'm not waiting around for you. There's something happening.'

'What the hell are you talking about?'

'Felicity wasn't kidnapped for fun. She's leverage for something her dad's involved in.'

'Like what?'

Storey hesitated, then said, 'I'll tell you later,' and hung up.

Darren had managed to get to his feet, leaning against the sink and massaging his thighs, trying to get his circulation going.

Storey said, 'What happened? I thought we told you to get lost.'

'I had a text from Billy. Said he needed to see me, urgent-like. I thought I could find out what the fuck he was doing, so I said okay and he told me where to meet him. It was some park, next to the ticket office. Ten o'clock, when it was dark. When I got there he was nowhere to be seen and that big fucker Lionel showed up and grabbed me and put me in the back of his car.'

'Billy's dead.'

'Ah, shit.'

'They used his phone to text you.'

'Is my uncle out there?'

'You should thank him. He's the only reason we're here.'

Darren ran the tap and threw some water on his face, then dried it with a paper towel. He stared at himself in the mirror.

He said, 'What a fuck-up. I've got to start again.'

'Good idea,' Storey said, and opened the door for him.

Next Storey called the Doyles. Charlotte answered and he told her the short version of what had happened and that he was bringing Felicity home.

She was no less angry than Jackie West had been.

'Is that what all the secrecy was about?' she said. 'Don't you think you might have told me what was going on? I think you're sacked.'

'Okay, but is Bran there? I think something's going to happen.'

'What?'

'I don't know. But Frank Ivory didn't take your daughter for fun. She was going to be leverage for something.'

The line was quiet, then she said, 'He's not here. He's gone off with the Tates.'

'Where?'

'I don't know. Nobody tells me anything. I just sit at home and wait for people to call me up and make me angry.'

'Do you want to talk to Felicity?'

'What a stupid question. Put her on.'

———

Storey waved Felicity over and handed her his phone, then joined Norton, who'd been talking quietly with Darren. He noticed that Norton had taken off his jacket and rolled up his sleeve and was looking at his bicep.

'Bastard just nicked me with his knife,' he said.

'Well you got him, didn't you? Do you think he's going to make it?'

'Look at him lying there, I doubt it. That's me up shit creek.'

'I'm a witness to your self-defence. Lionel was unarmed so I'm further up the creek than you are.'

He told Norton what Charlotte had said about Doyle going with the Tates but not knowing where. He turned to Darren. 'Did you hear them say anything? Mention any places?'

'Nothing. They put me in there last night, untied me this morning so I could eat and have a piss, then tied me up again. Next thing I heard was Fliss arguing with them next door but I couldn't do anything.'

Norton nodded, said, 'If Frank Ivory's involved I bet I know where he's gone. He'll be showing off to Bran.'

Storey saw it too, the symmetry. 'So the Tates come up to make a deal with Doyle to buy his land, but they've been teased by him once too often in the past, so they take out some insurance. They know Frank Ivory, who's been stealing Doyle's materials, and he says he knows what to do—get Lionel to take Darren prisoner, because of what he knows about Billy Jenkins, then take Felicity and hang on to her until the deal's signed. Everyone's a winner.'

'Except Doyle. Who sells his land in London cheaper than he would have wanted, while at the same time losing out to Swann, Lethbridge and Ivory and their new club, which has an advantage already because it's nearly finished.'

'All neat and tidy until we screw it up for them. Now where's this place?'

They decided Norton and Darren would stay with Lethbridge and Lionel to wait for the Emergency Services. Storey had gone downstairs and found Swann struggling to his feet and brought him back up, where he leaned against a wall looking pale-faced and defeated, avoiding Lethbridge's dark stare.

'Get Felicity out of here,' Norton said. 'Take her home, they can talk to her there, get a statement.'

'You'll be all right?'

'Best I've felt in a long while. Do you remember the directions?'

He was referring to the route that would take Storey to the other gym's site.

'I know where it is,' Storey said. 'And if everyone's there, I'll give them your regards.'

CHAPTER FORTY-SIX

I T TOOK STOREY longer than he thought to drive back to the Doyles' house and drop off Felicity. Her mother was standing outside wrapped in a padded jacket, and when her daughter climbed from the car they embraced, both crying — the first time Storey had seen any real emotion from Charlotte except the occasional flash of anger.

He left Felicity to explain what had happened because he was worried about Doyle and what he'd do if left by himself. He'd begun to see him more and more as a child with a child's impulses, alongside an inability to control them.

He remembered the directions that Norton had given him but now he was driving through a part of Coventry he didn't know well and had taken a couple of wrong turns before seeing the opening into the site that Norton had described. He parked on the roadside and walked carefully to the edge of the wooden hoarding that marked the boundary where the site met the pavement. Peering inside, he saw Doyle's large Mercedes SUV and Ivory's white truck.

So this was the right place.

He watched for a few moments but couldn't see any activity. The building was further developed than Doyle's and the walls were finished, the windows covered with black plastic, meaning he couldn't see what was going on inside. What were they doing? If the Tates were going to buy Doyle's London plot, why had they come out here? And why had Frank Ivory come along?

Then he realised: of course, Ivory would want to turn the knife, let Doyle know that he was involved and that Felicity was being held as collateral until he signed the sales contract on the land. It was another part of his revenge fantasy.

But now she was free Doyle didn't need to give in to the threat and sign unless he really wanted to. Did he?

————

He walked across the packed dirt of the lot and edged up to the front door, which he saw was slightly open. Putting an ear to the crack he heard voices—Doyle seemed to be arguing with both Charlie Tate and Frank Doyle. Trust him: when he was outnumbered, he was bound to become even more aggressive.

He still had the Glock in his jacket pocket. He put his hand inside the pocket and pushed the door open slowly. The voices were coming from his right, through a doorway that didn't yet have a door fitted. The light inside flickered as though it were coming from candles or lanterns, which made sense: he guessed the electricity hadn't been connected yet. He moved towards the room and saw the rounded backs of the Tate cousins, and past them the tall blond bodyguards, who each held one of Bran Doyle's arms. He was facing Frank Ivory, and now he heard Frank say, 'So you see, you don't hold any cards in this game right now. Do you?'

Which seemed the perfect time for him to pull out the Glock, stick it into Charlie Tate's back and say loudly, 'That's not true, Frank. There's a joker in the pack.'

————

Of course they all swivelled towards him, except Charlie, who knew exactly what it was sticking into the fat above his waist. He said, 'Don't anyone do anything! He's got a shooter in my back.'

Bran Doyle had been the last to turn, and when he saw Storey he broke out a grin.

'Fuck sake,' he said. 'I wondered when you'd turn up.'

Storey looked around the room, which was about fifteen metres square, twice the size of Doyle's gym's largest space. Big enough for a boxing ring and some rows of seating and still leave space to build dressing rooms behind. Currently it was just a large square space with a concrete floor and a couple of windows. He could see piles of cardboard boxes stacked in one corner, their sides showing cartoon images of a sink, taps, a microwave, glasses. He realised they were gearing up to fit out the bar, which he supposed would be next door. Two camping lanterns with glass bowls stood on the floor and one stood on a white plastic garden table in the middle of the room, and he smelled the familiar odour of paraffin.

'What's going on?' he asked Doyle over the top of Charlie Tate's head.

'I've said I'm not gonna sign the paper, but they've got Felicity somewhere. Taken her as fucking insurance. Can you believe it? These head-cases don't know how to win a fair fight. I've gotta sign now, haven't I?'

Storey shrugged. 'Not necessarily.'

'What do you mean?'

'It's only a threat if they've actually got Felicity, isn't it? If they haven't got her, what's the problem?'

Now Ivory spoke up, 'What are you saying?'

'What do you think?'

'Spit it out. Have you done something to my Lionel?'

Storey took a firm grip of the Glock and pushed Charlie Tate further into the room. He said, 'It's bad news, Frank.'

The men all backed away from him but Ivory stepped forward, saying, 'What's happened? Where's Lionel?'

'Sorry, Frank. He had an accident.'

'What do you mean?'

'He tried to stop a bullet, but it didn't work.'

'You fucker!' Ivory said, moving forward quickly, but was held back by Bert Tate and one of the bodyguards.

'He brought it on himself, Frank. He literally pulled the trigger. I had nothing to do with it except I happened to be holding the gun.'

'I don't believe you. Lionel wouldn't have tried anything if he'd known you had a shooter.'

'Strikes me you have no idea what Lionel was capable of.'

'Shut the fuck up. When this is over I'm coming for you.'

'I'm not going anywhere, Frank.'

Storey looked at the faces in front of him. He hadn't planned this far ahead and he didn't know what to do now.

Then Ivory surprised him. He shook himself away from Bert Tate and the bodyguard and pulled down his jacket sleeves. He stood more upright and put a smile back on his face, then said to Doyle, 'Bran, let's make a deal. You and me are fighters. We're in a fucking gym. Let's fight for it. Winner takes all.'

'All what? If you hadn't noticed, you're screwed.'

'Details. Charlie, you got that paper?'

Charlie Tate looked over his shoulder at Storey, who nodded, then reached into his jacket pocket and pulled out an envelope and passed it to Ivory.

'What are you going to do?' Charlie said.

'Doyle signs this bloody contract and we put it on the table over there. If he wins, we rip it up and you don't bother him again about selling the land. Forget it. It's over. You go back to London with nothing but your dick in your hand. He doesn't get a penny from us and has to go somewhere else for the money he needs.'

'What about if you win?'

'If I win, we take the paper and he sells you the plot for ten grand, say, as a gesture of good will—and he stops work on his own gym.'

Everyone looked at Doyle, Storey thinking this was the sticking point. The gym was Doyle's baby, he'd already risked his financial security on building it. He was older than Ivory and not in condition for a real fight. Would he take another risk when he didn't have to? Should he let him?

He said to Ivory, 'What do you get out of it?'

284

Ivory said, 'I get to knock his block off, don't I? And with my investment in this place I make more money if his is closed.'

Ivory and Doyle stared at each other, then Ivory said, 'Deal?'

Doyle shrugged. 'Why not? You ain't beaten me yet. You better ask these jokers, though.'

Charlie said, 'You sure about this, Frank?'

'Look at him. He's an old man. I've got five years on him. And I never stopped boxing, teaching Lionel ... which reminds me, Storey, you're next. Gun or no gun.'

'Give it your best shot,' Storey said.

Doyle said to the Tates, 'So come on. You gonna take a flutter on the fancy man here?'

Charlie looked at Bert, who hesitated a moment then said, 'Deal.'

It was then Storey remembered what Charlotte had told him about Doyle's heart condition. He said, 'Bran—'

'Shut up. I know what I'm doing. Where's that paper?'

Ivory handed him the envelope which Doyle tore open, taking out the two pages inside. He looked them over quickly, then said, 'You got a pen inside those fancy suits?'

Bert reached into his pocket and came out with a pen that Doyle took, then leaned on the table and signed the document on both pages. He threw the pen back at Bert, who dropped it but bent quickly to retrieve it.

'Right,' Doyle said. 'When do we start?'

The Tates and the two bodyguards moved away from Doyle and Ivory, starting to clear a space. Storey put the Glock in his pocket and moved to the door. He wasn't going to turn his back on any of them.

Bert picked up the lantern from the table while Charlie pushed it against the wall, under the windows. Storey watched them make a larger space in the centre of the room by pushing stray boxes further back and standing the other two lanterns safely against the walls. At the last moment Charlie picked up one of the lanterns and stood it on top of a couple of cardboard boxes so the room was better lit.

Ivory had taken off his cream jacket and laid it on the table and was now rolling up the sleeves of his black shirt. Doyle had peeled off his tee-shirt to show his chunky torso with only a slight roll of fat around the waist. Storey thought he wasn't in bad condition for a man just over sixty. Perhaps he used the swimming pool and tennis court behind his house to keep trim.

There were a couple of scars across his chest probably related to his heart problem, but otherwise he seemed strong. Storey wondered whether he was as strong as he looked. This was going to be bare-knuckle fighting, potentially lethal, but in the end it was Doyle's choice. Maybe it was the kind of finality they all needed after thirty years.

Now Ivory was trying a couple of punches, leading with the right, uppercut with the left, bouncing back and forth on his toes. He was five years younger than Doyle and he still had some elasticity in his physique.

Doyle said, 'Stop showing yourself up, Frank. Wait till I'm standing there.'

'Come on then, stop pissing about and let's get this over.'

'Don't you want to know the rules?'

'What rules?'

'One of us winds up on the floor, the other one's the winner.'

'Good enough.'

Then Doyle turned to Charlie Tate and said, 'Hey, this is just like old times, ain't it? Shouldn't you be wiping him down and whispering in his ear, telling him to gouge me in the eye and kick me in the balls?'

'Shut the fuck up, Doyle. You're gonna get your arse kicked. Right, Frank?'

'Right.'

Doyle glanced at Charlie, then looked at Storey and winked. He said, 'Got 'em rattled already.'

At last Doyle and Ivory squared up, each raising their fists, both right-handers, and started moving clockwise on the concrete floor, their feet scuffling slowly. Doyle's body was pale and solid in the flickering shadows. Ivory's black shirt, the sleeves rolled up, was like a negative to Doyle's physique, filling an opposite space. They were like planets circling an invisible sun.

Storey glanced at the Tates and the two bodyguards, all of them engrossed, perhaps even enjoying the idea of the deal being dependent on the fight. He looked over at the table and saw the contract was still there—he wouldn't have been surprised if Charlie Tate had slyly pocketed it.

Now Frank Ivory shot out a right hand but Doyle saw it coming and moved his head slightly and the punch slid by.

'Good one, Frank,' he said. 'Always had a quick right hand.'

Storey was fascinated by Doyle's movement—his torso moved left and right from the waist as he shuffled, giving Ivory a moving target. He hadn't thrown a punch yet, just the occasional feint, bobbing his head, keeping in motion.

Ivory was more solid, more fluent, as though he was happy to move in a slow circle and take whatever Doyle might throw at him.

He led with his right again and Doyle slipped it again, but then Ivory followed with an uppercut from his left and then tried an overhand right, both shots grazing Doyle's face but not making solid contact.

'Go on, Frank!' Charlie shouted. 'Nail the bastard!'

Ivory seemed to be relaxing into it. He rolled his neck left and right, then shook his hands out before putting them back into position.

'That's right,' Doyle said, 'get yourself comfy.'

And immediately launched a right hand straight punch that Ivory saw only at the last minute, turning his head so that Doyle's fist caught him above the ear. He grimaced and backed off but Storey thought he wasn't too hurt.

Ivory said, 'That your one punch, Bran? You all done now?'

Doyle was grinning, still moving, head bobbing, fists clenching and unclenching. He said, 'I've got more. Been saving them up for you.'

They continued to move, breathing more heavily now, Storey thought, their age catching up with them. Doyle was dogged, obviously the one who did the chasing. Storey remembered the films he'd seen, Doyle emerging from his corner like an attack dog and smashing his opponent before he was settled. That was a few decades ago. Looking at the wrinkles on Doyle's face and the solidity of his torso, it was no surprise he was taking things easier.

He wondered what would happen if Doyle lost. Would he give up the land so easily? Would he just take the money and let it go?

On the other hand, if he won, would the Tates let him keep it? Or would they have another go at persuading him?

Given the expression on Doyle's face, he wasn't about to let anything go. His eyes were pinpricks, following Ivory's movements like a cat watching the tiniest motions of its prey.

There was a flurry and suddenly Doyle was retreating, Ivory putting together a combination of right jabs and a left-handed blow to Doyle's body that seemed to wind him, knocking air from him and bending him at the waist.

And then Ivory was attacking, his face a mask of concentration, his right hand coming quickly, knocking Doyle further and further back so he was now pressed against the corner, hands raised, the hard slap of Ivory's knuckles drawing blood from the corner of Doyle's eye. He bent down, his hands lashing out in defence, but Ivory was relentless, throwing punches from all angles, and Doyle sagged, his head down, his hands getting lower and lower as Ivory punished him. Storey thought the end was only a few seconds away.

He felt himself wanting to push forward and defend the man, pull Ivory away and protect Doyle from getting his head stoved in ... but he held back. This was a prehistoric fight—they had to finish it themselves or it would be meaningless.

And as Storey was thinking this, Doyle found new strength. He caught Ivory with a right that knocked him back, then an uppercut that seemed to come from the depth of his stomach and jolted Ivory's head upwards, giving Doyle the space to move away from the corner.

At which point he took aim with his massive right fist and smacked it into the side of Ivory's jaw.

Storey heard the smack and saw Ivory's face shift to the left under the impact. He saw the shock in Ivory's eyes and then watched as the man began to lose control of his limbs, his knees buckling, his shoulders drooping, his hands falling limp at his side.

Then his legs went one way and his body went the other and he fell awkwardly to the floor, staggering at the last second into the corner piled high with cardboard boxes.

'Fuck!' Charlie yelled, stepping forward and shouting down at Frank Ivory's dull-eyed face. 'You stupid bastard, you've just fucked us over!'

It was at this point things started to fall apart.

Storey had seen that as he staggered and fell into the cardboard boxes, Ivory had dislodged one of the paraffin lanterns, which now wobbled crazily before falling to the concrete and smashing.

There was a whoomp! and the flames spread over the nearest boxes irresistibly, the paraffin spilling out and catching fire. The rolls of paper towels next to the boxes started to crackle as their plastic wrapping was attacked by the flames, and within seconds the paper inside was alight. Black smoke was fanned by the open doorway and started to rise upwards.

Storey had the sense that everyone knew what had happened but they all reacted differently. There was a moment's pause as they considered the situation and what they should do. The two bodyguards, who as far as Storey could tell had neither said nor done anything, looked at each other and shrugged, then walked swiftly past him to get outside. They avoided his eyes while giving him a wide berth. Whatever the Tates had paid them, it was too much.

Turning, Storey saw Bert Tate glance around to see if anyone was watching, step smartly to the garden table and pick up the document Doyle had signed. He then also moved quickly through the open doorway, shielding his face from the growing flames with a hand.

Storey had already moved towards Doyle, who had been putting on his tee-shirt and was now picking up his fleece jacket. The older man grinning at him. 'Did him again, didn't I?'

'You did,' Storey said, finding he had to shout to make himself heard above the sound of the burning cardboard and the spitting of all the packaging materials. 'We better get you out of here before all that paper and cardboard go up.' He grabbed Doyle's arm and started to lead him out.

Fifteen feet away, Charlie was still standing in the middle of the room looking down at Ivory, who was groggily raising himself to one elbow. Charlie saying, 'You were useless then and you're useless now,' and before Storey could stop him, Charlie had seized the third lantern from the table and flung it like a Molotov cocktail at the man on the floor. Ivory saw it coming at the last moment and tried to raise his free arm to protect himself.

It didn't help. The lamp smashed on his arm and the paraffin-fuelled flames leapt over it and spread on to his face, following the liquid. Ivory began to scream, waving his arms and flapping at his face and head. Charlie stood over him for a second then ran out after his cousin.

Storey arrived next to Frank a moment later, taking off his jacket and smothering Ivory's arm and face, then helping him to his feet, saying over his shoulder to Doyle, 'Take his other arm.'

Doyle moved around to the other side and between them they half-carried Ivory from the room, his hair still smoking, the skin on his cheek and neck already beginning to turn pink and peel. He looked up at Storey with his eyes wild, the corner of his lips blackened. Any sounds he made were drowned by the noise of the burning cardboard boxes and their contents.

Outside, the cold air hit them and Storey breathed deeply. He and Doyle lowered Ivory to the floor. Storey didn't know what he expected to see, but it wasn't three police cars pulling up in the lot, with another coming through the gate. As he watched, two policemen climbed from the first and gave chase to the Tate cousins, who were running towards the exit and looking in their dark suits like baby bears heading towards their first taste of freedom.

The two bodyguards stood to one side and watched.

CHAPTER FORTY-SEVEN

AFTER THE FIRE engine arrived the officer in charge said Doyle and Storey could go home. They'd come around later for statements.

Storey asked how they'd known to arrive at the gym. The man tapped the side of his nose and said, 'State secret,' then wandered off to watch the firemen douse the last embers. From what he could see, Storey thought the place would need rebuilding—if Swann or Lethbridge were still interested. Whatever happened, it would be some time before the place would rise again.

Back at Doyle's place there were more police cars. Storey was driving his own car and Doyle peered through the windscreen and said, 'Oh, shit.'

'It's going to be a long night.'

Doyle turned to him. 'Do you think I did the right thing?'

'Which one of all the things you did tonight are we talking about?'

'Taking on Frank Ivory. Fighting him again.'

'You won, didn't you?'

'Yeah, but it was a fucking risk, wasn't it? I could have lost everything.'

'Did you think you might lose?'

'Not really. Frank was never a winner. Well he won't be so 'andsome now, will he? Poor bugger.'

He'd been taken away from the gym in an ambulance but it looked to Storey as if half of his face and some of his neck had been burned. It wasn't pretty.

'Anyway,' Doyle said, 'if I won how come I feel like shit?'

Storey had no answer to that.

As they parked, Charlotte and Norton came out of the entrance, Charlotte running the last few steps towards Doyle and embracing him. She gripped his shoulders and stepped back to look up at his face, her eyes searching for damage.

'You mad bastard,' she said. 'They told me you'd been in a fight. Did you win?'

'Do I ever lose?'

She linked her arm through his and led him indoors. 'You can tell me all about it. And I don't want to hear any lies …'

As they went inside, Norton approached Storey and held out a hand, which Storey shook.

Norton said, 'I should never have doubted you.'

'Yes, you should. I wasn't entirely straight with you or the Doyles.'

'What do you mean?'

Storey explained what Jackie West had told him before he accepted the job. He'd known there were listening devices in the house and that Doyle was under surveillance.

Norton stood looking across the deck towards the dark pond. A full moon cast long and static shadows from the distant trees over the pond's furthest rim, but the water itself shuddered slightly, reflecting the moonlight in jagged lines.

When Storey had finished, Norton said, 'So we were all acting under false pretences. You, me, Swann and Lethbridge, Frank Ivory. Even Felicity, bless her, and Darren, too. Pretending to be a suitor for Doyle's sake. What a farce.'

Storey thought about Kate, the decorator who began working for Doyle while thinking of ways to destroy him. Only to change her mind when she really knew the man and his family.

He said, 'It's tough work being honest with people.'

'Is that more of your Chinese philosophy?'

'I'm thinking of making it into a tee-shirt.'

Now another car drove through the gateway and pulled up in front of them. Jackie West climbed out and walked over, looking up at the house and around at the deck, the pond, the distant trees.

'Looks bigger in real life than on Google,' she said.

Storey introduced her to Norton, who shook her hand then went inside.

She looked Storey up and down. 'You all right? You smell of smoke.'

'How did you know where we were, Doyle and me?'

'Tracker on his car. He had both of his Mercs serviced a month ago and we fitted them then.'

'You could have told me.'

'None of your business. You didn't take my advice so you were on your own.'

He saw something in her face, despite the darkness. He said, 'You're enjoying this, aren't you?'

'What's not to like? That sleazebag Ivory is out of action. We've got the Tates and they're spilling their guts already about the kidney harvesting. Alf Chamberlain's been picked up—'

'Hold on, how's all this come about? Why are they coughing up so soon?'

'We got them on tape, didn't we, talking about it. Making arrangements to meet Chamberlain as soon as they'd finished with Doyle. So we're playing Charlie off against Bert and vice versa. No real love lost there, it seems.'

'You told me the surveillance was over.'

'Apparently, according to my boss, I over-stated the case. When the Tates came here earlier today we reactivated the devices. The Tates and Doyle were having a nice conversation in the sitting room when Doyle got up and left—looking for you, I think. When he was out of the room the others started talking about when they were going to meet Chamberlain and whether he was going to meet his quota. The words "girl" and "kidney" were uttered. Very careless of them.'

Storey felt a great tiredness come over him. He wanted to go back to his house but it was still occupied by Felicity and Nicki. He would have to carry on in the cottage, at least for a short while. Still be the driver. Still deal with Doyle's impulsiveness and Charlotte's casual flirting.

Something occurred to him.

'You haven't said anything about Lionel. I shot him. Well, strictly speaking he forced it on himself.'

'You keep telling yourself that,' Jackie West said, almost laughing. 'It's how you soothe your conscience. Besides, you won, didn't you?'

He stared at her. Remembering what Doyle had said: *If I won, how come I feel like shit?*

ALSO BY KEITH DIXON

The Sam Dyke Series

Altered Life The
Private Lie The
Hard Swim The
Bleak
The Strange Girl
The Secret Sharers
The Innocent Dead
The Second Guess (short story)

Paul Storey Crime Thrillers

Storey

Standalone Novels

A French Darcy – a Romance
Actress – a Contemporary novel

Essays on Writing

The Idle Writer
Crime Writing Confidential

Blog

www.cwconfidential.blogspot.com

Webpage

http://www.keithdixonnovels.com

Subscribe

If you subscribe to the newsletter you'll receive the second
in the Sam Dyke series, *The Private Lie,* for free, plus news of
forthcoming work and the occasional free gift.